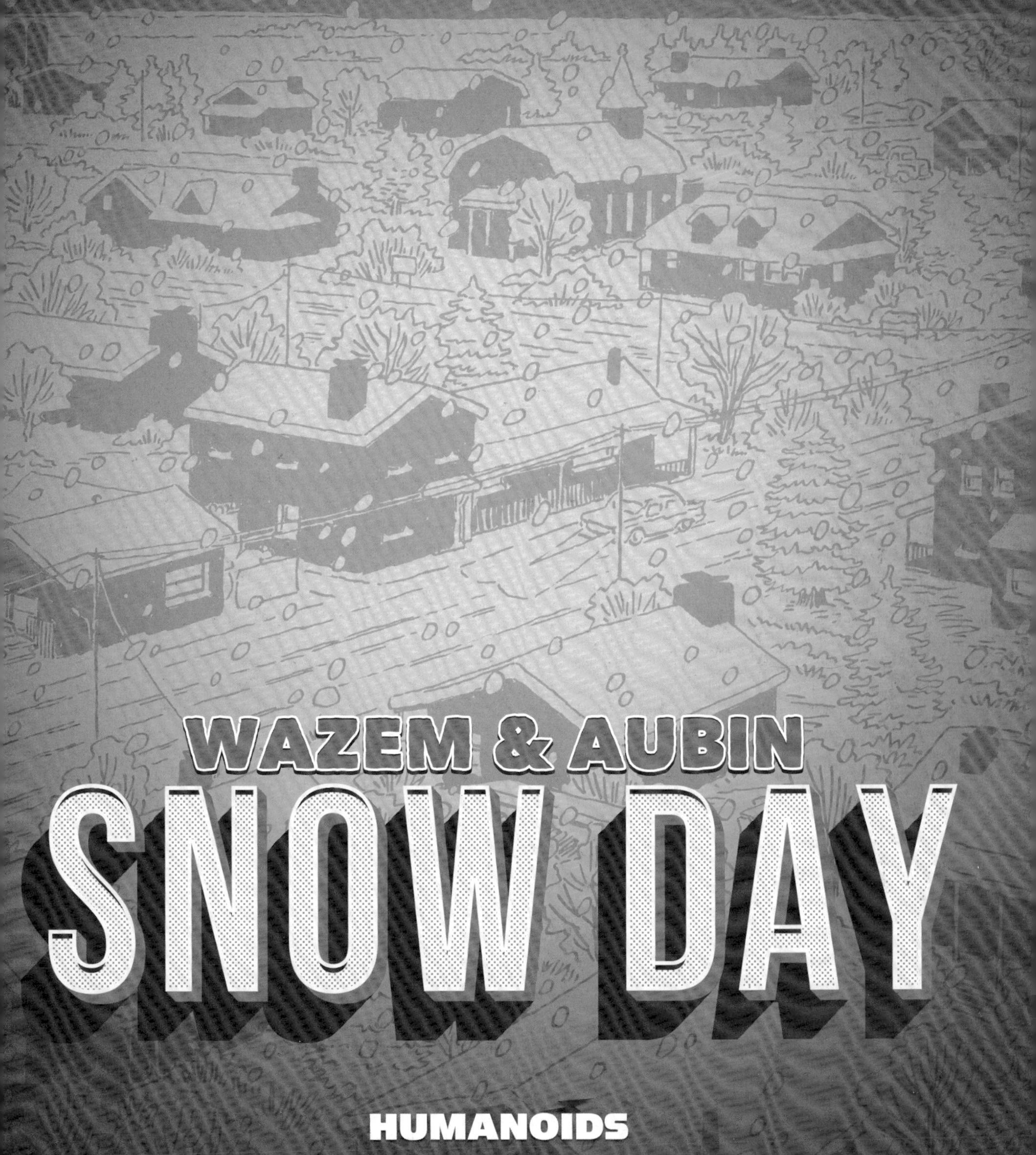

WAZEM & AUBIN

SNOW DAY

HUMANOIDS

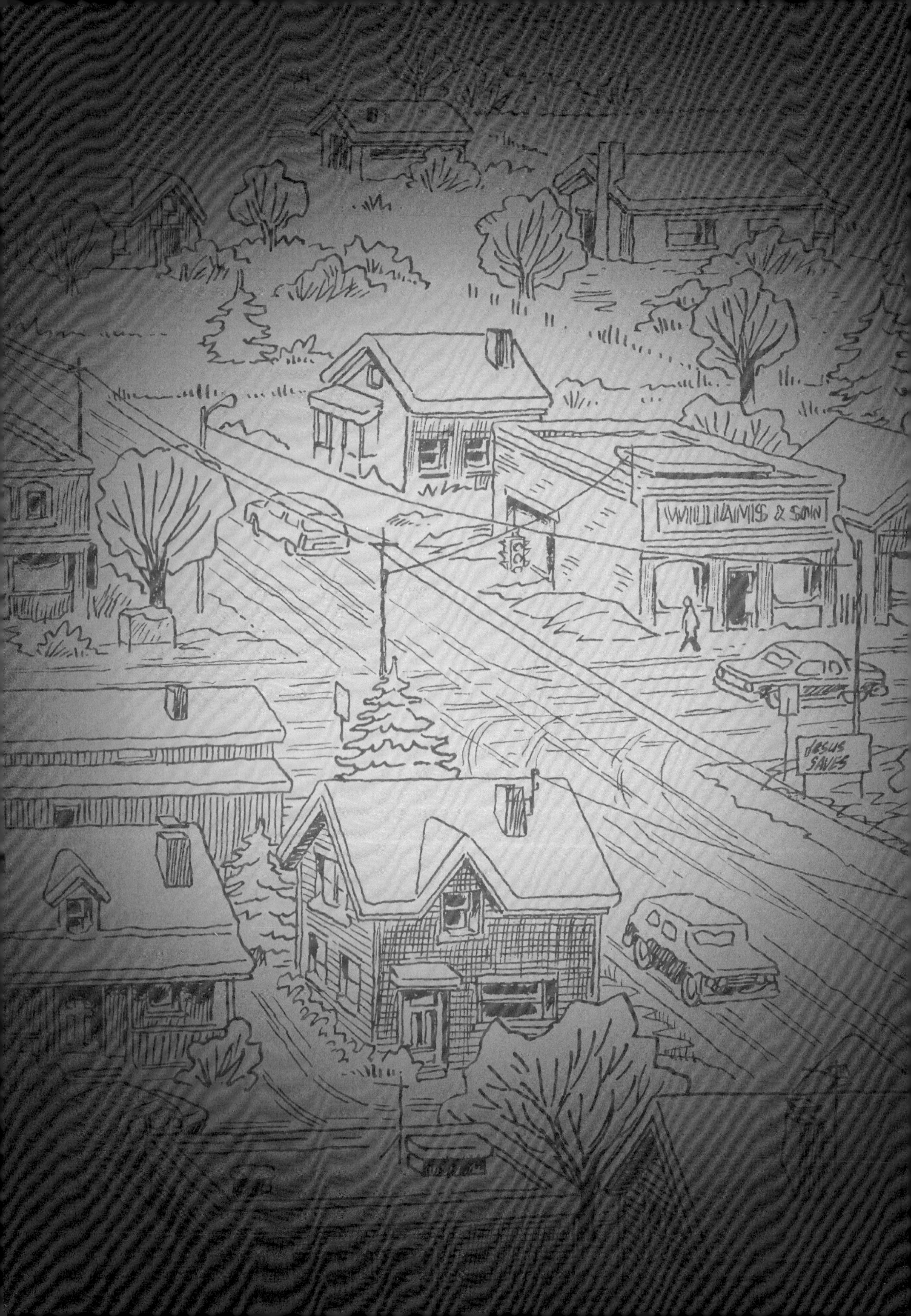
WILLIAMS & SON
Jesus SAVES

PIERRE WAZEM
Writer

ANTOINE AUBIN
Artist

MARK BENCE
Translator

•

**ALEX DONOGHUE
& TIM PILCHER**
U.S. Edition Editors

JERRY FRISSEN
Book Designer

•

Fabrice Giger, Publisher

Rights & Licensing - licensing@humanoids.com
Press and Social Media - pr@humanoids.com

SNOW DAY
This title is a publication of Humanoids, Inc. 8033 Sunset Blvd. #628, Los Angeles, CA 90046.
Copyright © 2017 Humanoids, Inc., Los Angeles (USA). All rights reserved.
Humanoids and its logos are ® and © 2017 Humanoids, Inc.

Originally published in French by Les Humanoïdes Associés (Paris, France).

By the same writer:

KOMA
with Frederik Peeters
ISBN: 978-1-59465-147-2

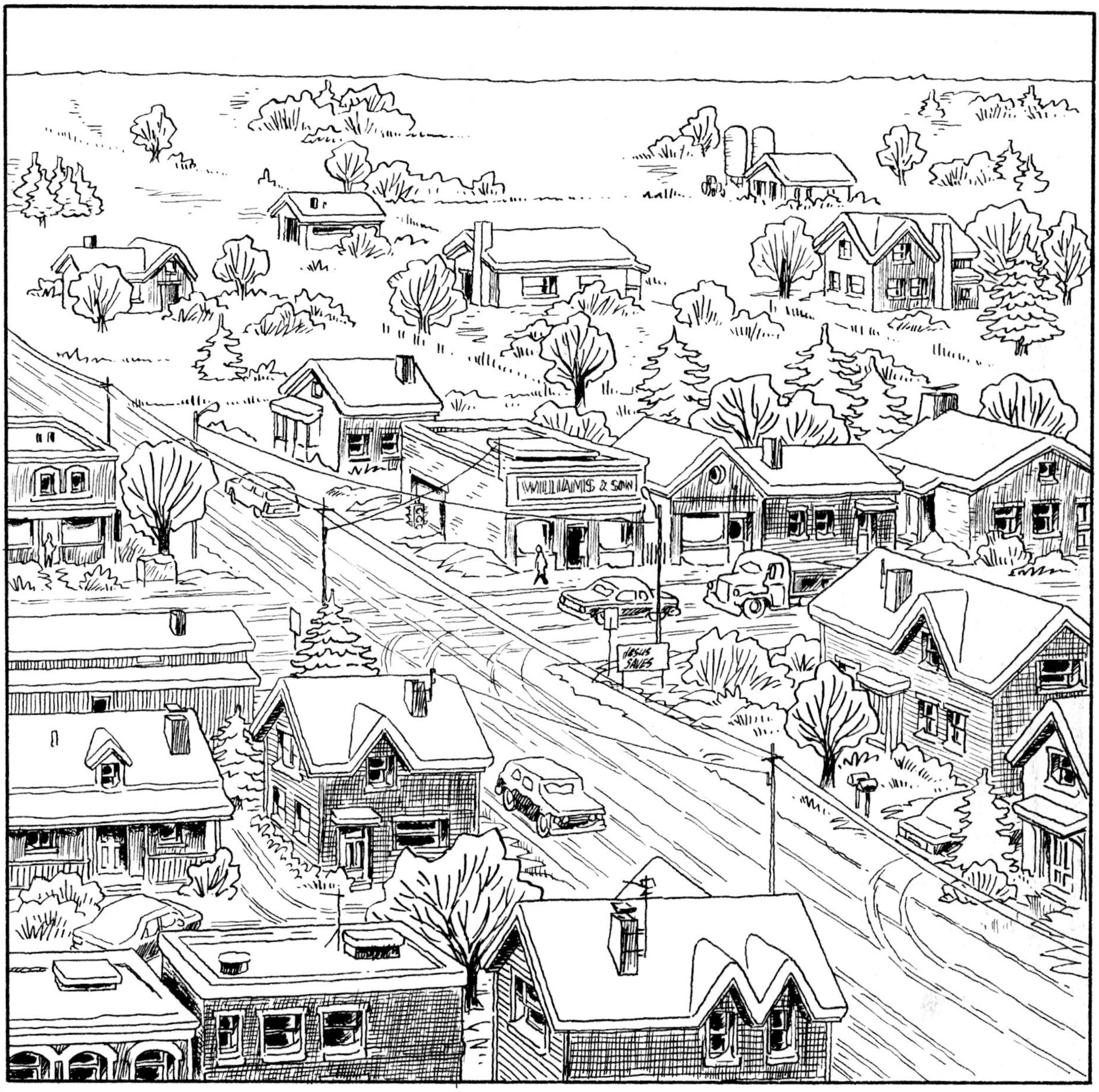
WILLIAMS & SON
JESUS SAVES

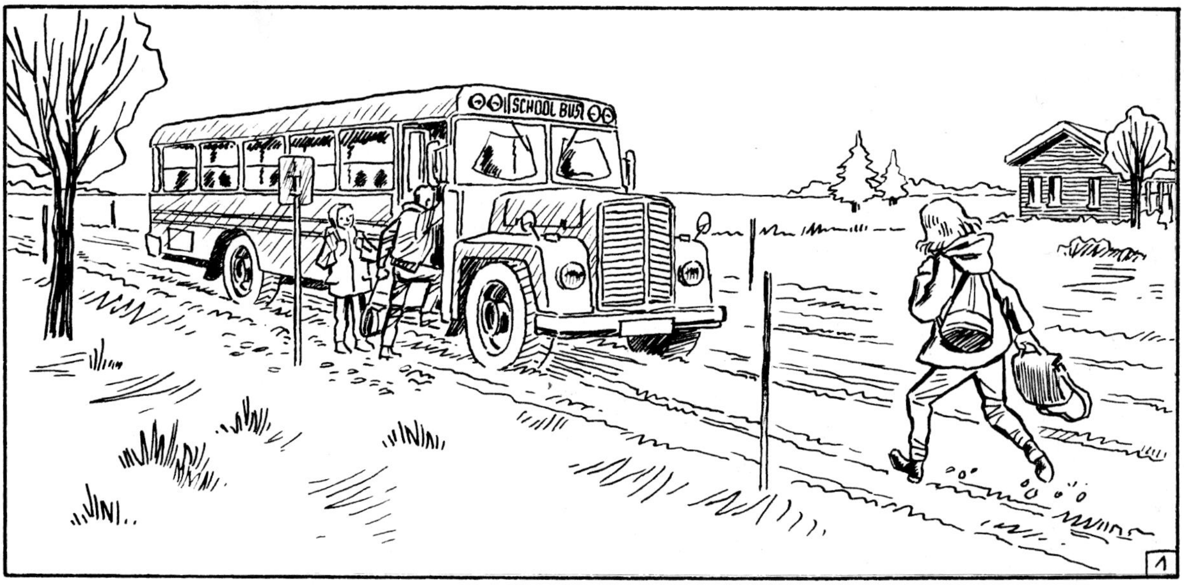
SCHOOL BUS

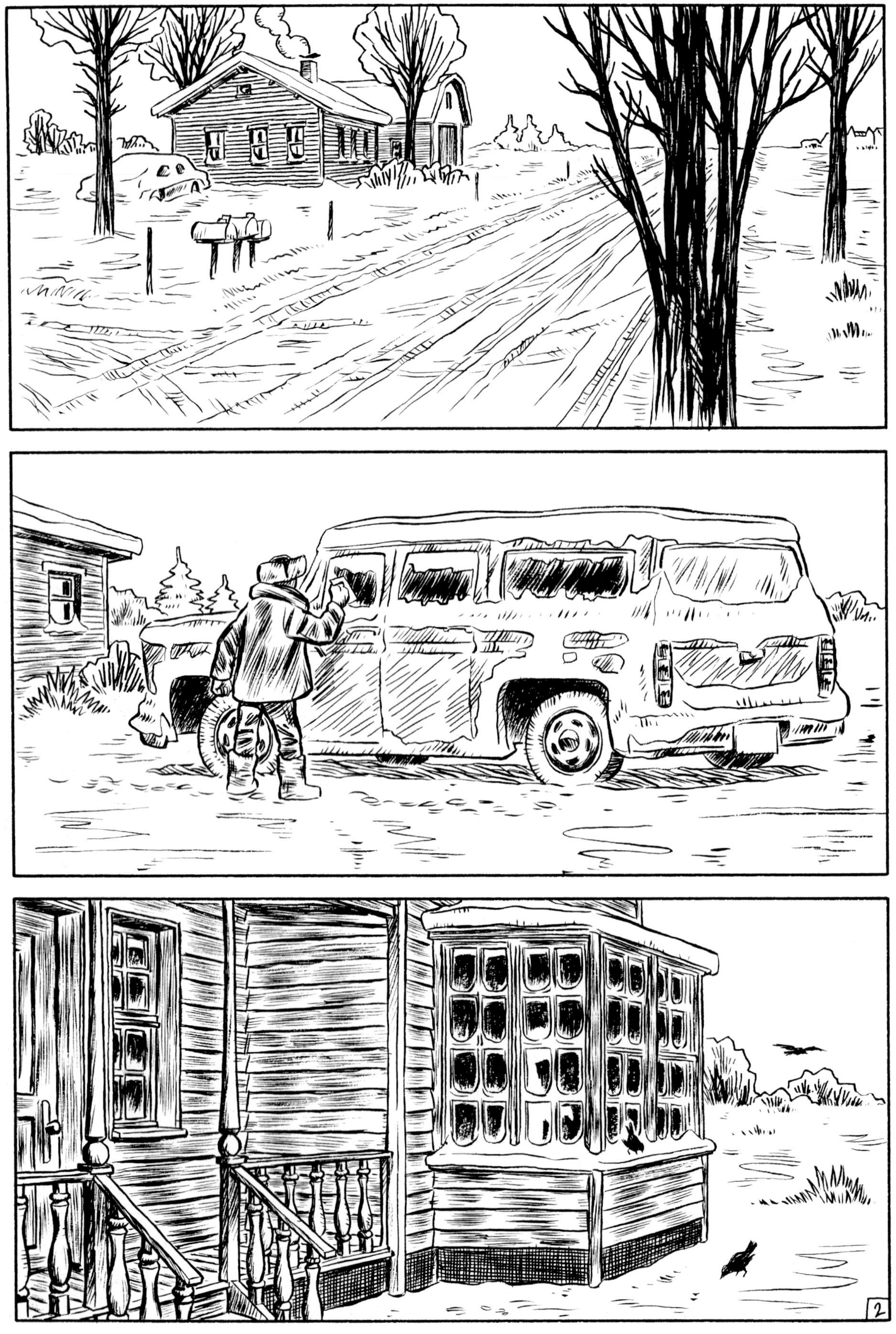

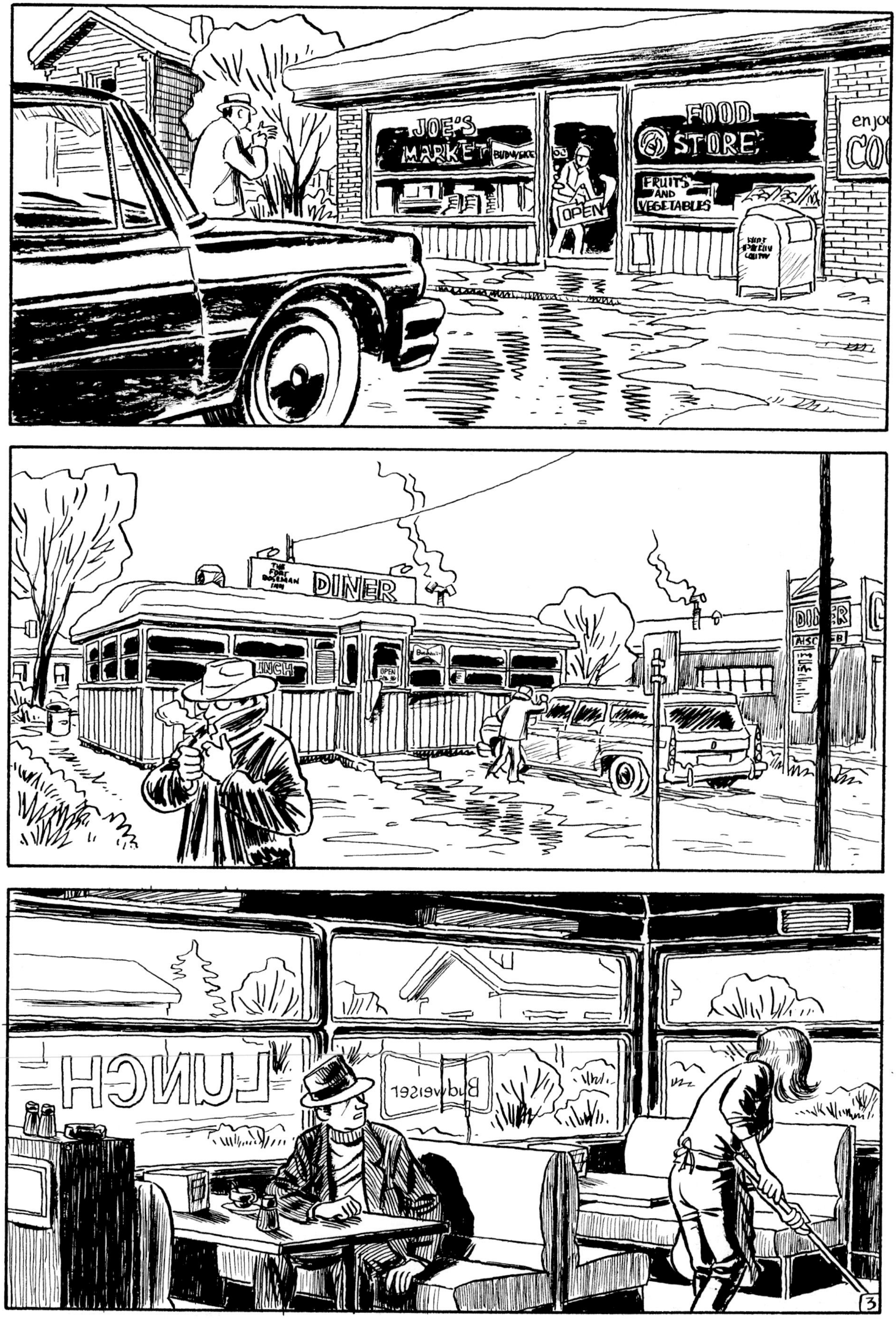
JOE'S MARKET
FOOD STORE
FRUITS AND VEGETABLES
OPEN
DINER
LUNCH

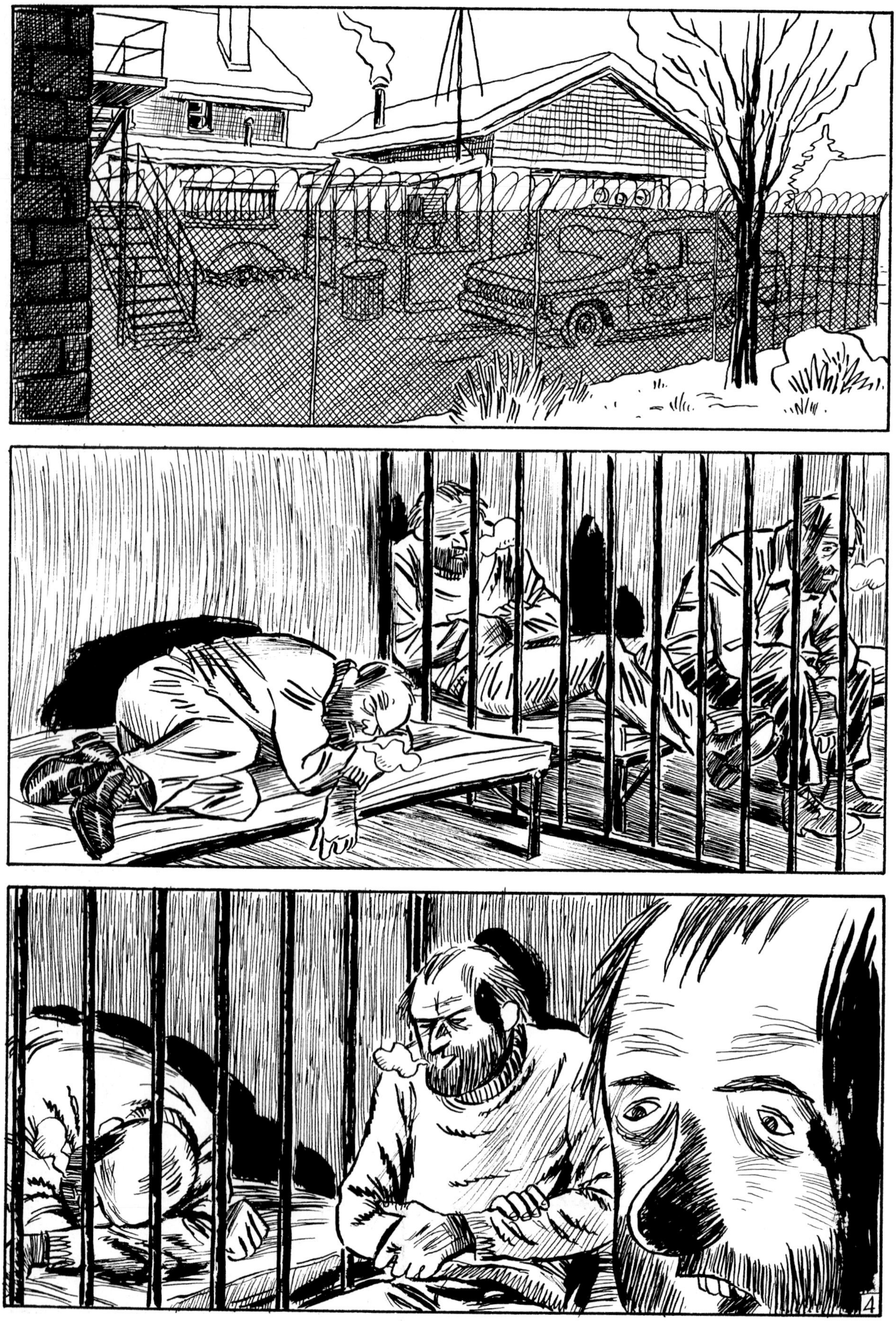

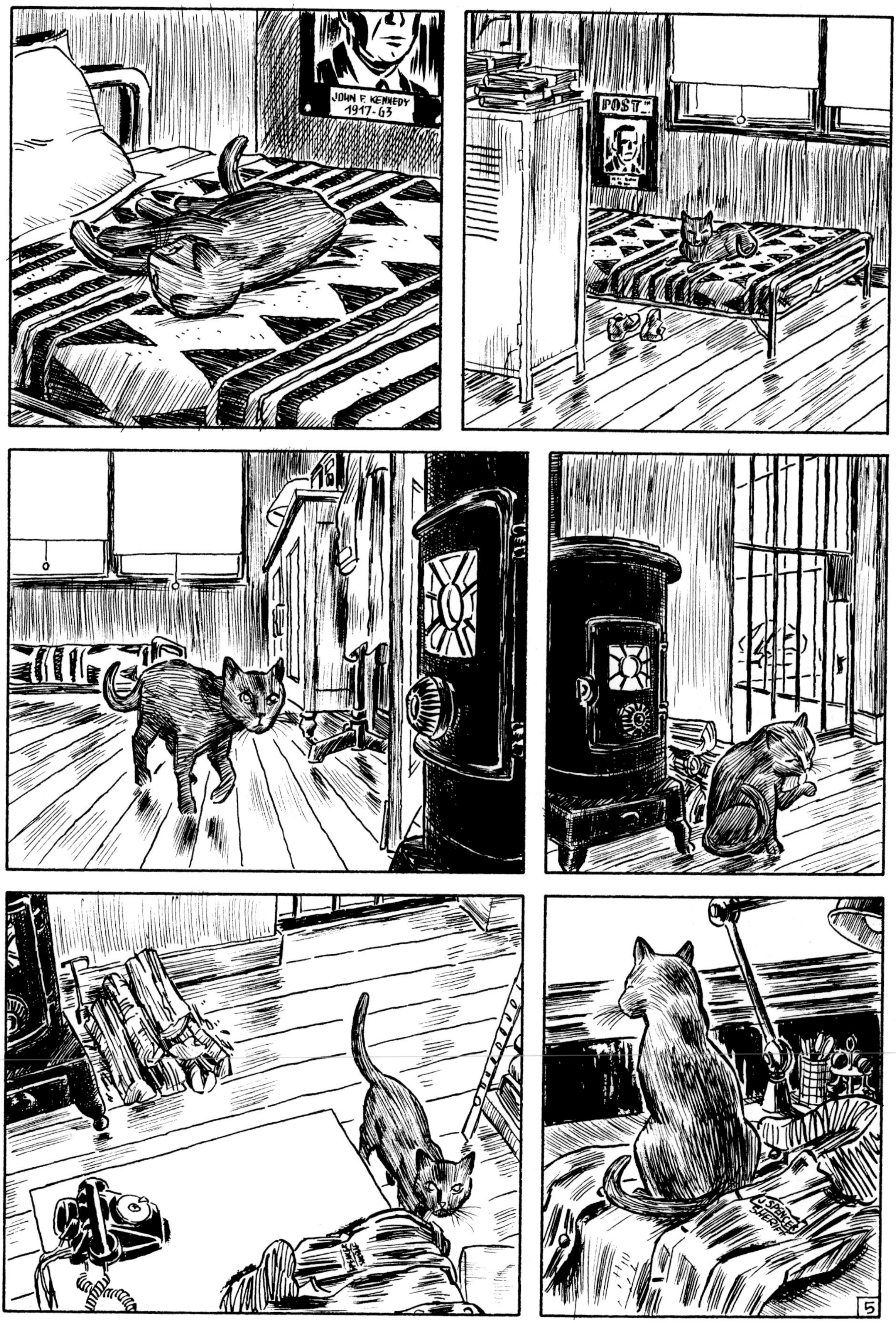
JOHN F. KENNEDY
1917-63
POST
J. SPENCER
SHERIFF

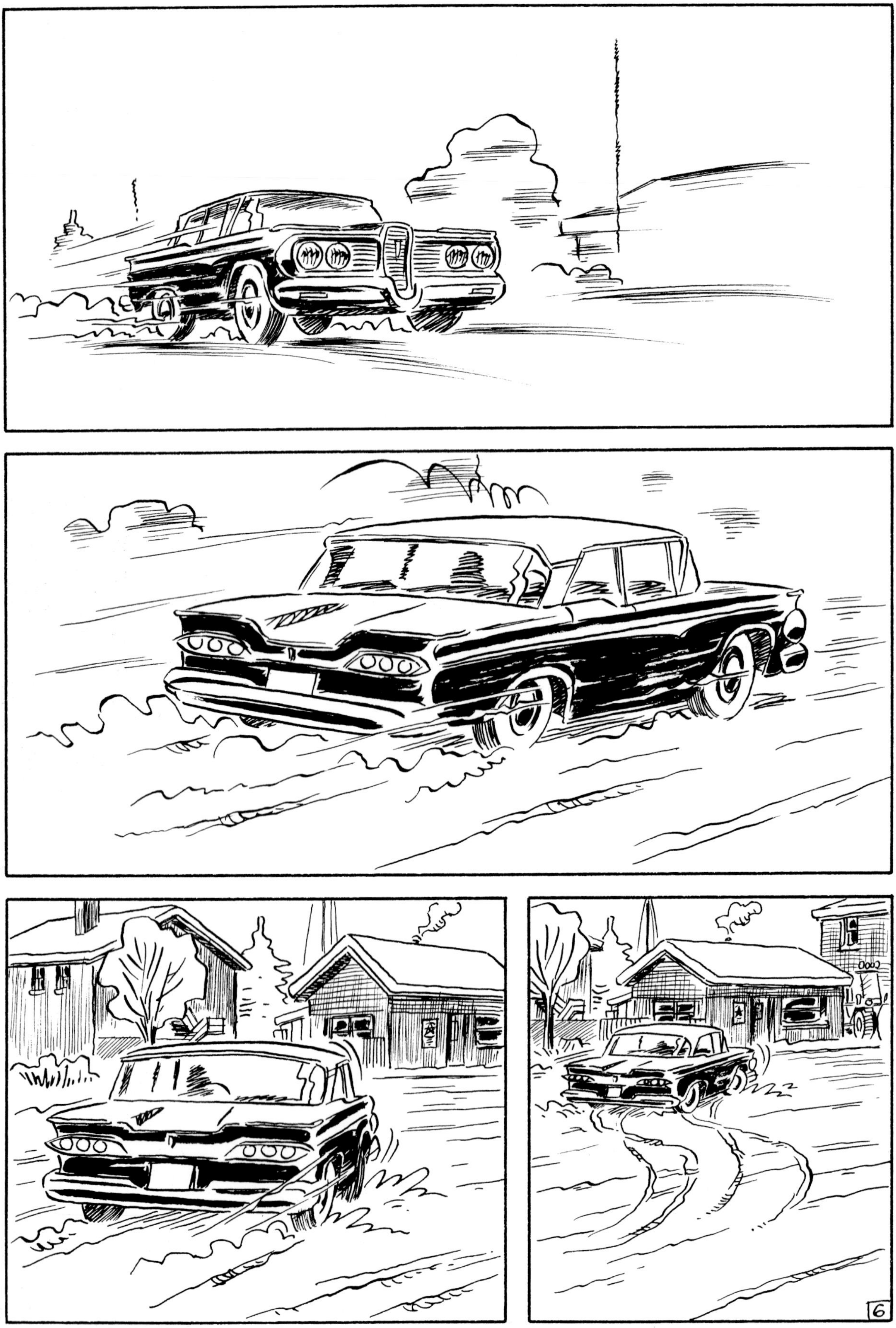

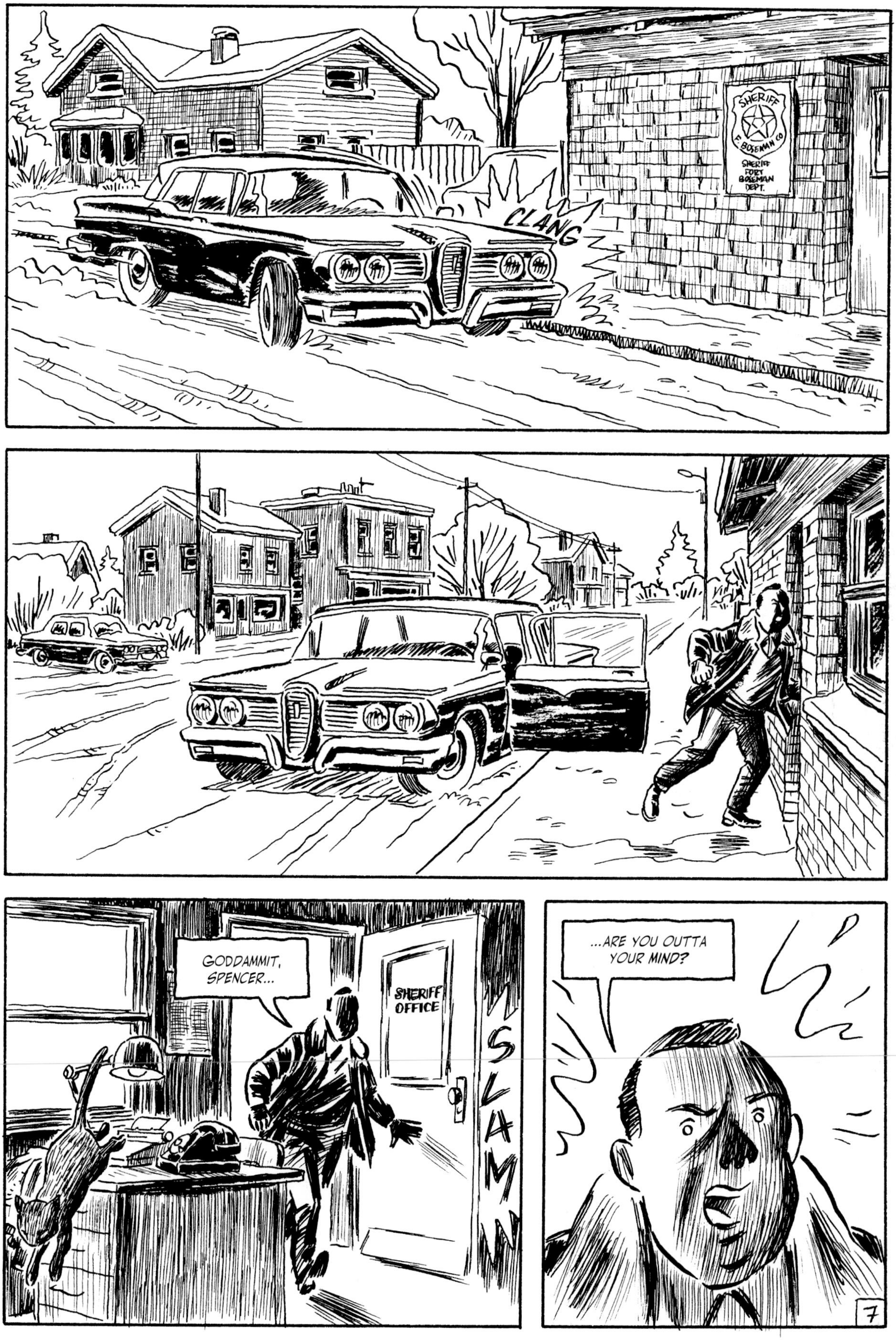
CLANG
SHERIFF
F. BOSEMAN CO.
SHERIFF
FORT
BOSEMAN
DEPT.
GODDAMMIT, SPENCER...
SHERIFF OFFICE
SLAM
...ARE YOU OUTTA YOUR MIND?

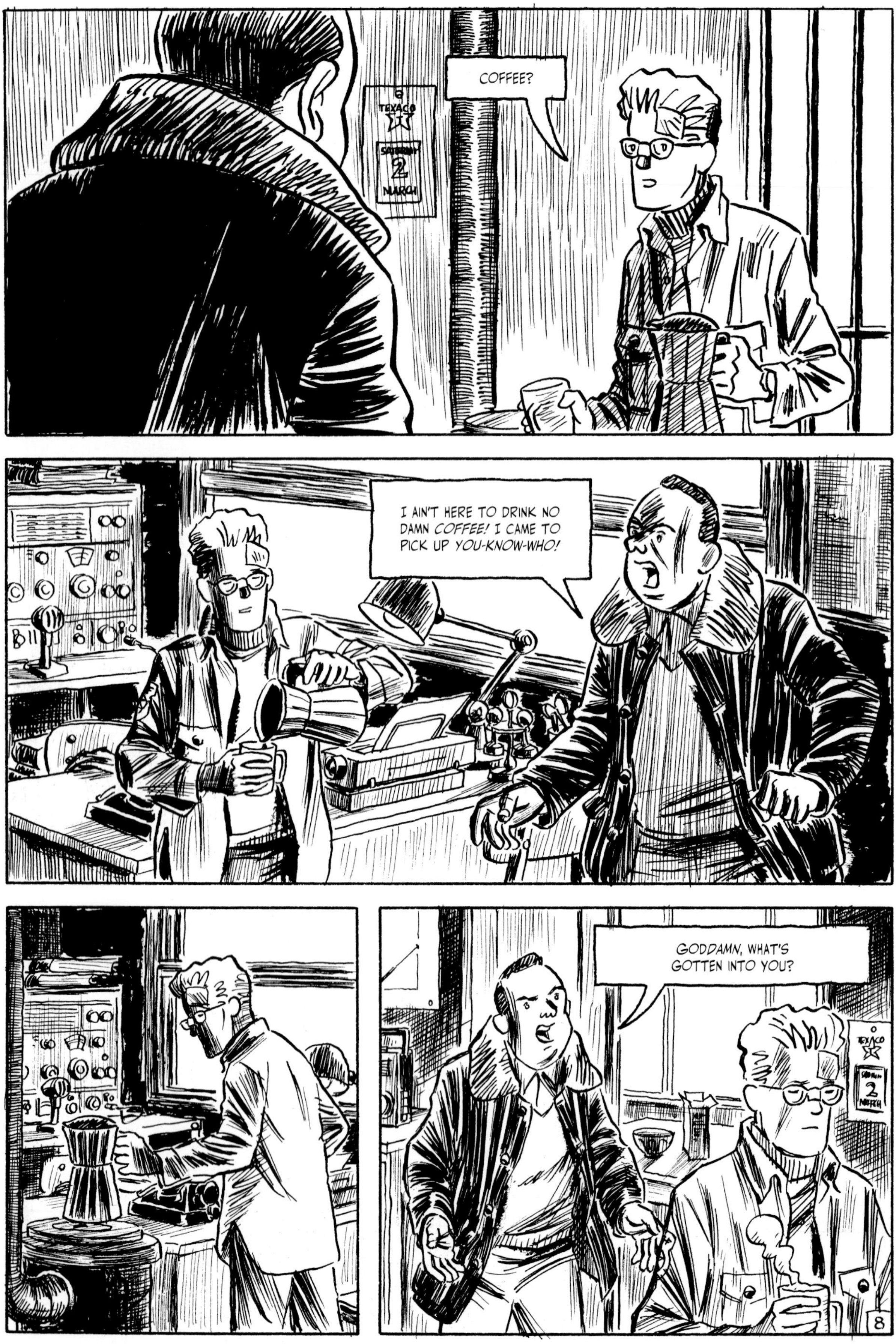
COFFEE?
I AIN'T HERE TO DRINK NO DAMN *COFFEE!* I CAME TO PICK UP *YOU-KNOW-WHO!*
GOD*DAMN*, WHAT'S GOTTEN INTO YOU?

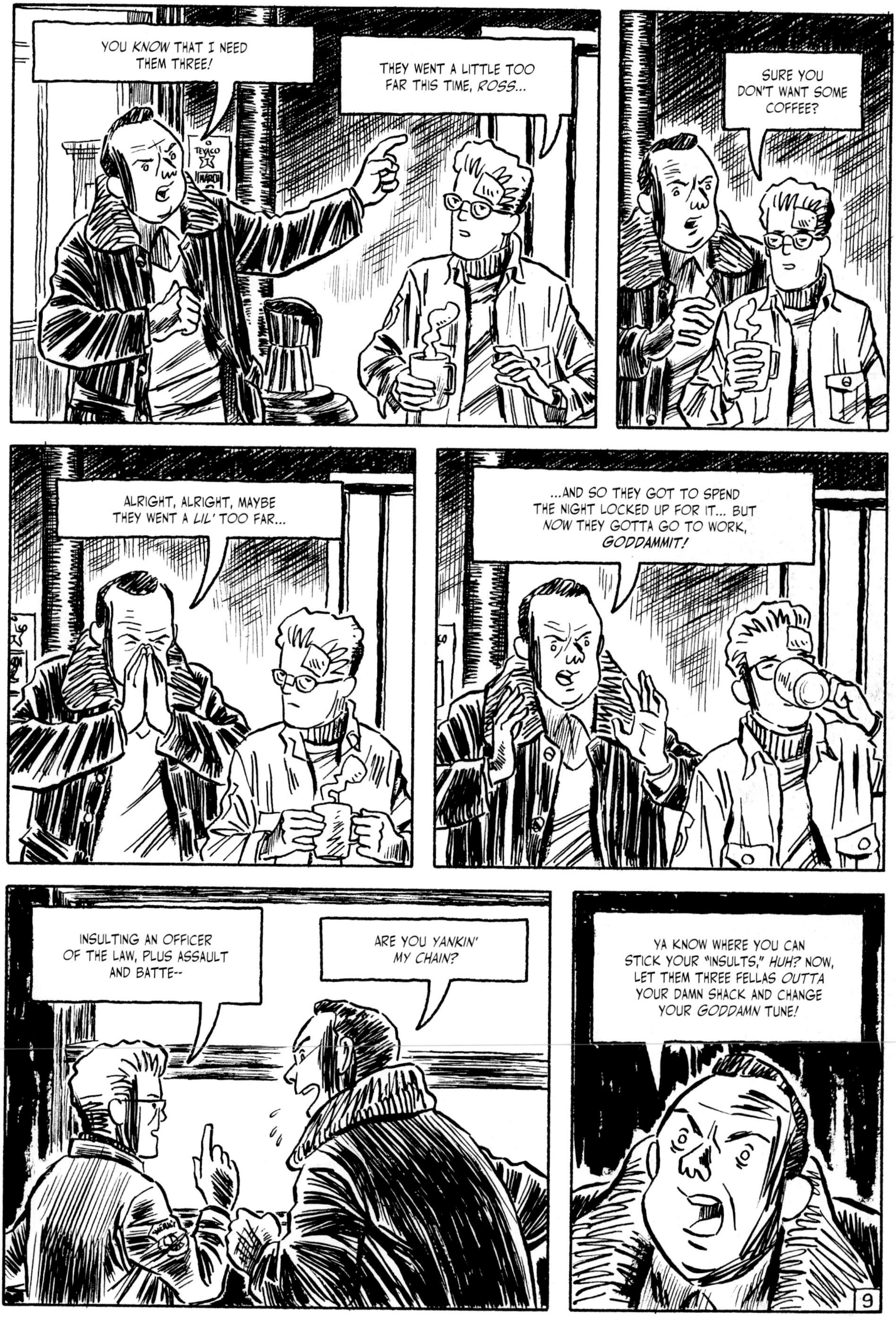
YOU *KNOW* THAT I NEED THEM THREE!
THEY WENT A LITTLE TOO FAR THIS TIME, *ROSS*...
TEXACO
SURE YOU DON'T WANT SOME COFFEE?
ALRIGHT, ALRIGHT, MAYBE THEY WENT A *LIL'* TOO FAR...
...AND SO THEY GOT TO SPEND THE NIGHT LOCKED UP FOR IT... BUT *NOW* THEY GOTTA GO TO WORK, *GODDAMMIT!*
INSULTING AN OFFICER OF THE LAW, PLUS ASSAULT AND BATTE--
ARE YOU *YANKIN'* *MY CHAIN?*
YA KNOW WHERE YOU CAN STICK YOUR "INSULTS," *HUH?* NOW, LET THEM THREE FELLAS *OUTTA* YOUR DAMN SHACK AND CHANGE YOUR *GODDAMN* TUNE!

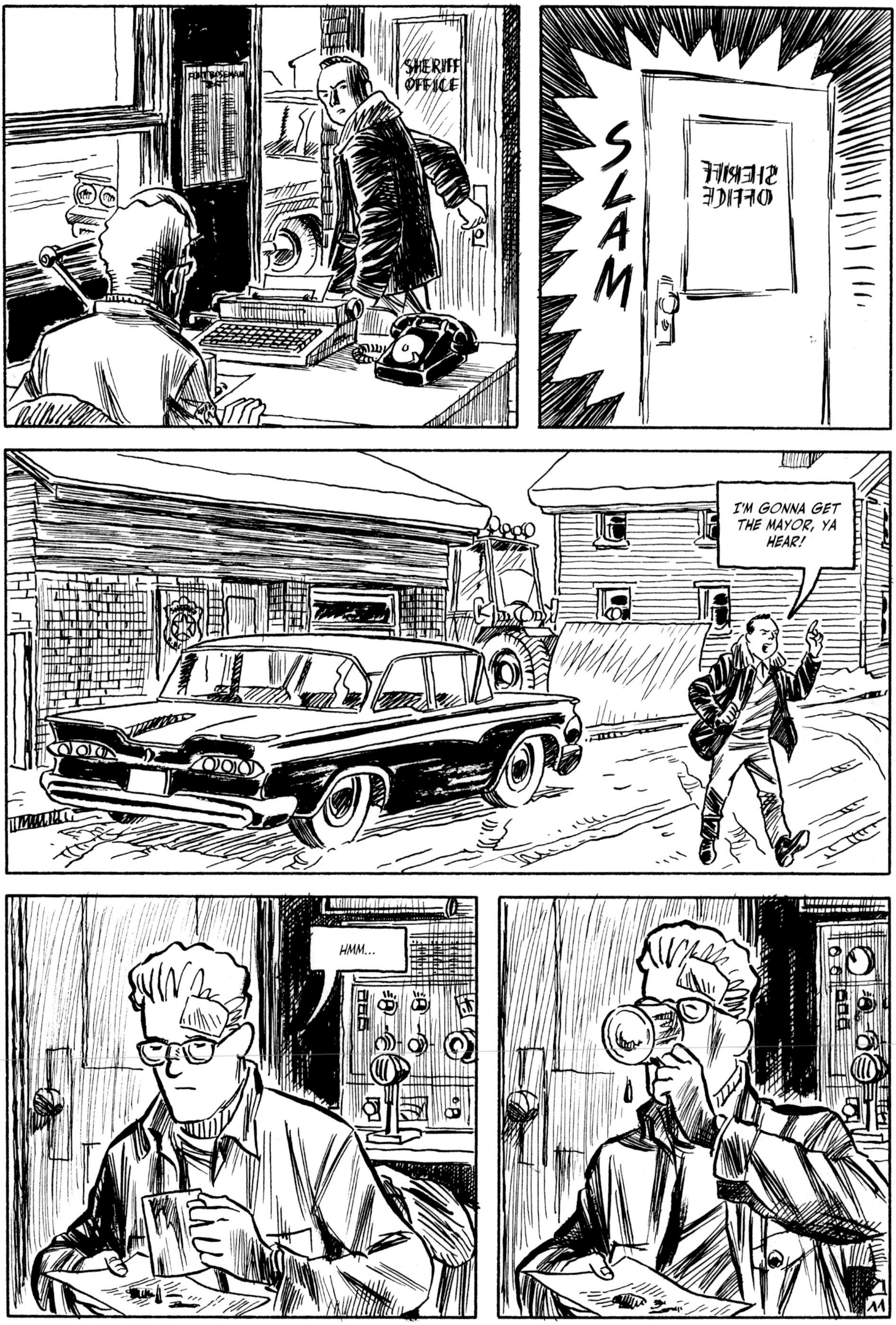
SHERIFF OFFICE
SLAM
I'M GONNA GET THE MAYOR, YA HEAR!
HMM...

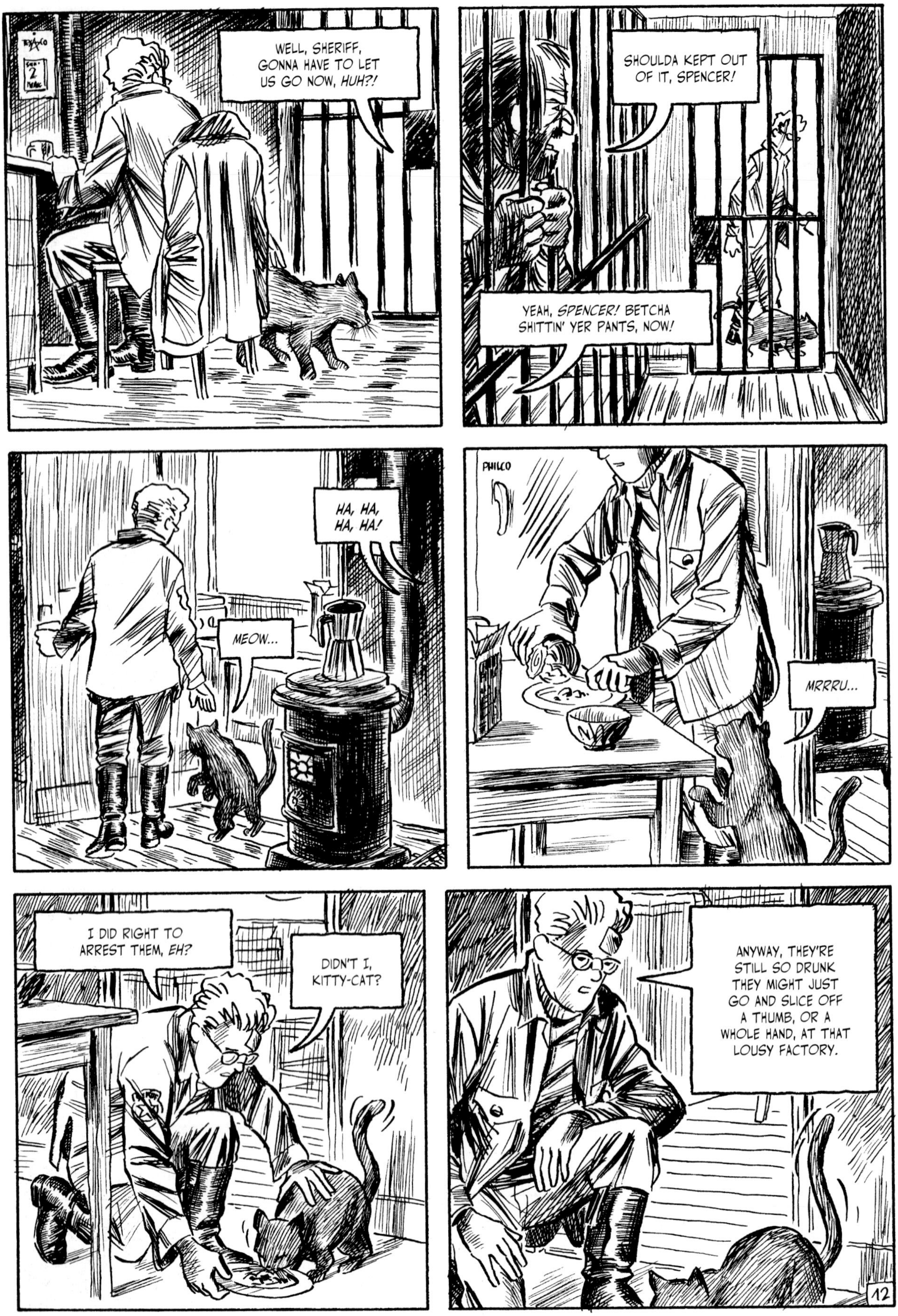
TEXACO
WELL, SHERIFF, GONNA HAVE TO LET US GO NOW, HUH?!
SHOULDA KEPT OUT OF IT, SPENCER!
YEAH, SPENCER! BETCHA SHITTIN' YER PANTS, NOW!
HA, HA, HA, HA!
MEOW...
PHILCO
MRRRU...
I DID RIGHT TO ARREST THEM, EH?
DIDN'T I, KITTY-CAT?
ANYWAY, THEY'RE STILL SO DRUNK THEY MIGHT JUST GO AND SLICE OFF A THUMB, OR A WHOLE HAND, AT THAT LOUSY FACTORY.

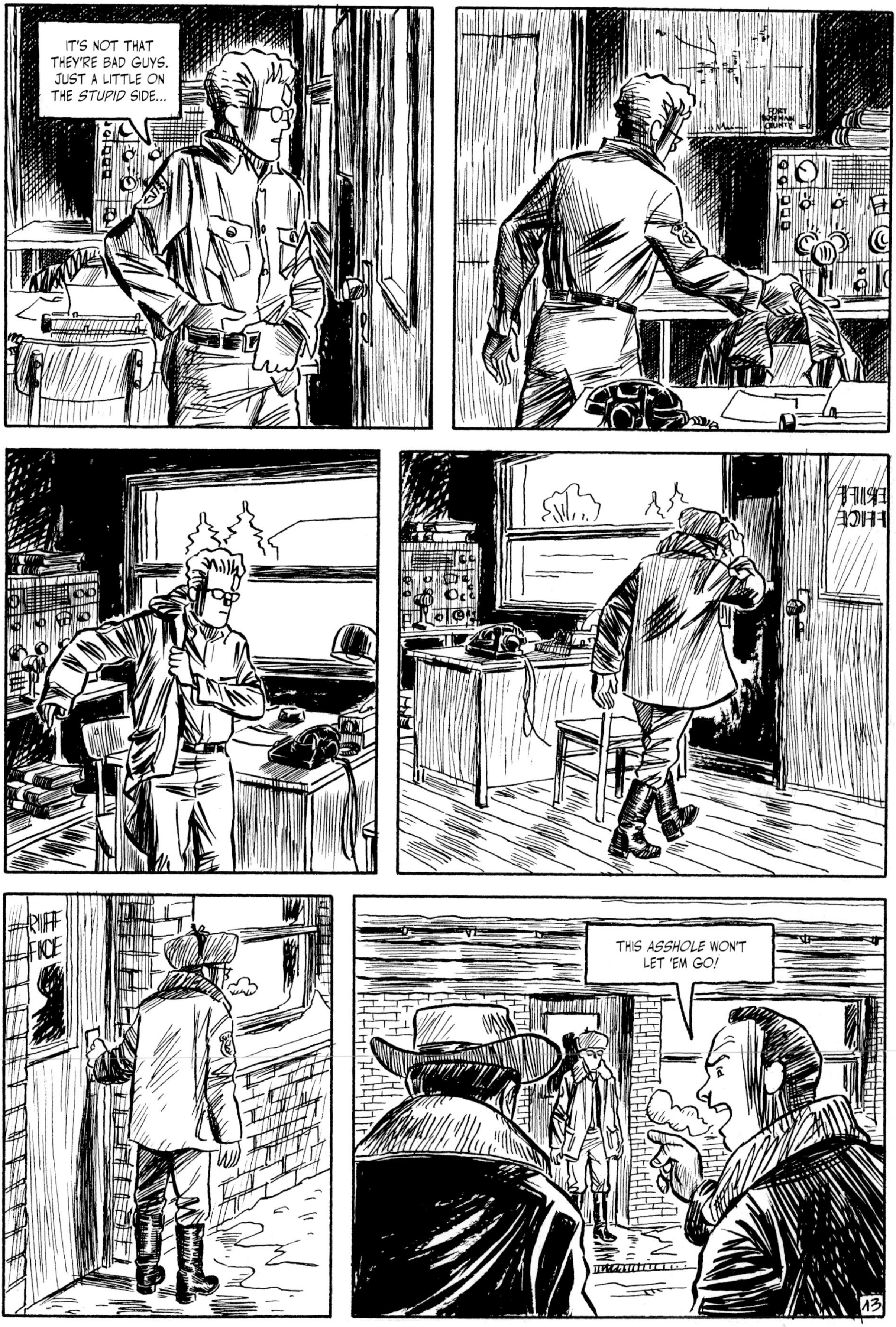
IT'S NOT THAT THEY'RE BAD GUYS. JUST A LITTLE ON THE *STUPID* SIDE...
THIS *ASSHOLE* WON'T LET 'EM GO!

14

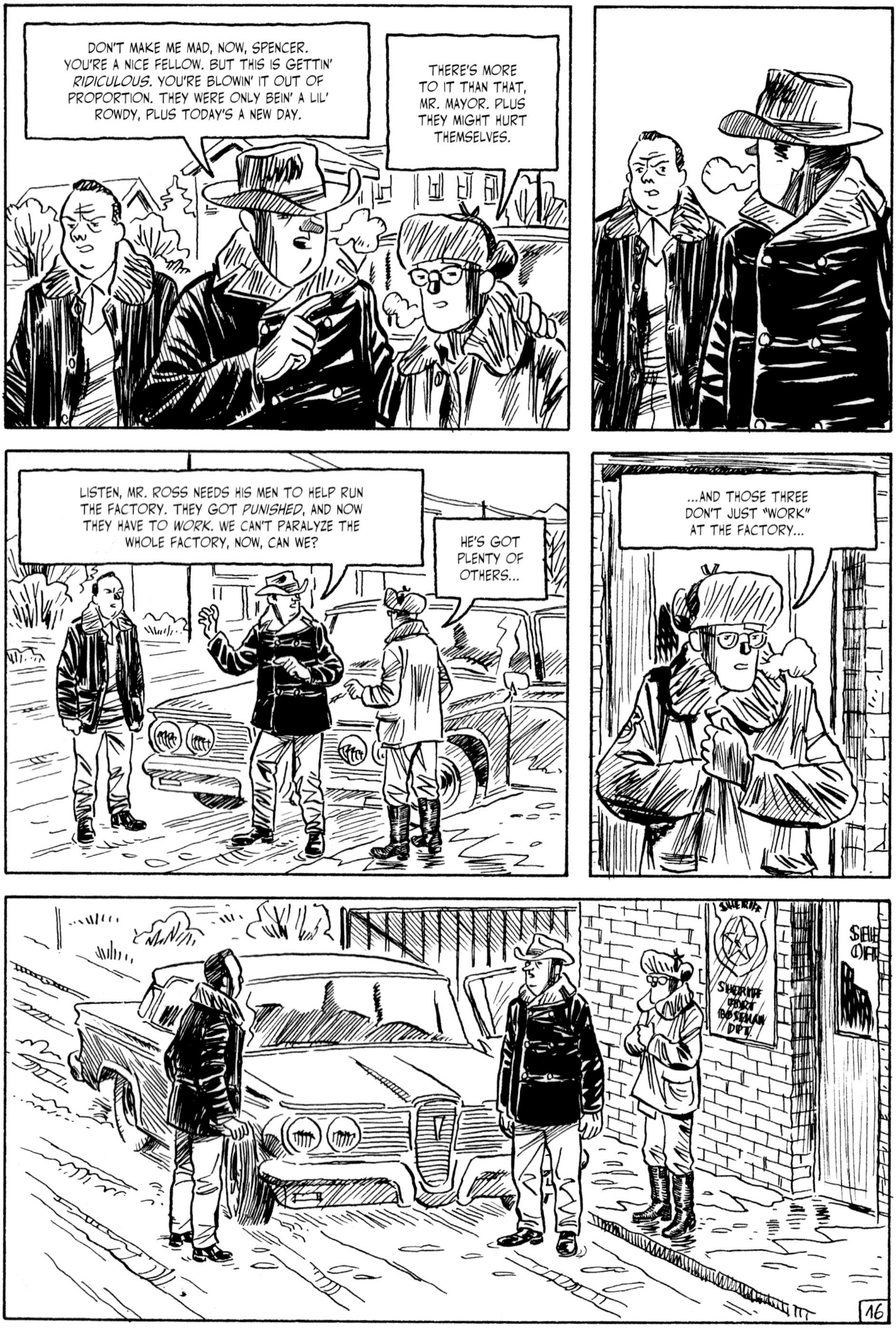
DON'T MAKE ME MAD, NOW, SPENCER. YOU'RE A NICE FELLOW. BUT THIS IS GETTIN' *RIDICULOUS*. YOU'RE BLOWIN' IT OUT OF PROPORTION. THEY WERE ONLY BEIN' A LIL' ROWDY, PLUS TODAY'S A NEW DAY.
THERE'S MORE TO IT THAN THAT, MR. MAYOR. PLUS THEY MIGHT HURT THEMSELVES.
LISTEN, MR. ROSS NEEDS HIS MEN TO HELP RUN THE FACTORY. THEY GOT *PUNISHED*, AND NOW THEY HAVE TO *WORK*. WE CAN'T PARALYZE THE WHOLE FACTORY, NOW, CAN WE?
HE'S GOT PLENTY OF OTHERS...
...AND THOSE THREE DON'T JUST "WORK" AT THE FACTORY...
SHERIFF
SHERIFF FORT BOSEMAN DPT.

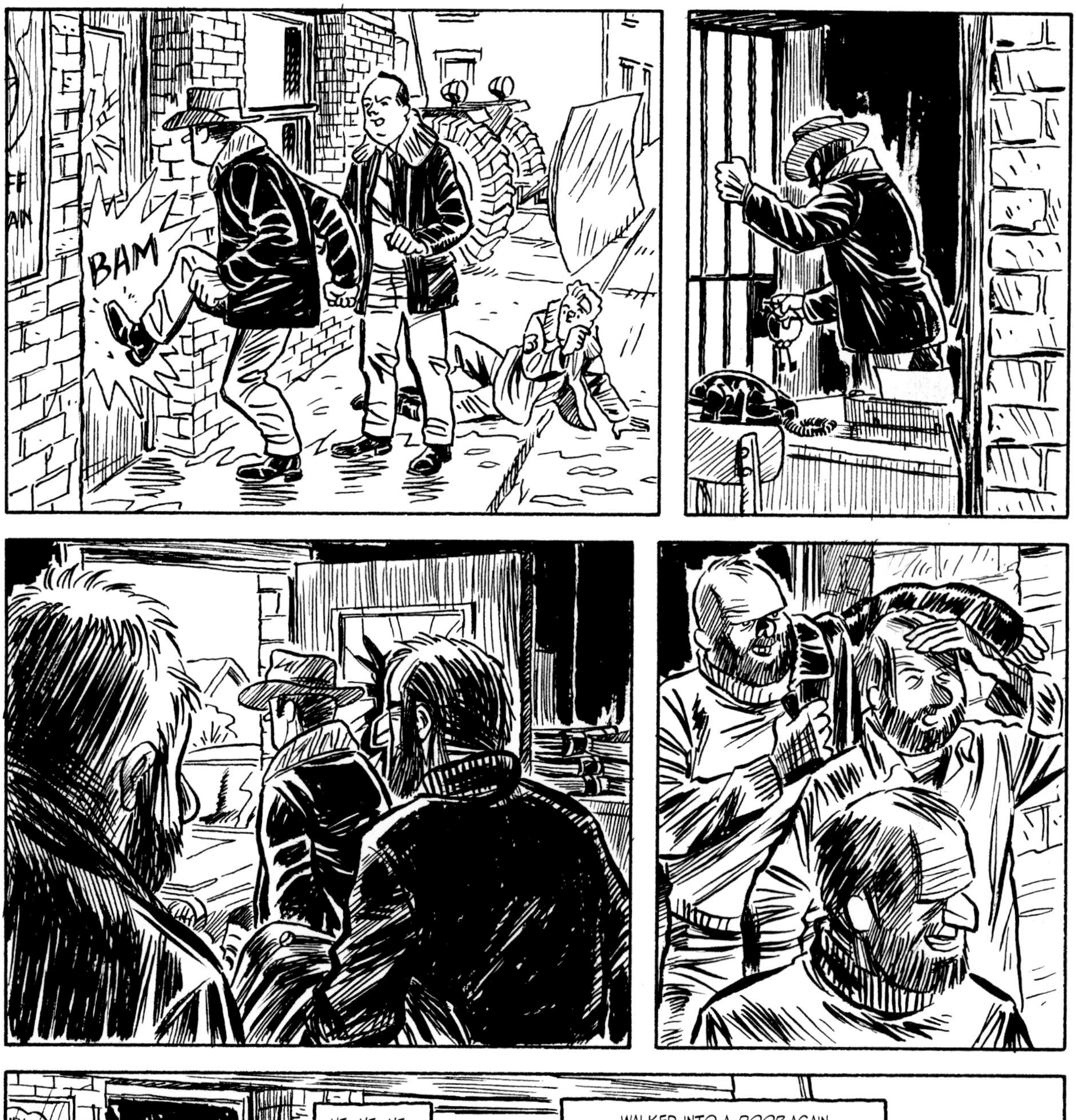
BAM
HE, HE, HE...
WALKED INTO A DOOR AGAIN, DID YA, SPENCER?

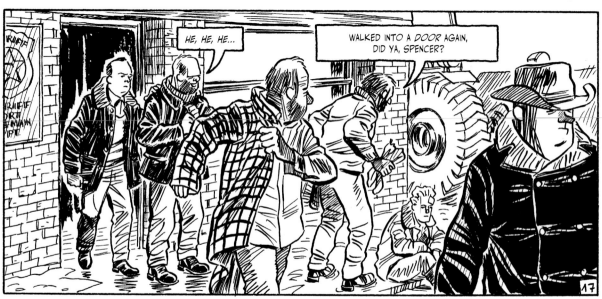

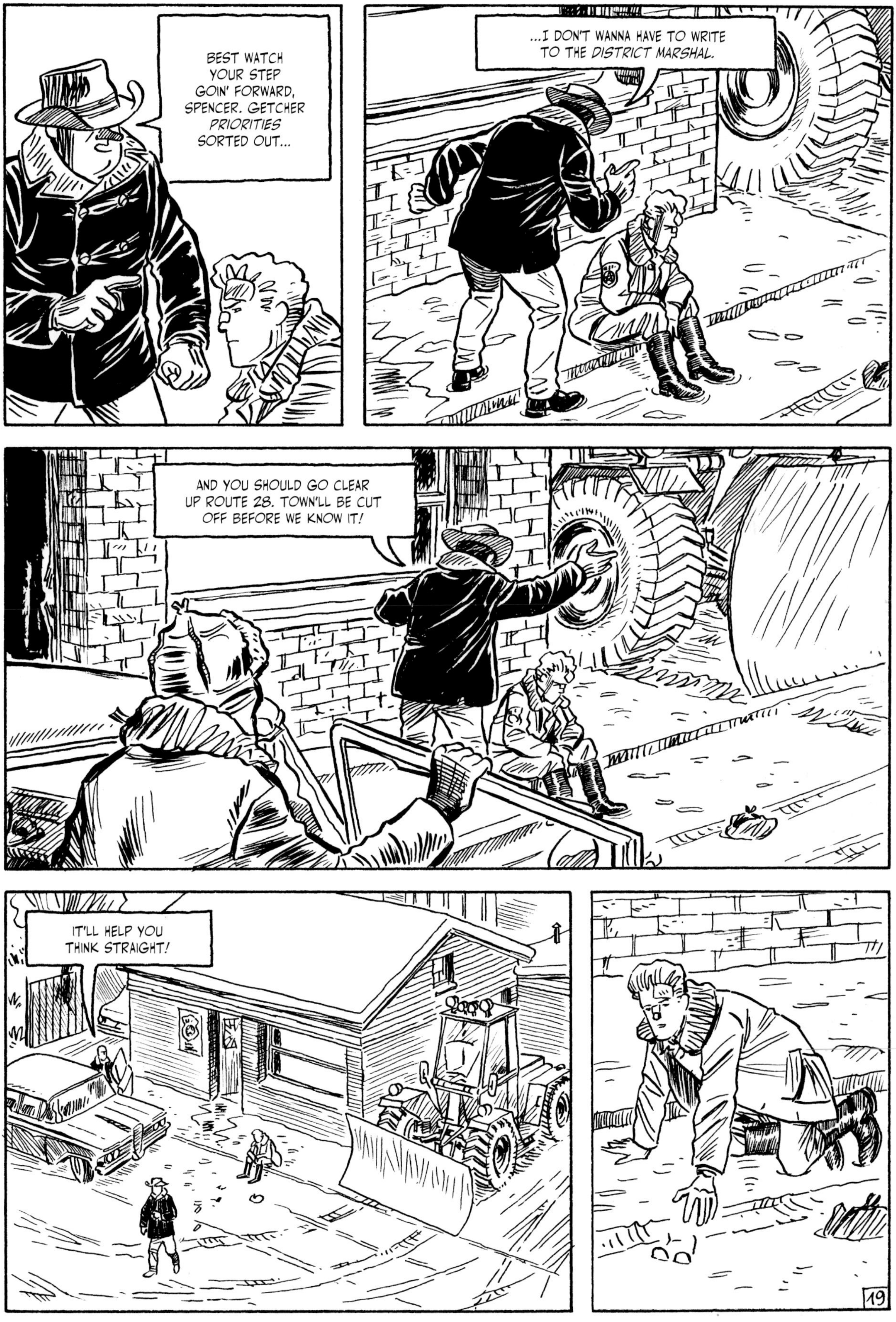
BEST WATCH YOUR STEP GOIN' FORWARD, SPENCER. GETCHER *PRIORITIES* SORTED OUT...
...I DON'T WANNA HAVE TO WRITE TO THE *DISTRICT MARSHAL.*
AND YOU SHOULD GO CLEAR UP ROUTE 28. TOWN'LL BE CUT OFF BEFORE WE KNOW IT!
IT'LL HELP YOU THINK STRAIGHT!

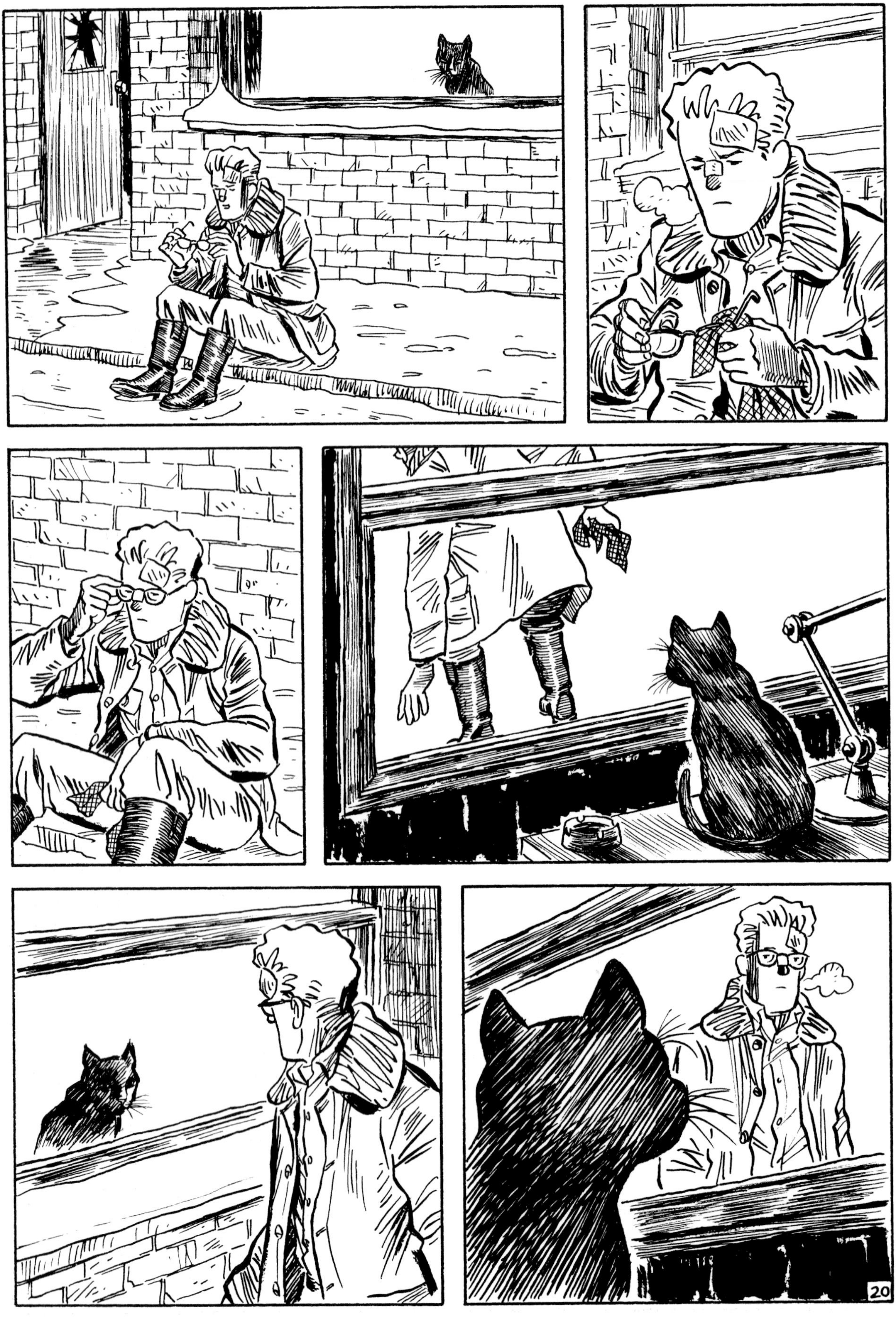

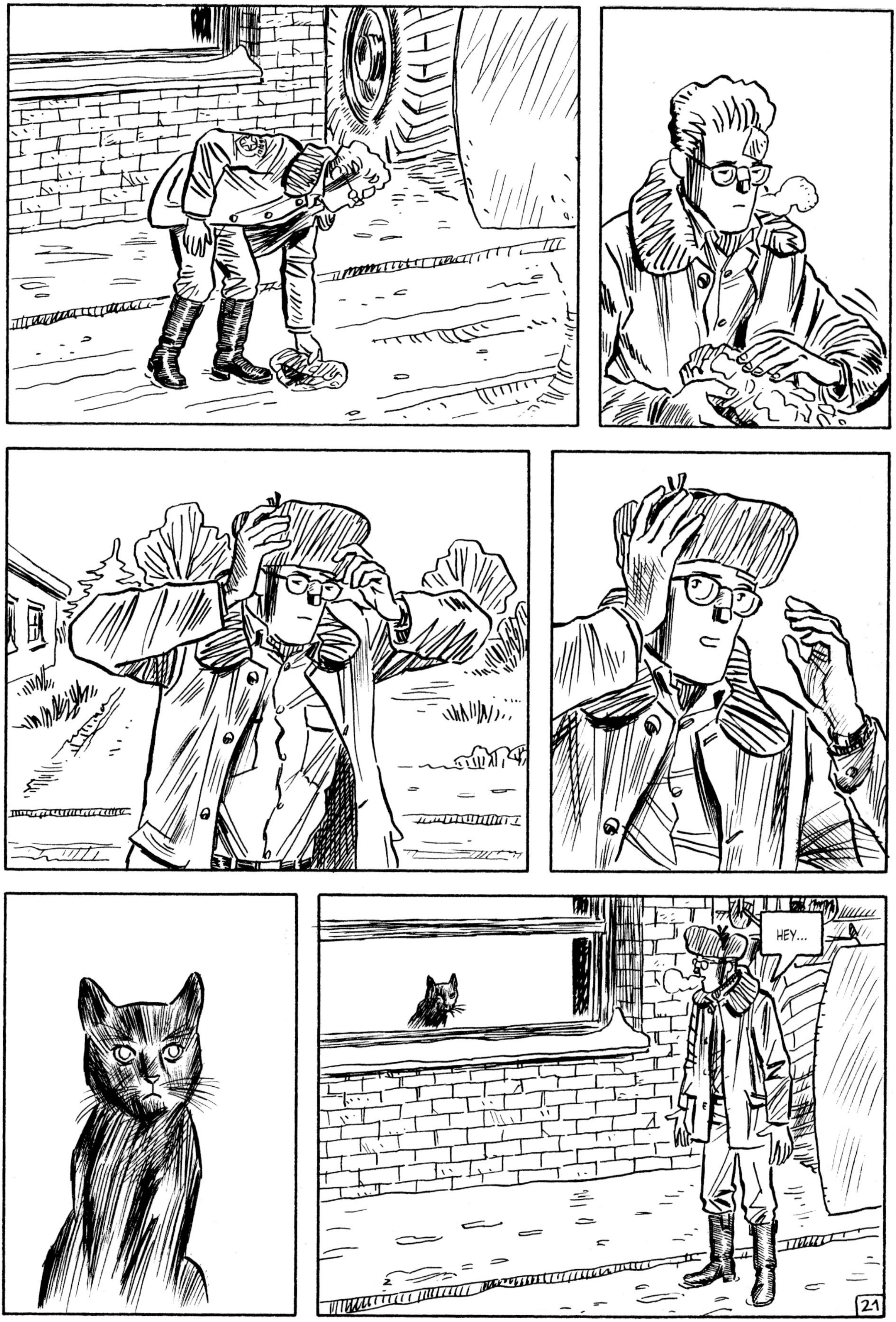
HEY...

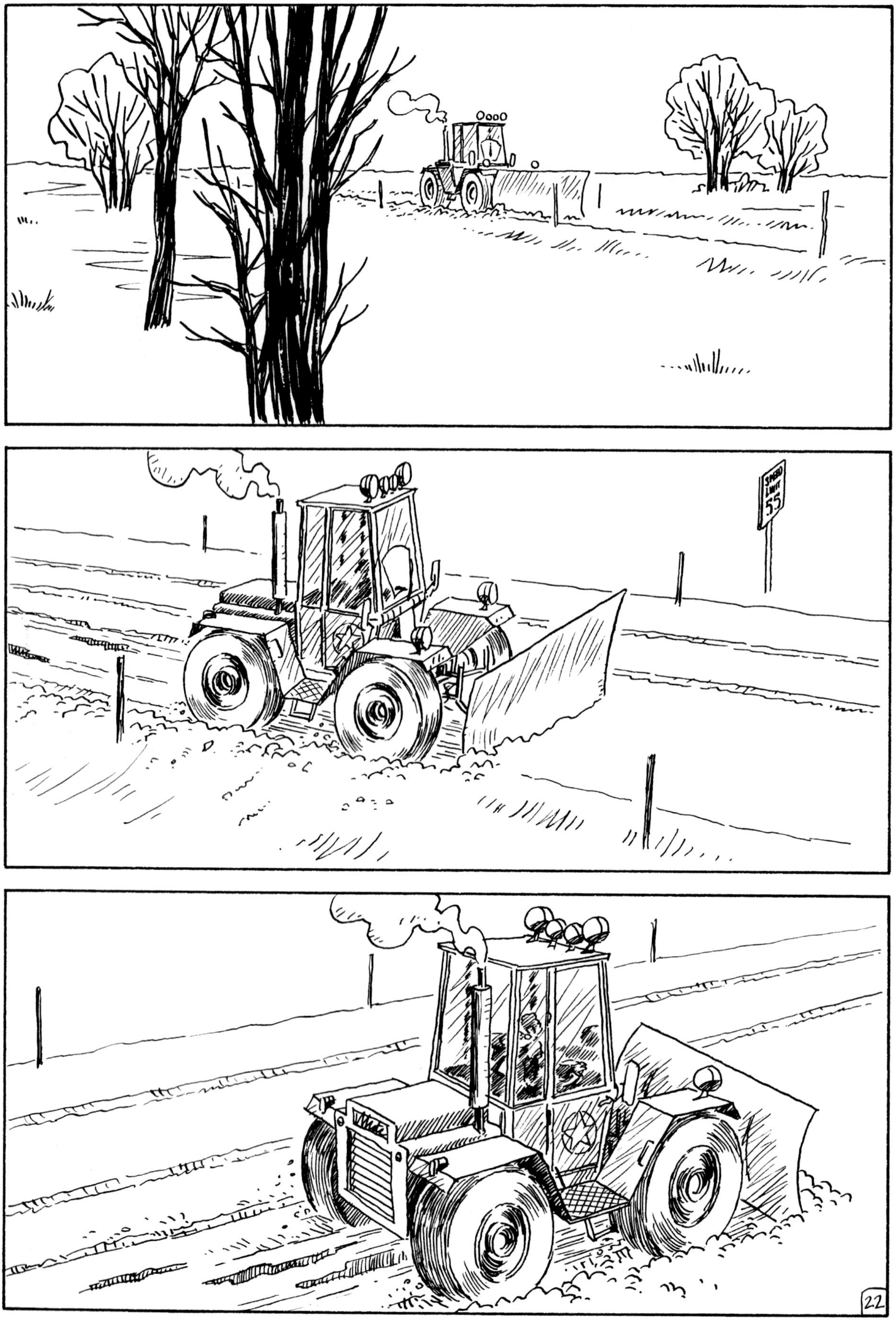
SPEED LIMIT
55

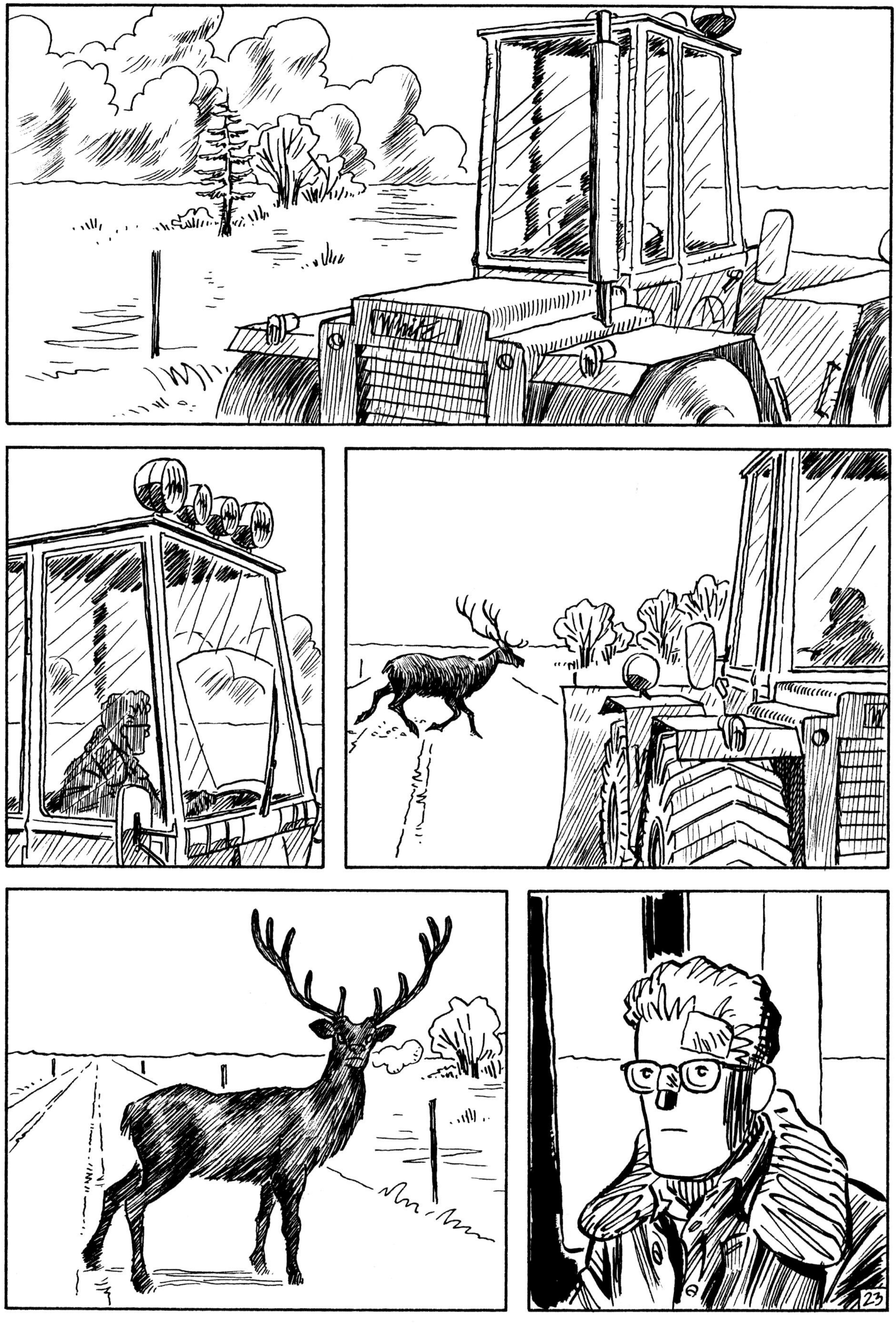

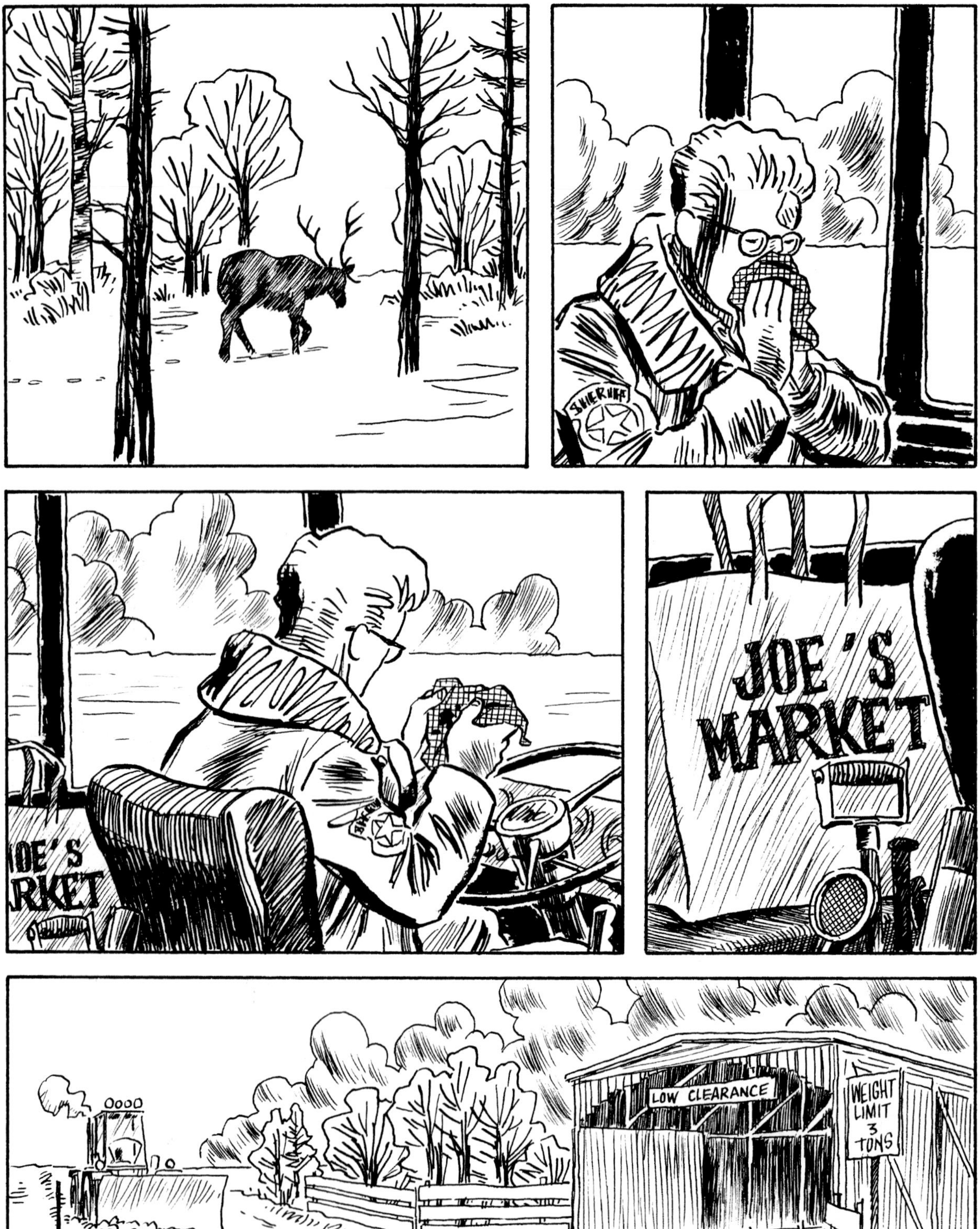
SHERIFF
JOE'S
MARKET
LOW CLEARANCE
WEIGHT
LIMIT
3
TONS

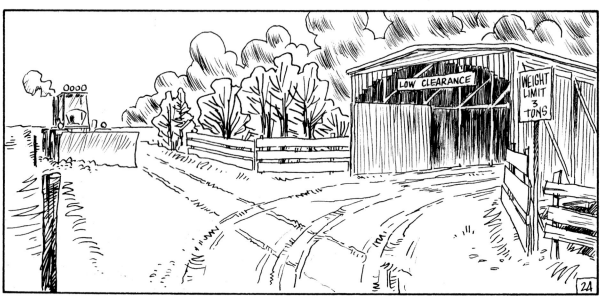

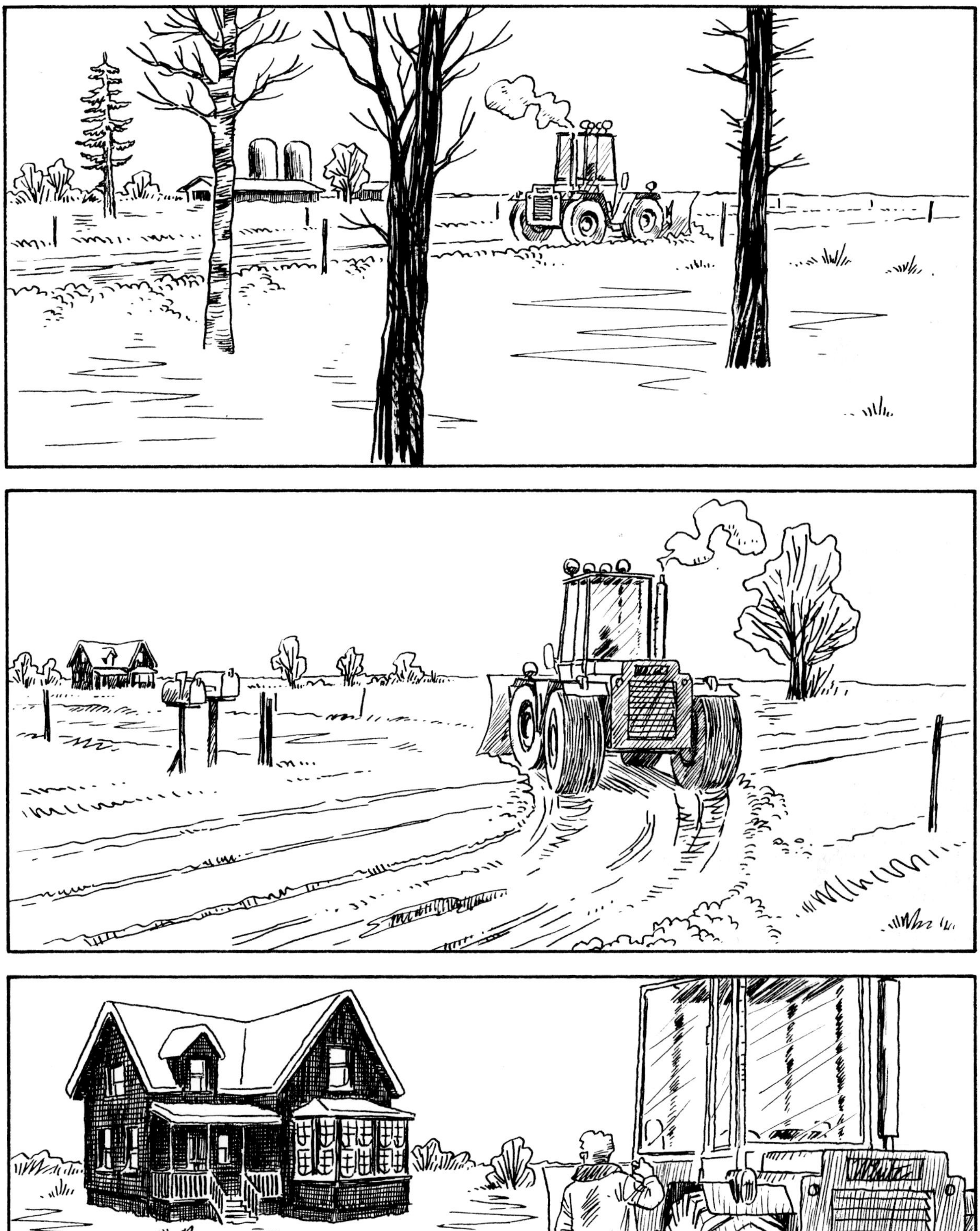

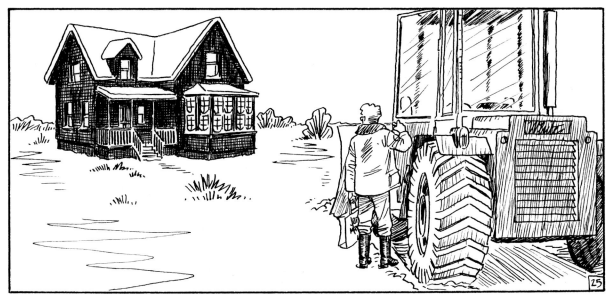

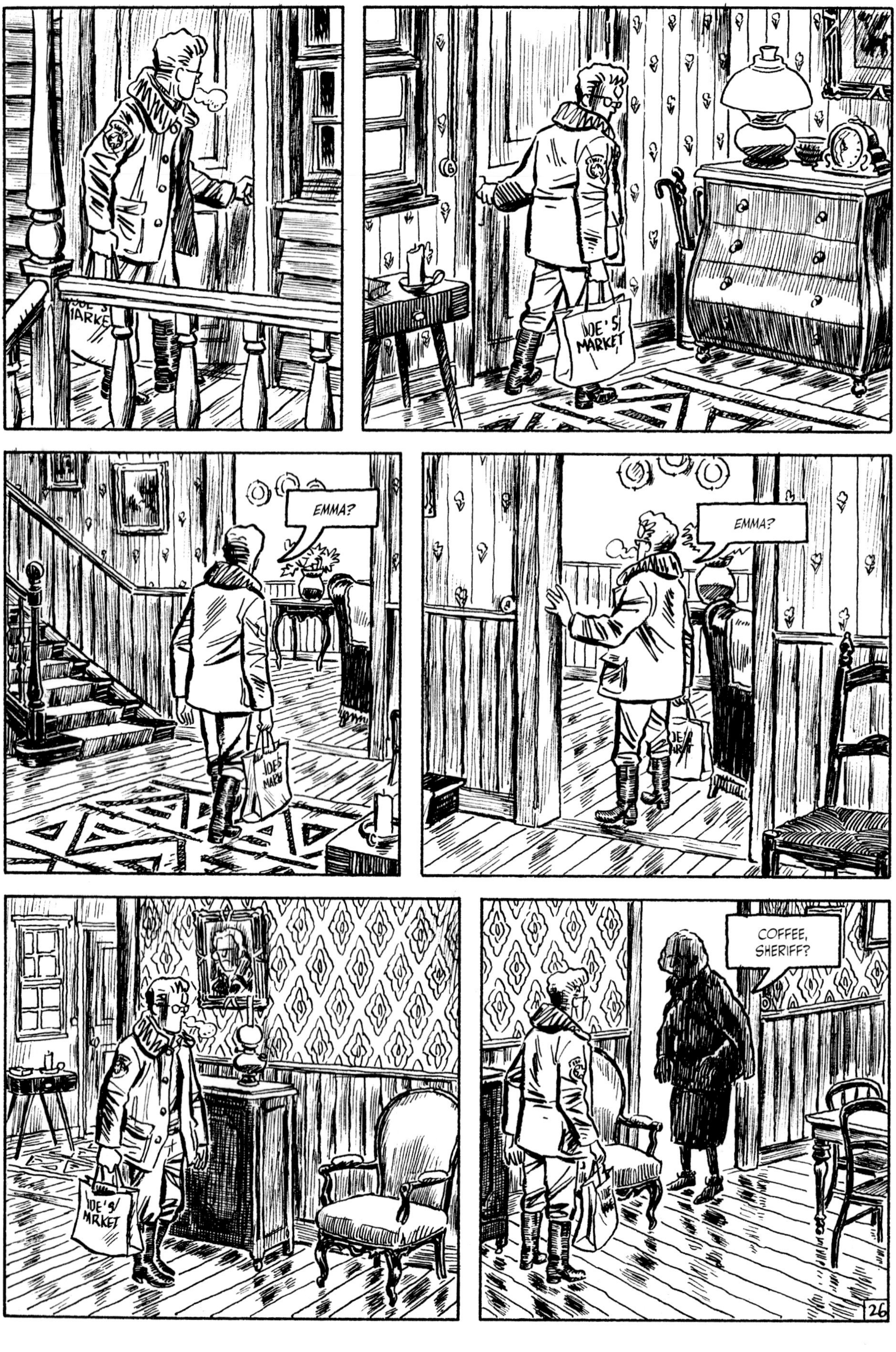
JOE'S MARKET
EMMA?
EMMA?
COFFEE, SHERIFF?

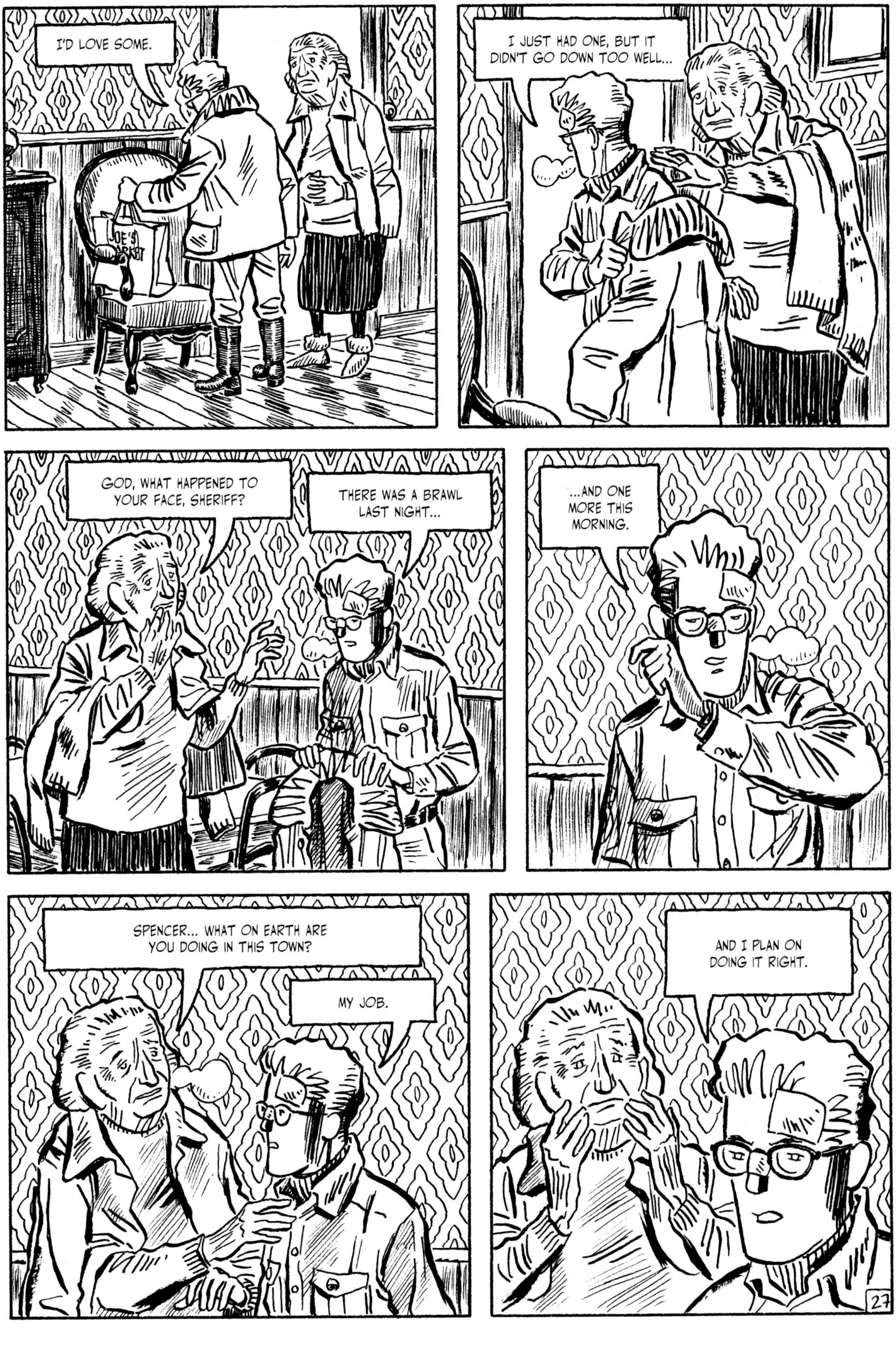
I'D LOVE SOME.
I JUST HAD ONE, BUT IT DIDN'T GO DOWN TOO WELL...
GOD, WHAT HAPPENED TO YOUR FACE, SHERIFF?
THERE WAS A BRAWL LAST NIGHT...
...AND ONE MORE THIS MORNING.
SPENCER... WHAT ON EARTH ARE YOU DOING IN THIS TOWN?
MY JOB.
AND I PLAN ON DOING IT RIGHT.

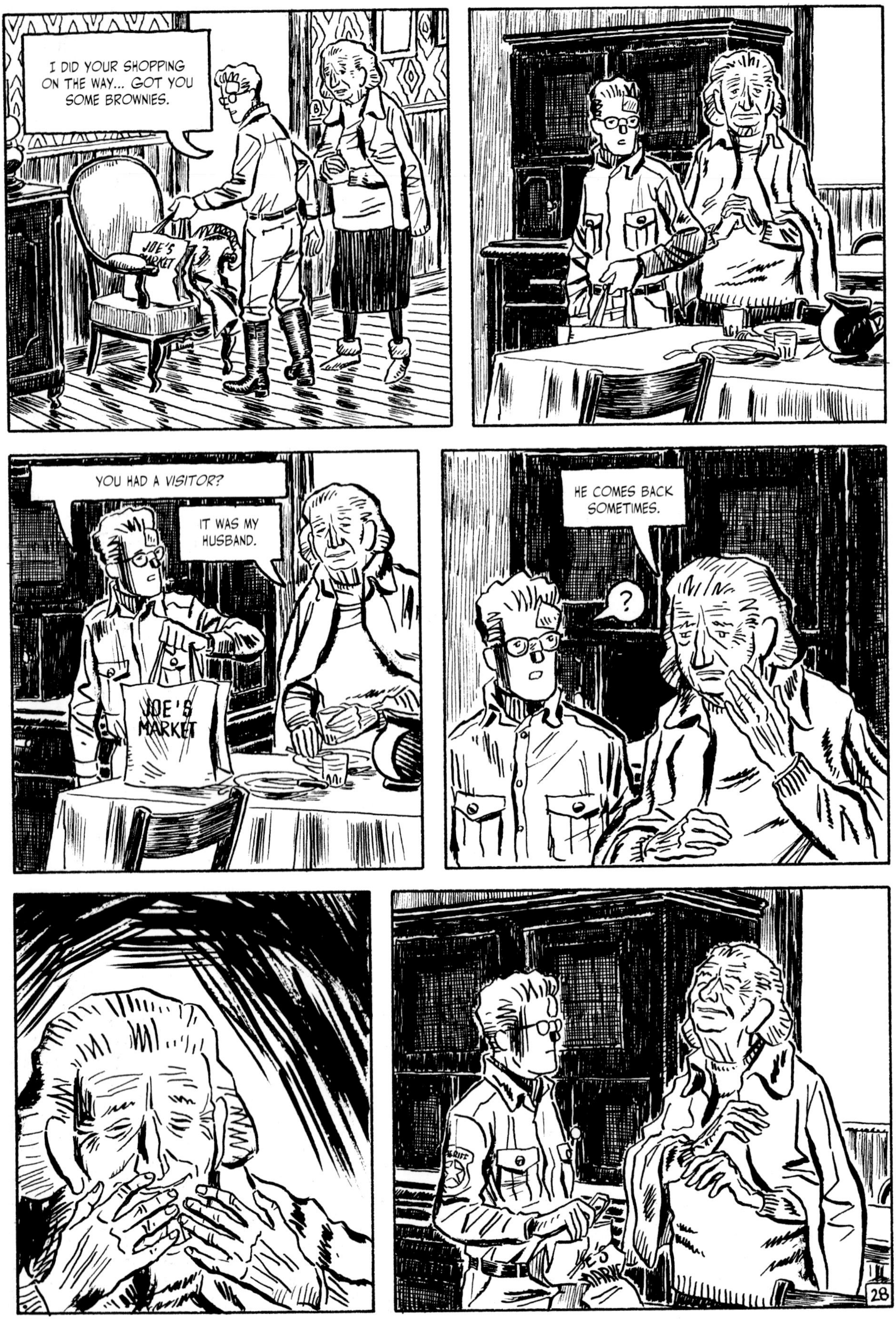
I DID YOUR SHOPPING ON THE WAY... GOT YOU SOME BROWNIES.
JOE'S MARKET
YOU HAD A *VISITOR?*
IT WAS MY HUSBAND.
JOE'S MARKET
HE COMES BACK SOMETIMES.
?

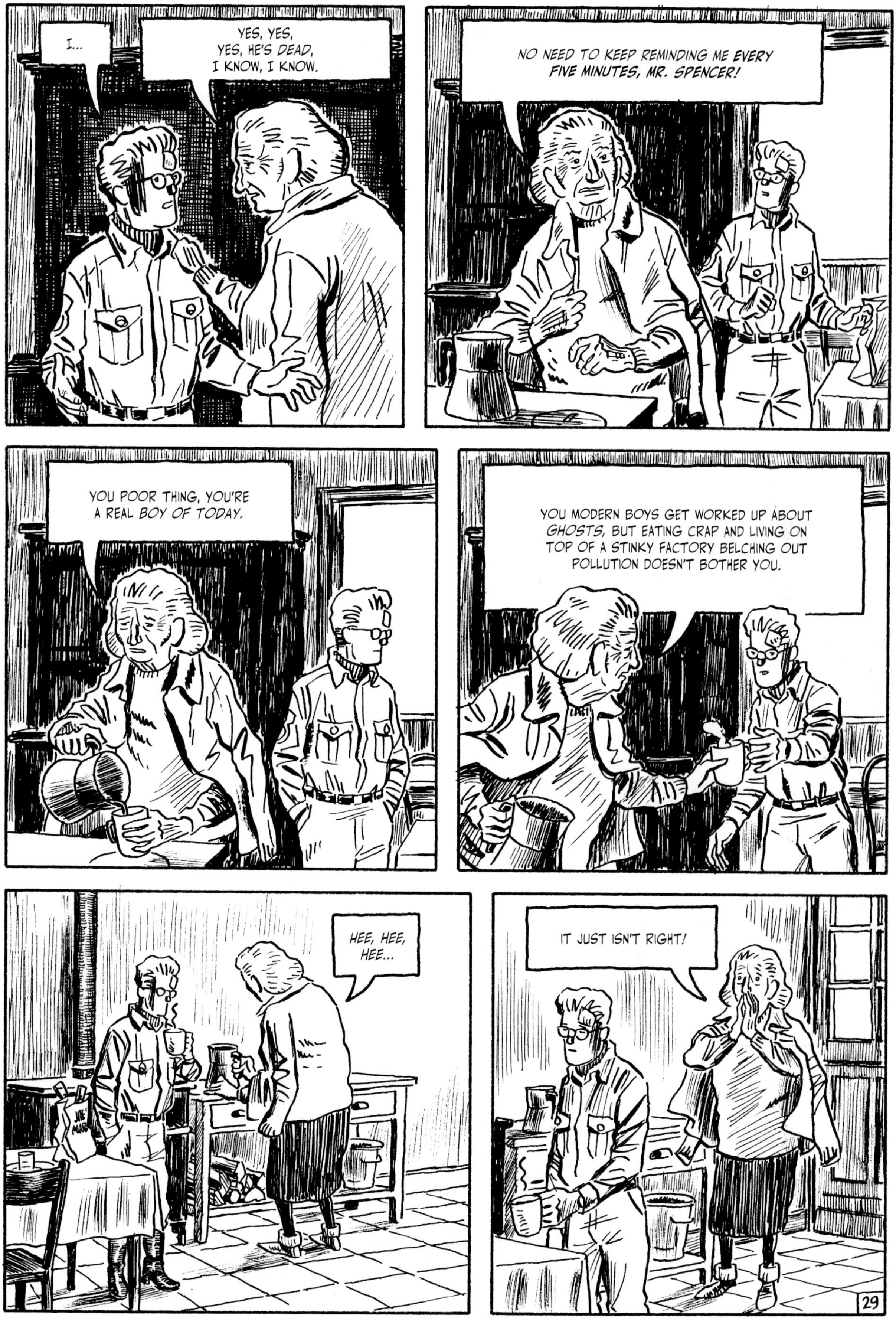
I...
YES, YES, YES, HE'S *DEAD*, I KNOW, I KNOW.
NO NEED TO KEEP REMINDING ME ***EVERY FIVE MINUTES, MR. SPENCER!***
YOU POOR THING, YOU'RE A REAL *BOY OF TODAY.*
YOU MODERN BOYS GET WORKED UP ABOUT *GHOSTS,* BUT EATING CRAP AND LIVING ON TOP OF A STINKY FACTORY BELCHING OUT POLLUTION DOESN'T BOTHER YOU.
HEE, HEE, HEE...
IT JUST ISN'T RIGHT!

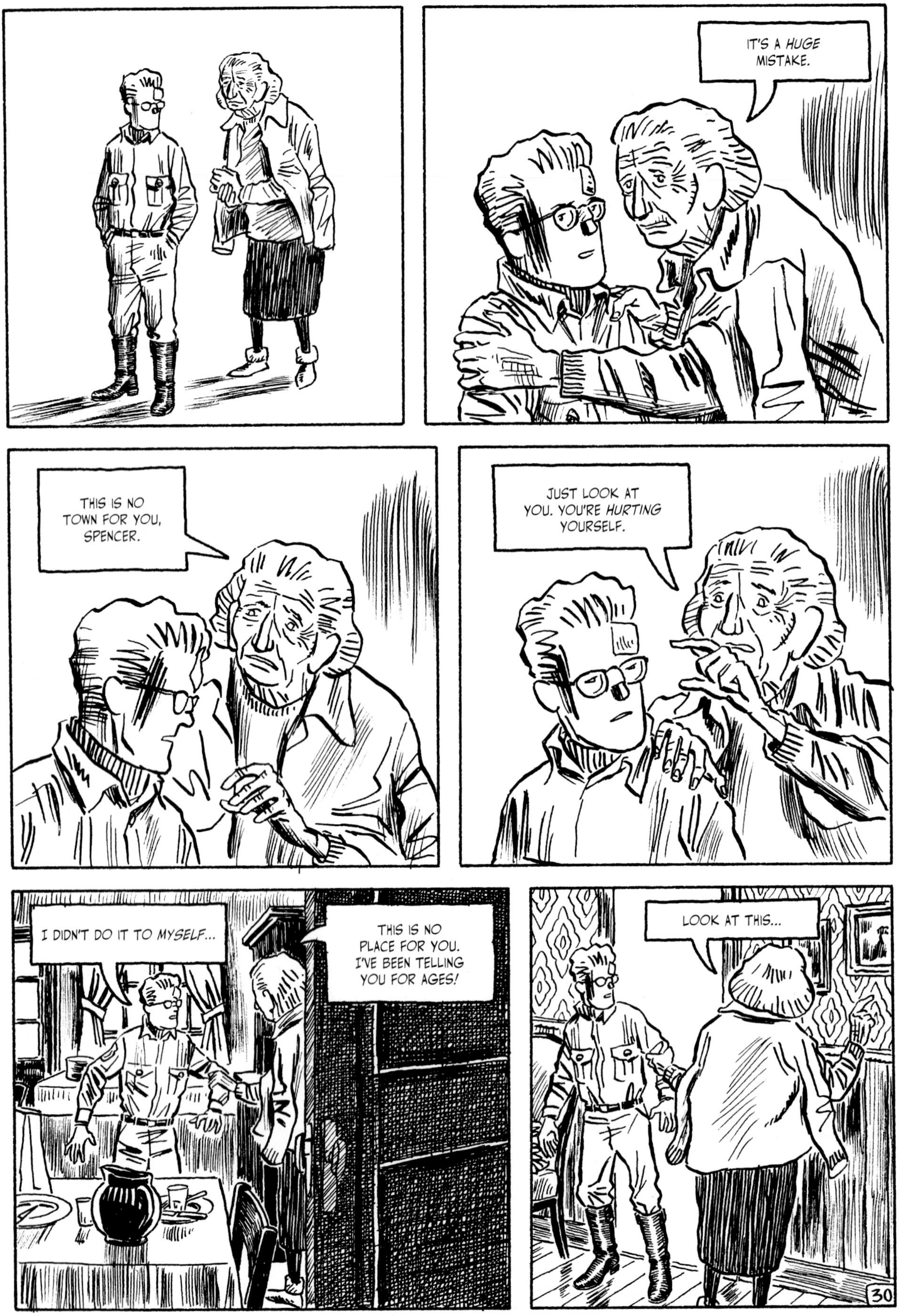
IT'S A *HUGE* MISTAKE.
THIS IS NO TOWN FOR YOU, SPENCER.
JUST LOOK AT YOU. YOU'RE *HURTING* YOURSELF.
I DIDN'T DO IT TO *MYSELF*...
THIS IS NO PLACE FOR YOU. I'VE BEEN TELLING YOU FOR AGES!
LOOK AT THIS...

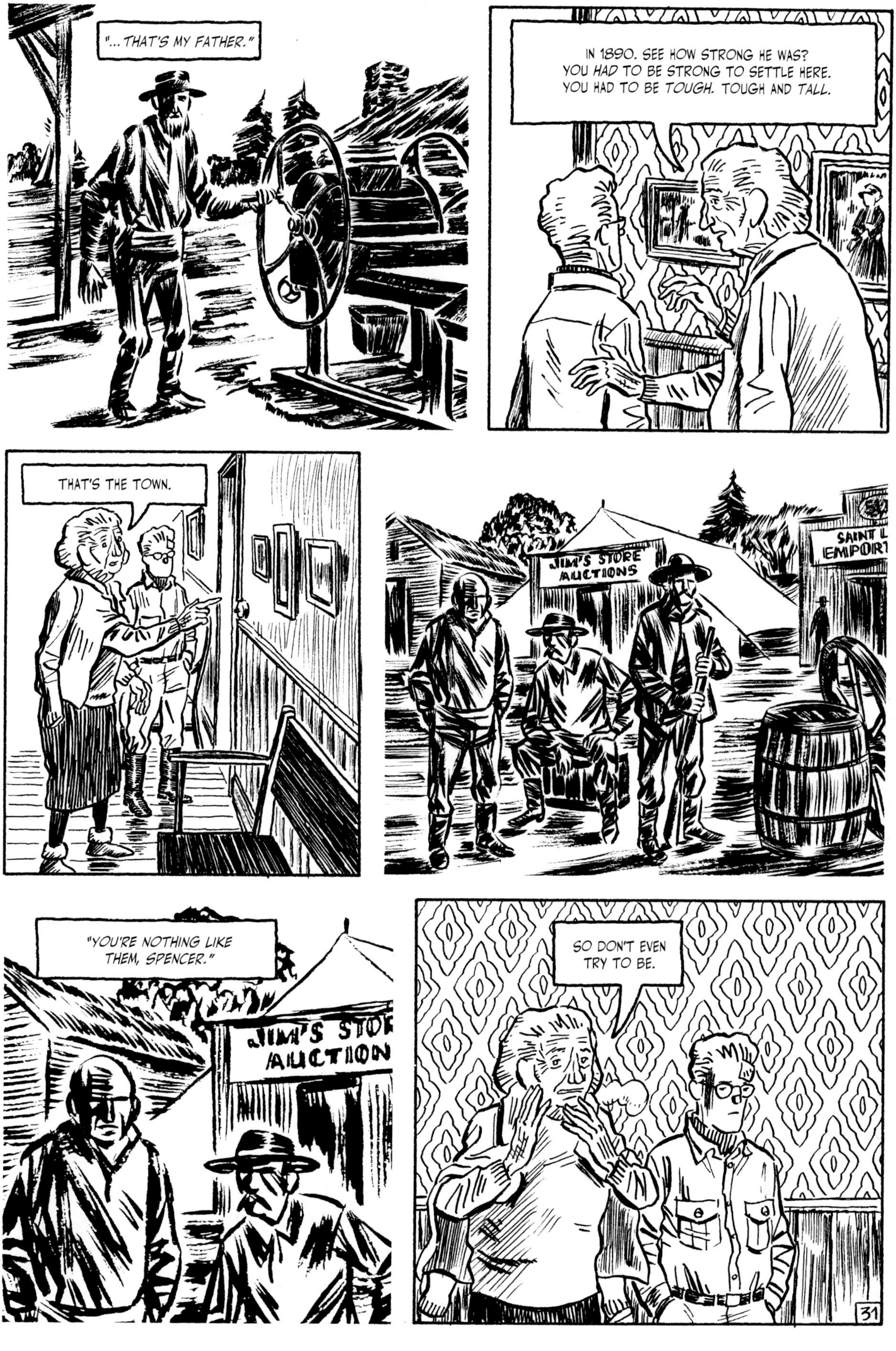
"...THAT'S MY FATHER."
IN 1890. SEE HOW STRONG HE WAS? YOU *HAD* TO BE STRONG TO SETTLE HERE. YOU HAD TO BE *TOUGH.* TOUGH AND *TALL.*
THAT'S THE TOWN.
JIM'S STORE AUCTIONS
SAINT L
EMPORT
"YOU'RE NOTHING LIKE THEM, SPENCER."
JIM'S STOR
AUCTION
SO DON'T EVEN TRY TO BE.

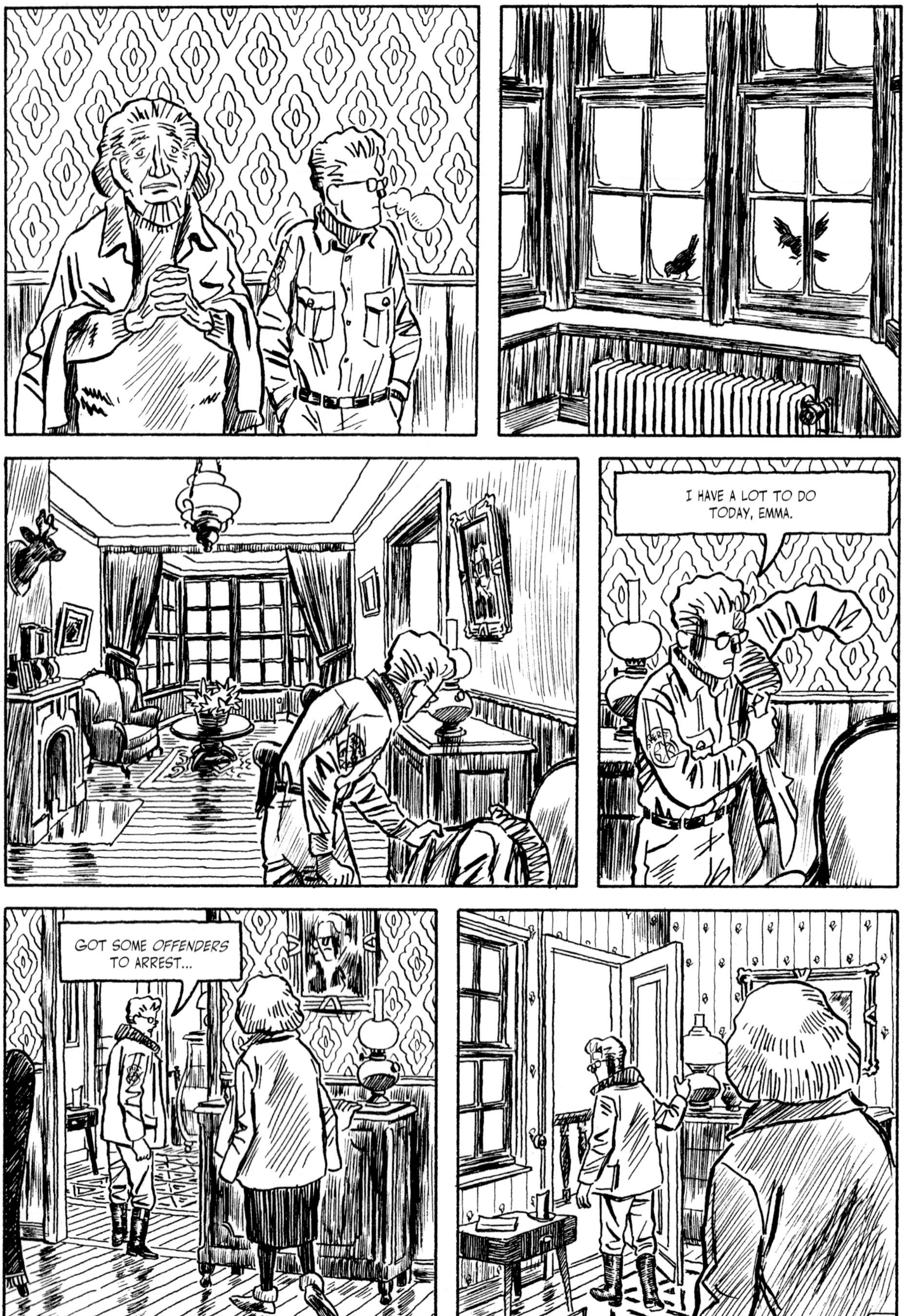
I HAVE A LOT TO DO TODAY, EMMA.
GOT SOME *OFFENDERS* TO ARREST...
SHERIFF

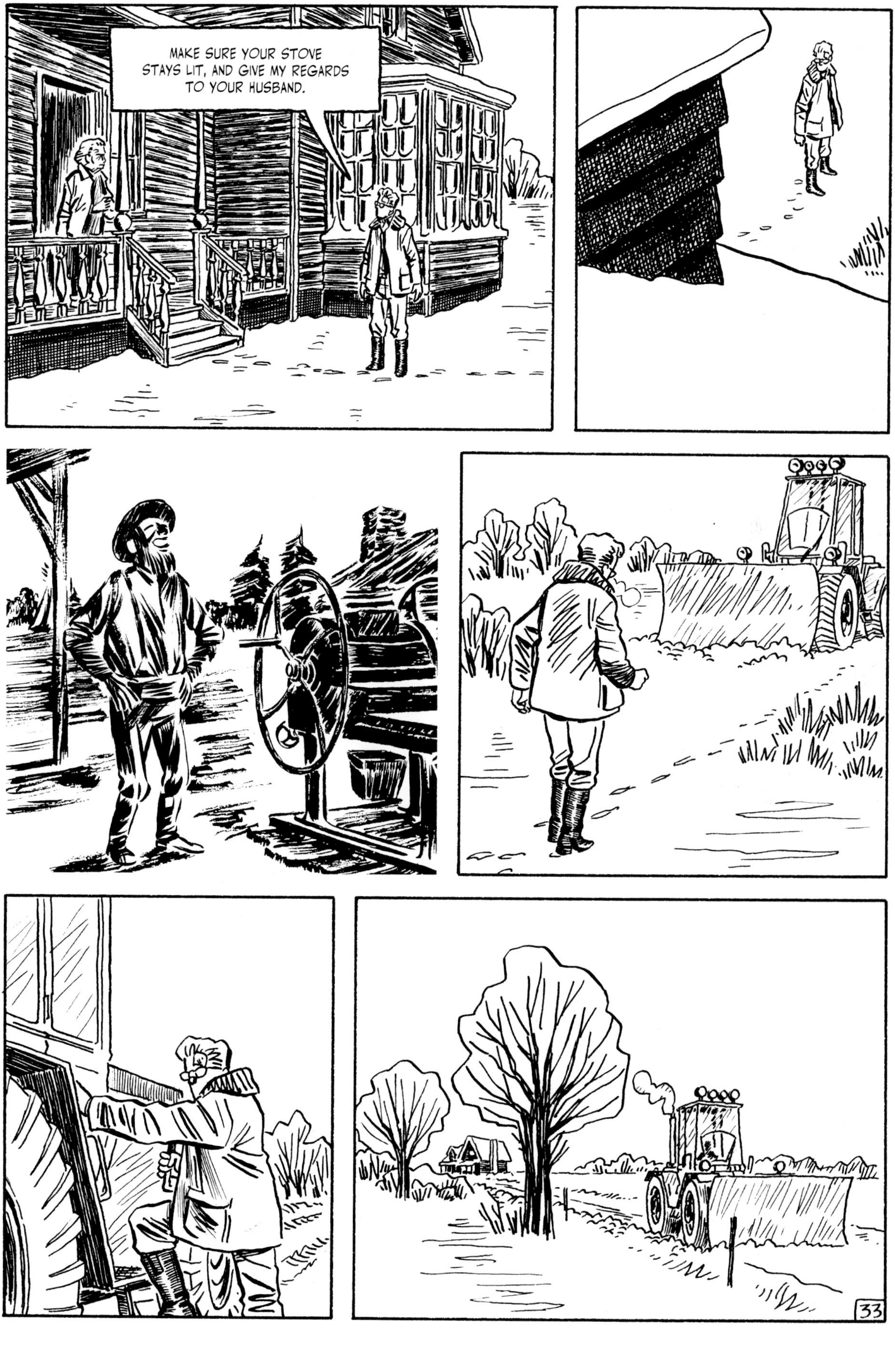
MAKE SURE YOUR STOVE STAYS LIT, AND GIVE MY REGARDS TO YOUR HUSBAND.
33

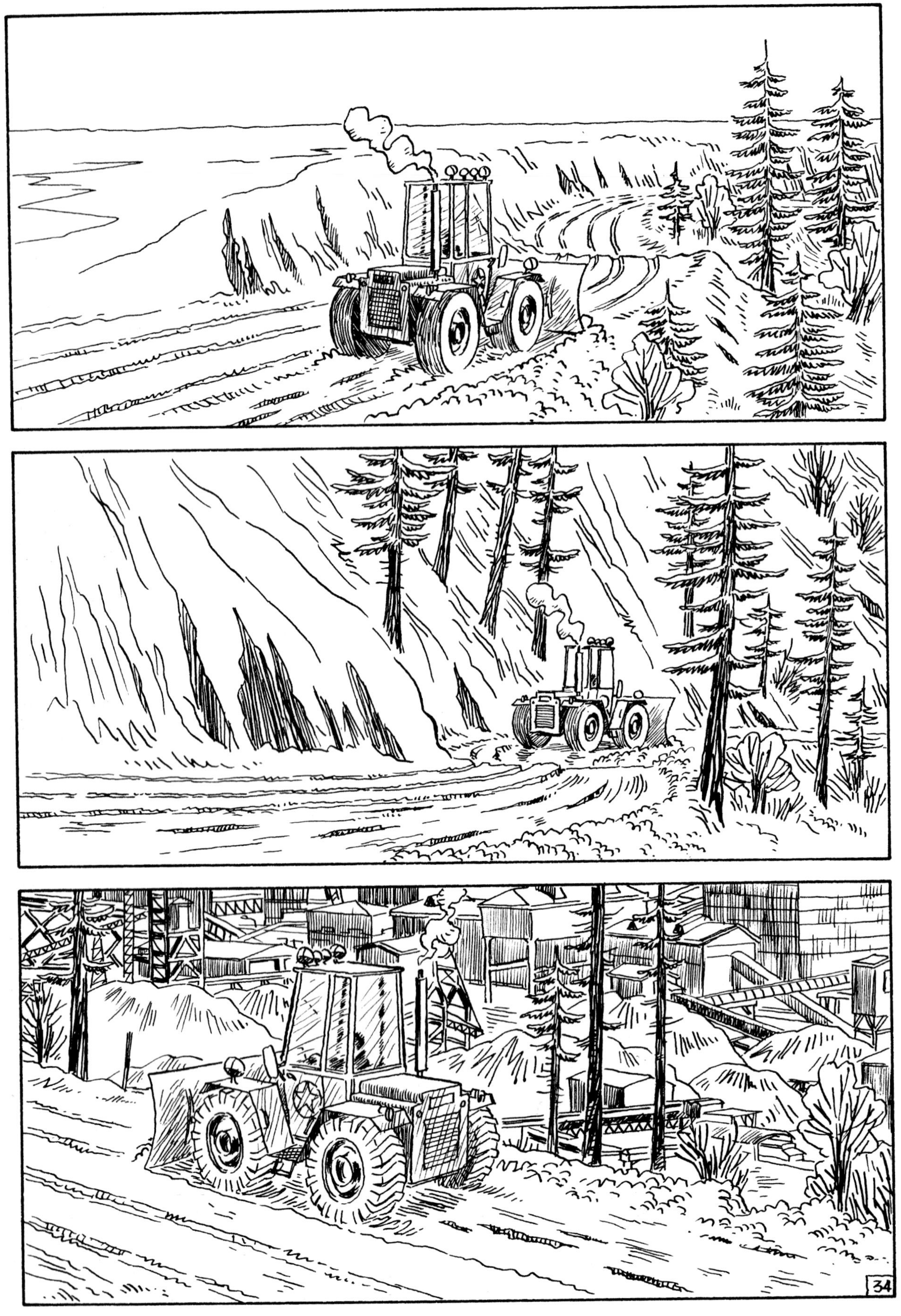

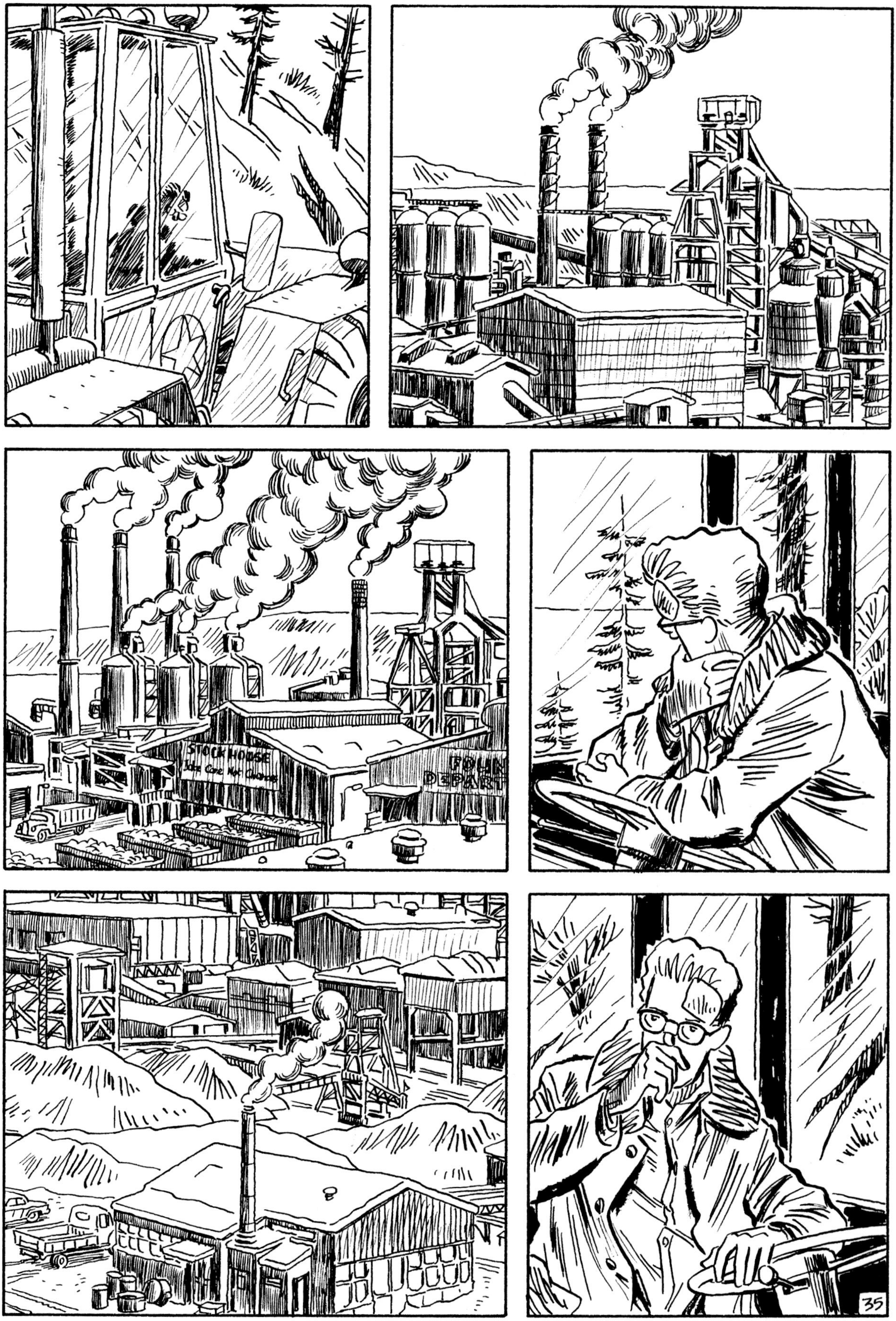
STOCK HOUSE

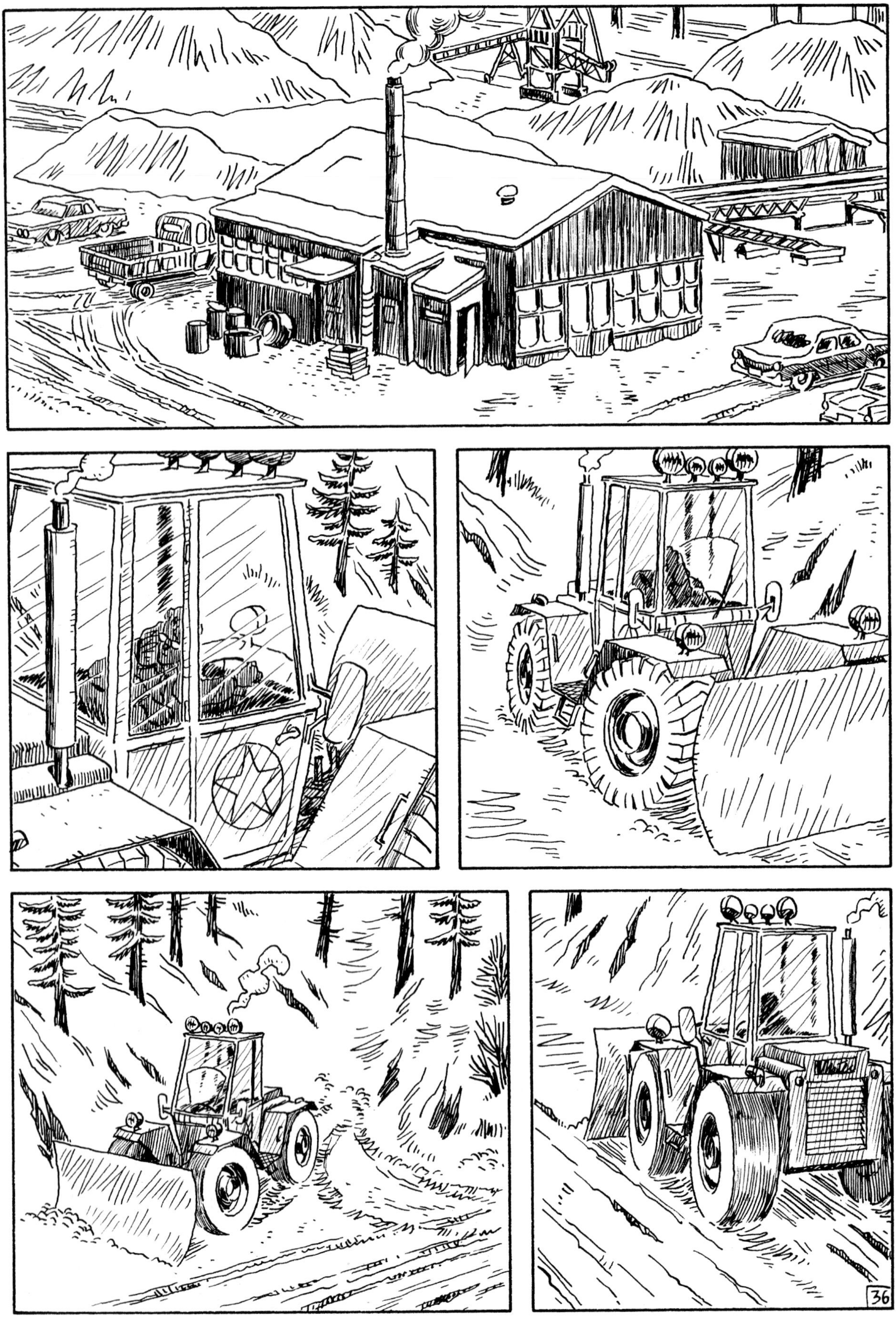

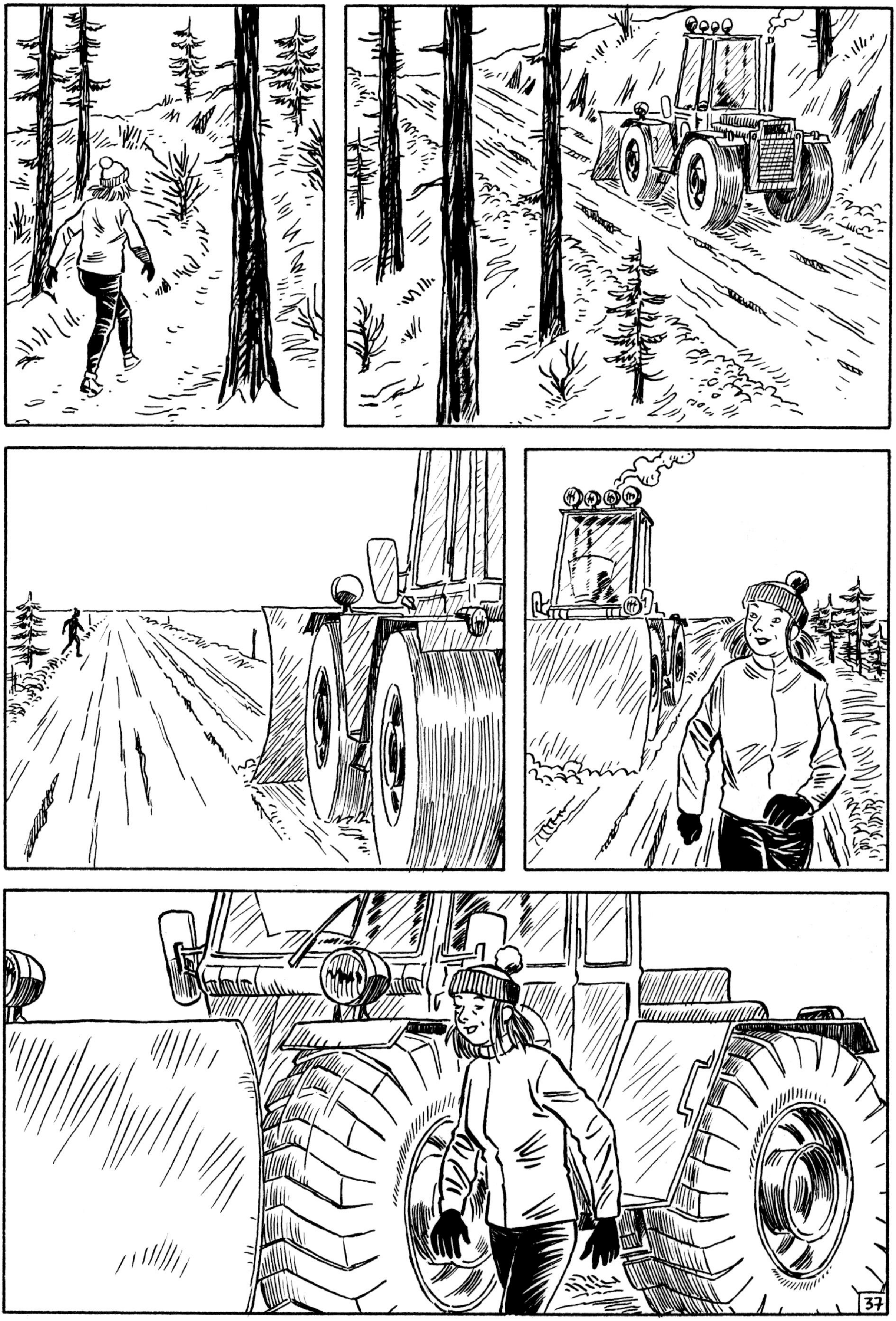

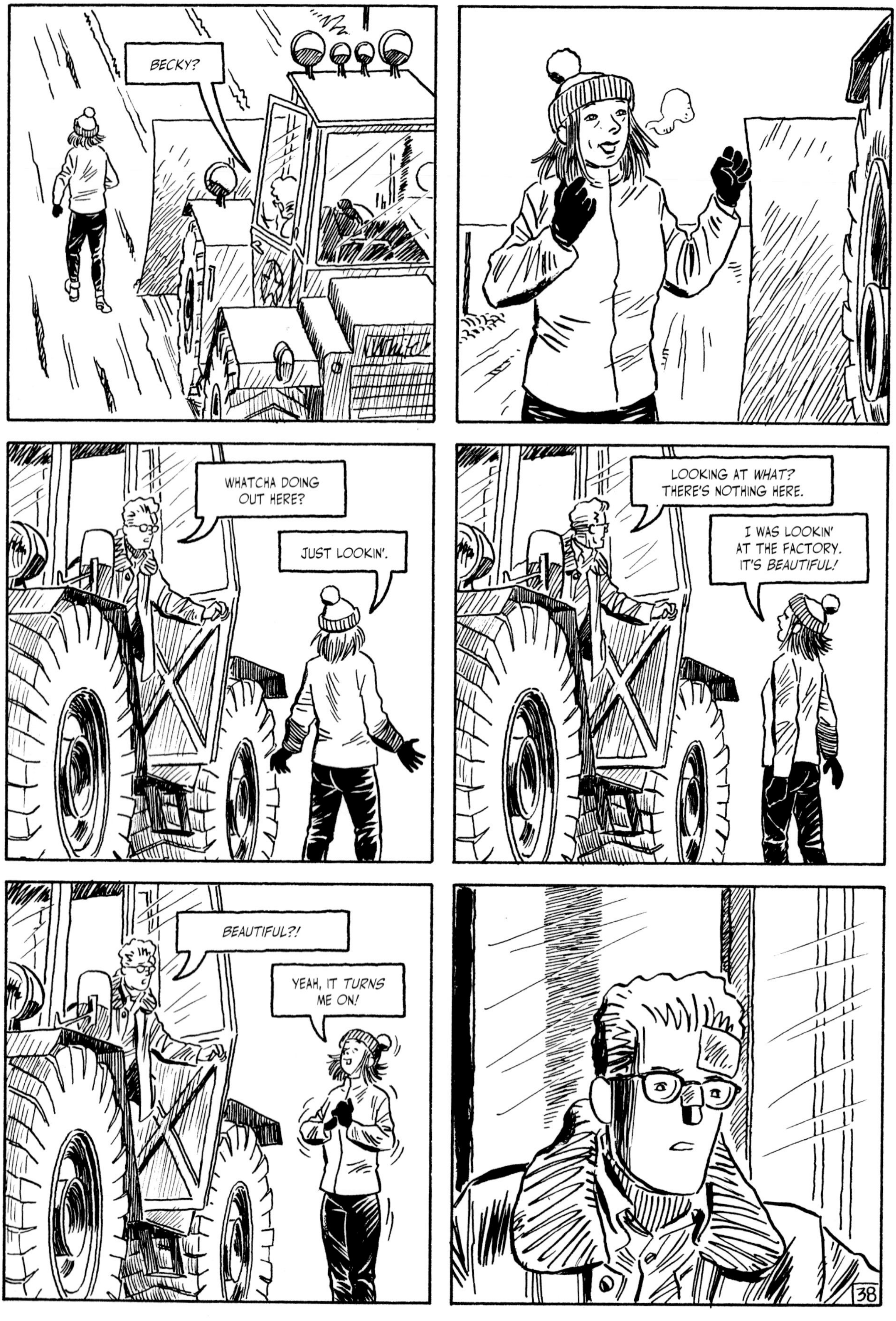
BECKY?
WHATCHA DOING OUT HERE?
JUST LOOKIN'.
LOOKING AT *WHAT?* THERE'S NOTHING HERE.
I WAS LOOKIN' AT THE FACTORY. IT'S *BEAUTIFUL!*
BEAUTIFUL?!
YEAH, IT *TURNS* ME ON!
38

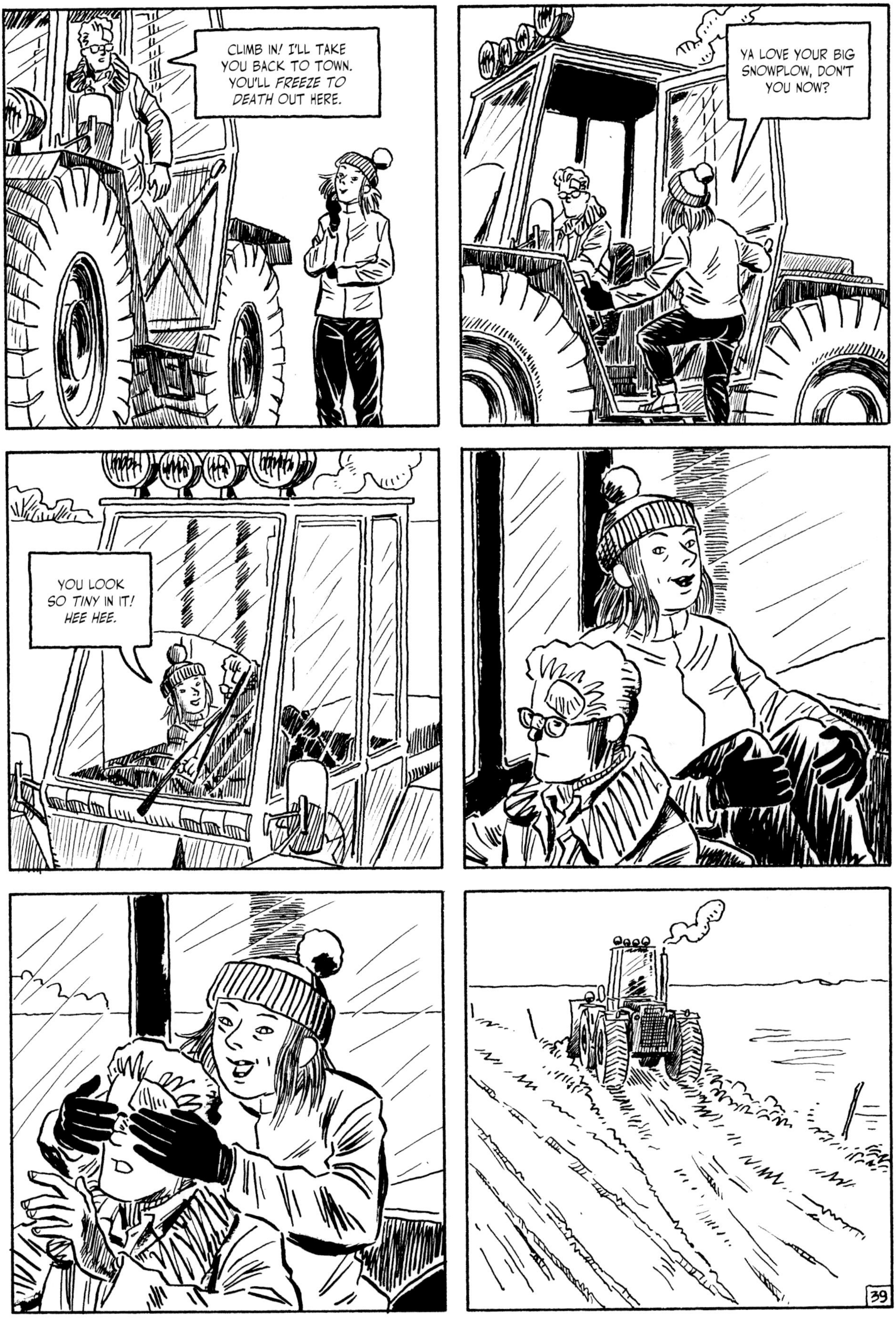
CLIMB IN! I'LL TAKE YOU BACK TO TOWN. YOU'LL *FREEZE TO DEATH* OUT HERE.
YA LOVE YOUR BIG SNOWPLOW, DON'T YOU NOW?
YOU LOOK SO *TINY* IN IT! *HEE HEE.*
39

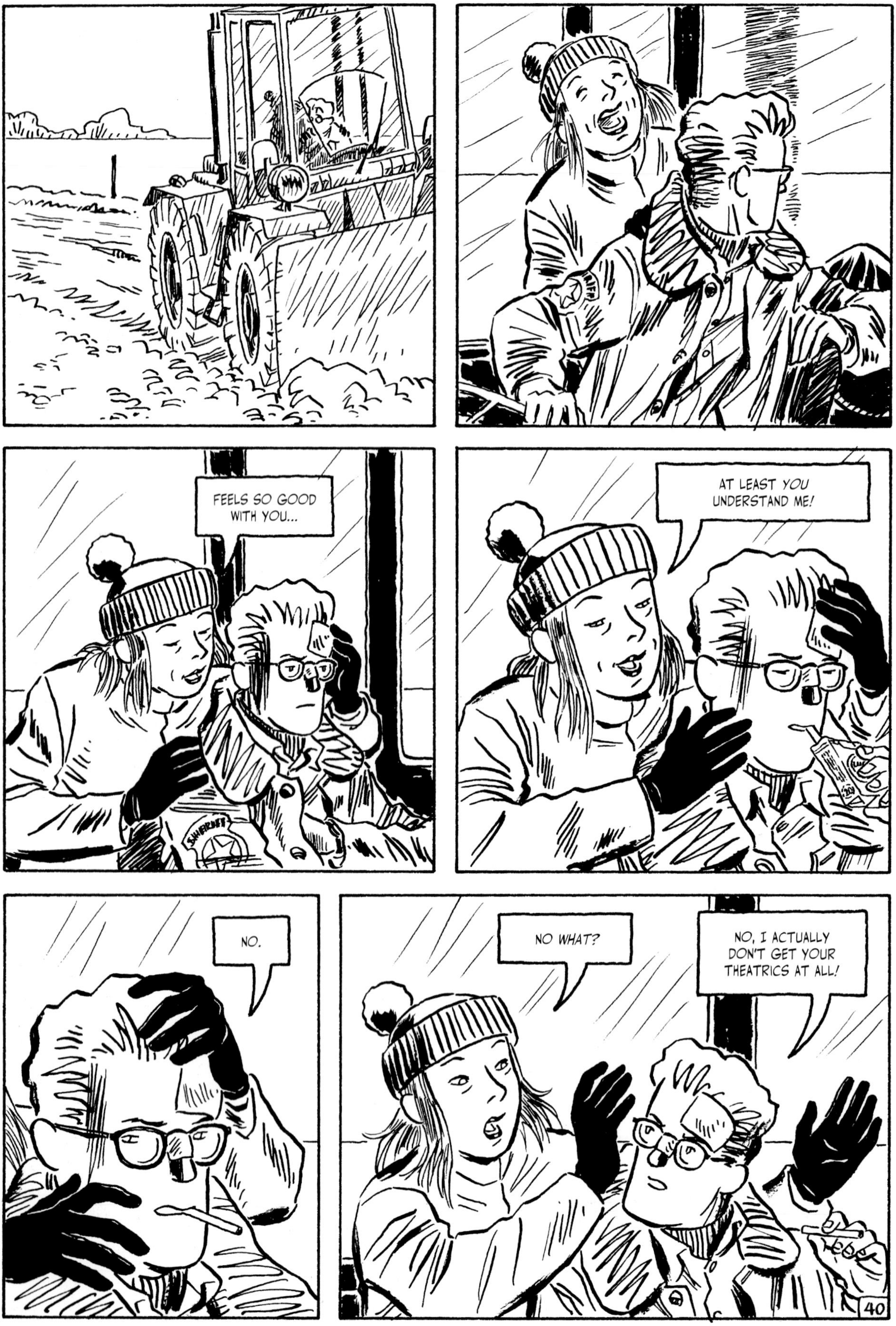
FEELS SO GOOD WITH YOU...
AT LEAST YOU UNDERSTAND ME!
NO.
NO WHAT?
NO, I ACTUALLY DON'T GET YOUR THEATRICS AT ALL!
40

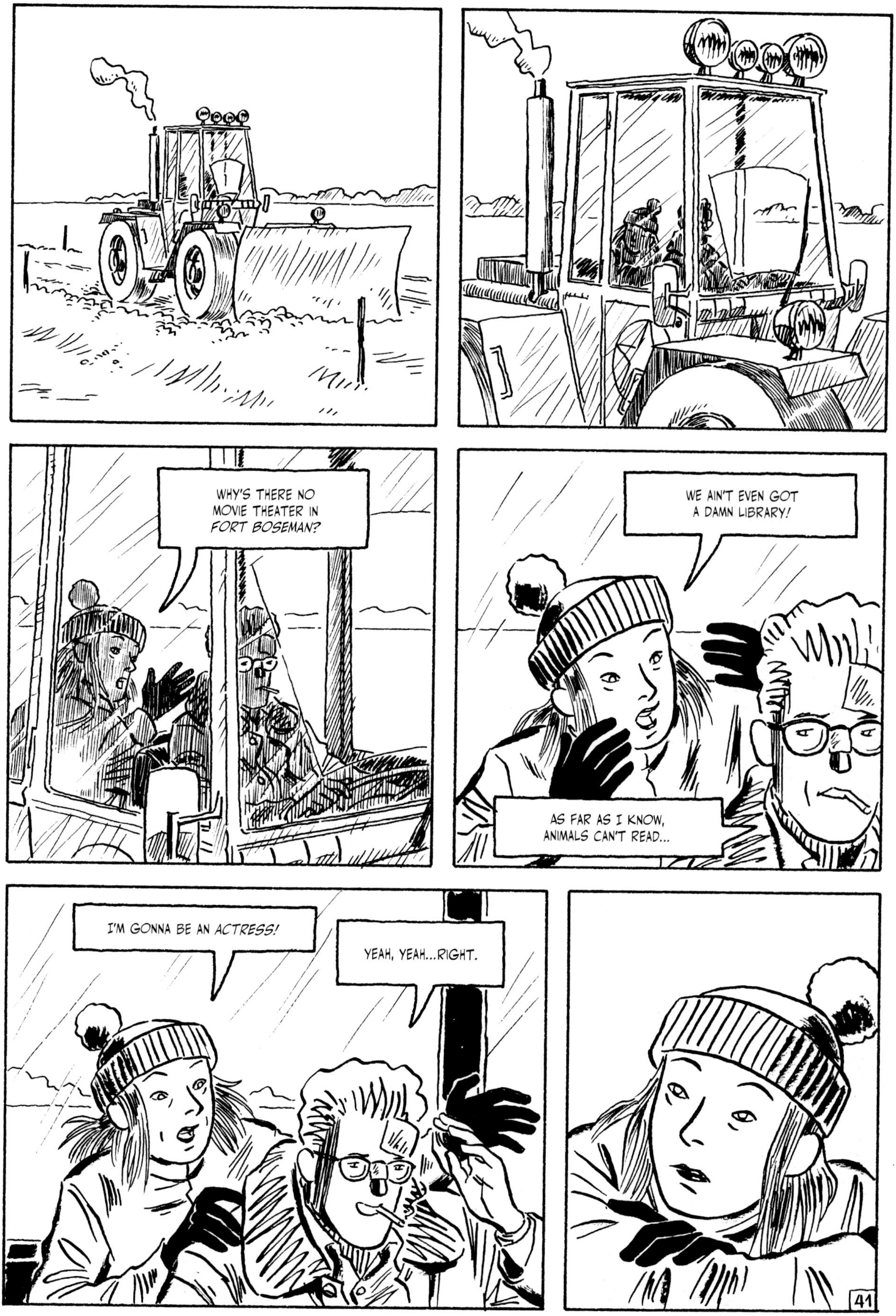
WHY'S THERE NO MOVIE THEATER IN *FORT BOSEMAN?*
WE AIN'T EVEN GOT A DAMN *LIBRARY!*
AS FAR AS I KNOW, ANIMALS CAN'T READ...
I'M GONNA BE AN *ACTRESS!*
YEAH, YEAH...RIGHT.
41

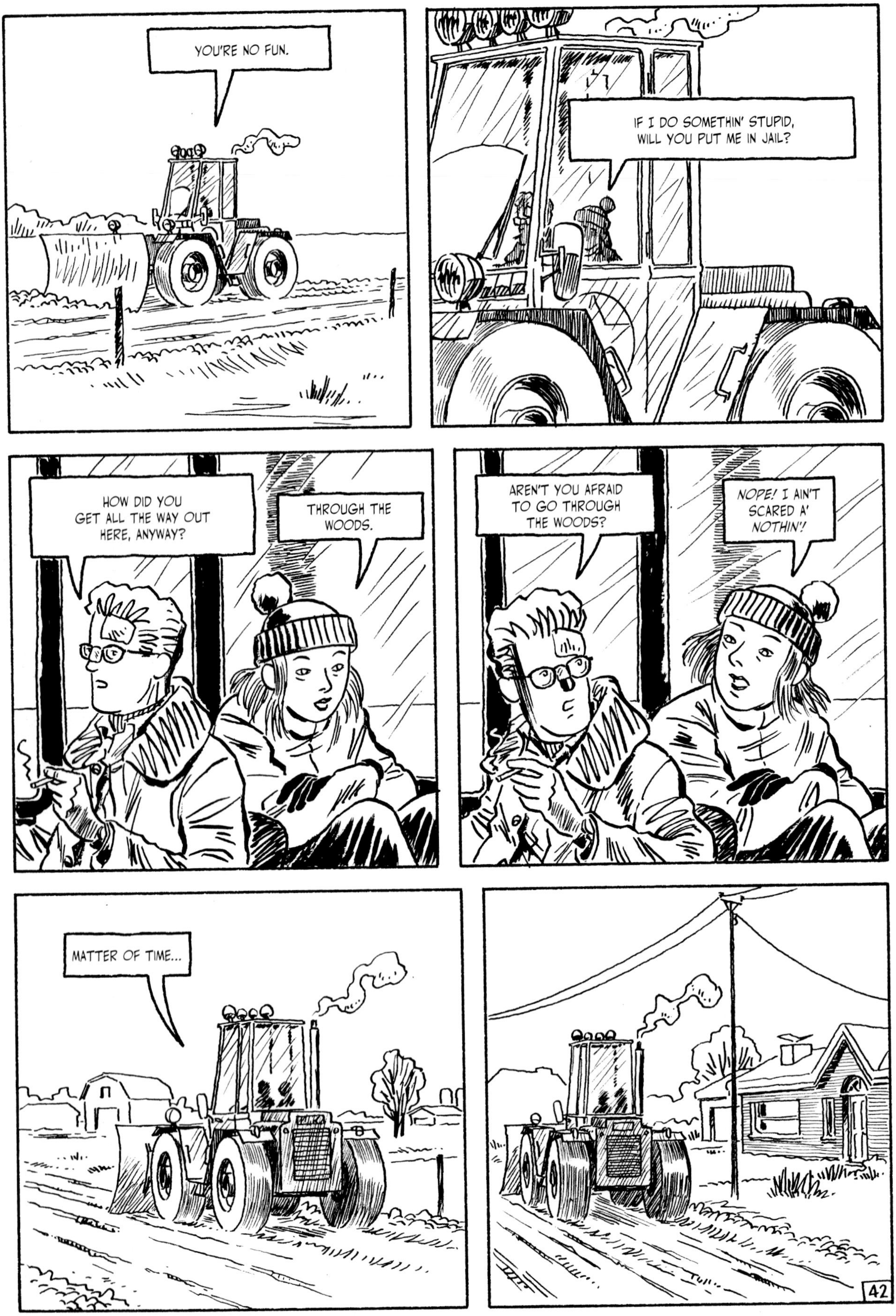

YOU'RE NO FUN.
IF I DO SOMETHIN' STUPID, WILL YOU PUT ME IN JAIL?
HOW DID YOU GET ALL THE WAY OUT HERE, ANYWAY?
THROUGH THE WOODS.
AREN'T YOU AFRAID TO GO THROUGH THE WOODS?
NOPE! I AIN'T SCARED A' *NOTHIN'!*
MATTER OF TIME...

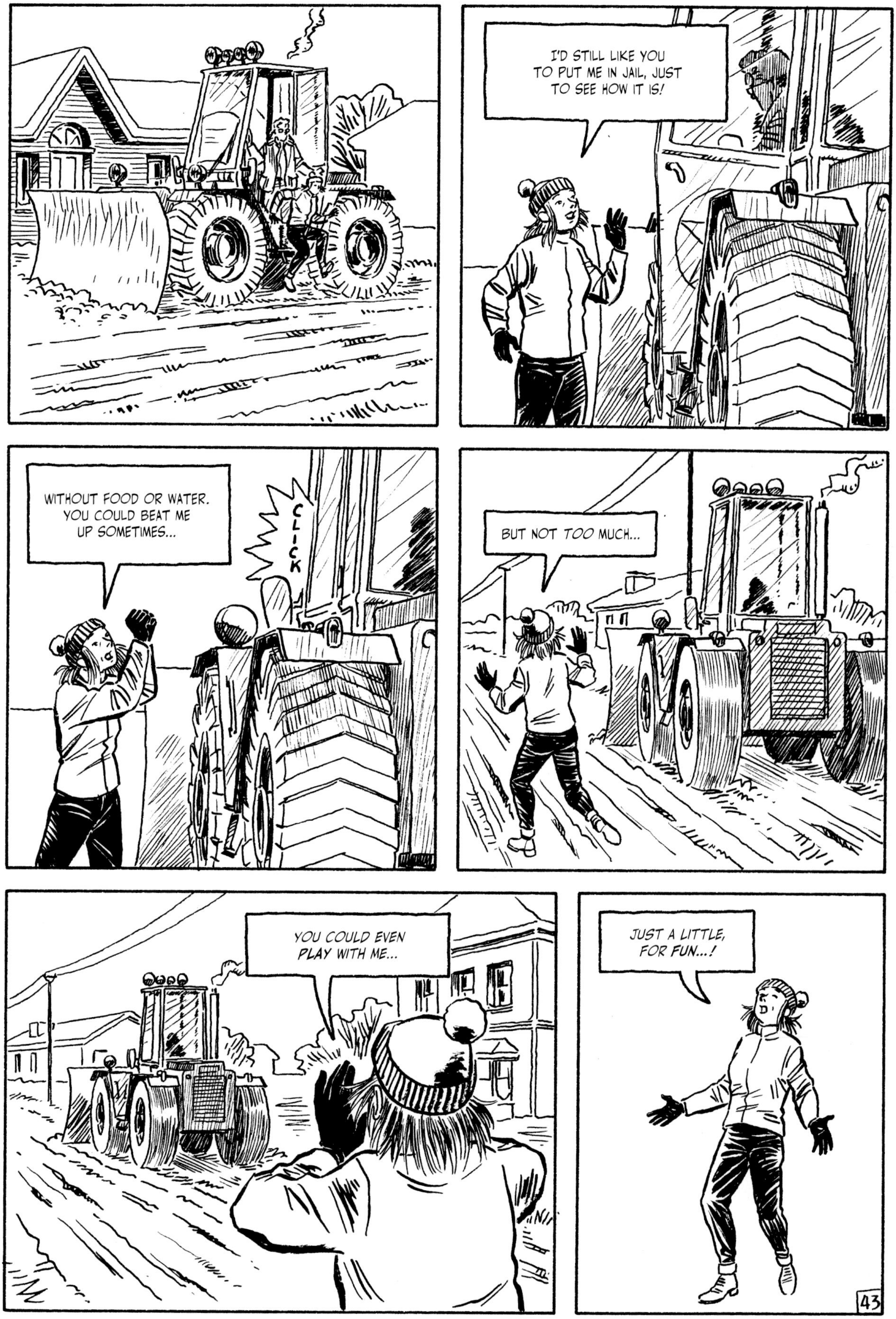
I'D STILL LIKE YOU TO PUT ME IN JAIL, JUST TO SEE HOW IT IS!
WITHOUT FOOD OR WATER. YOU COULD BEAT ME UP SOMETIMES...
CLICK
BUT NOT TOO MUCH...
YOU COULD EVEN PLAY WITH ME...
JUST A LITTLE, FOR FUN...!

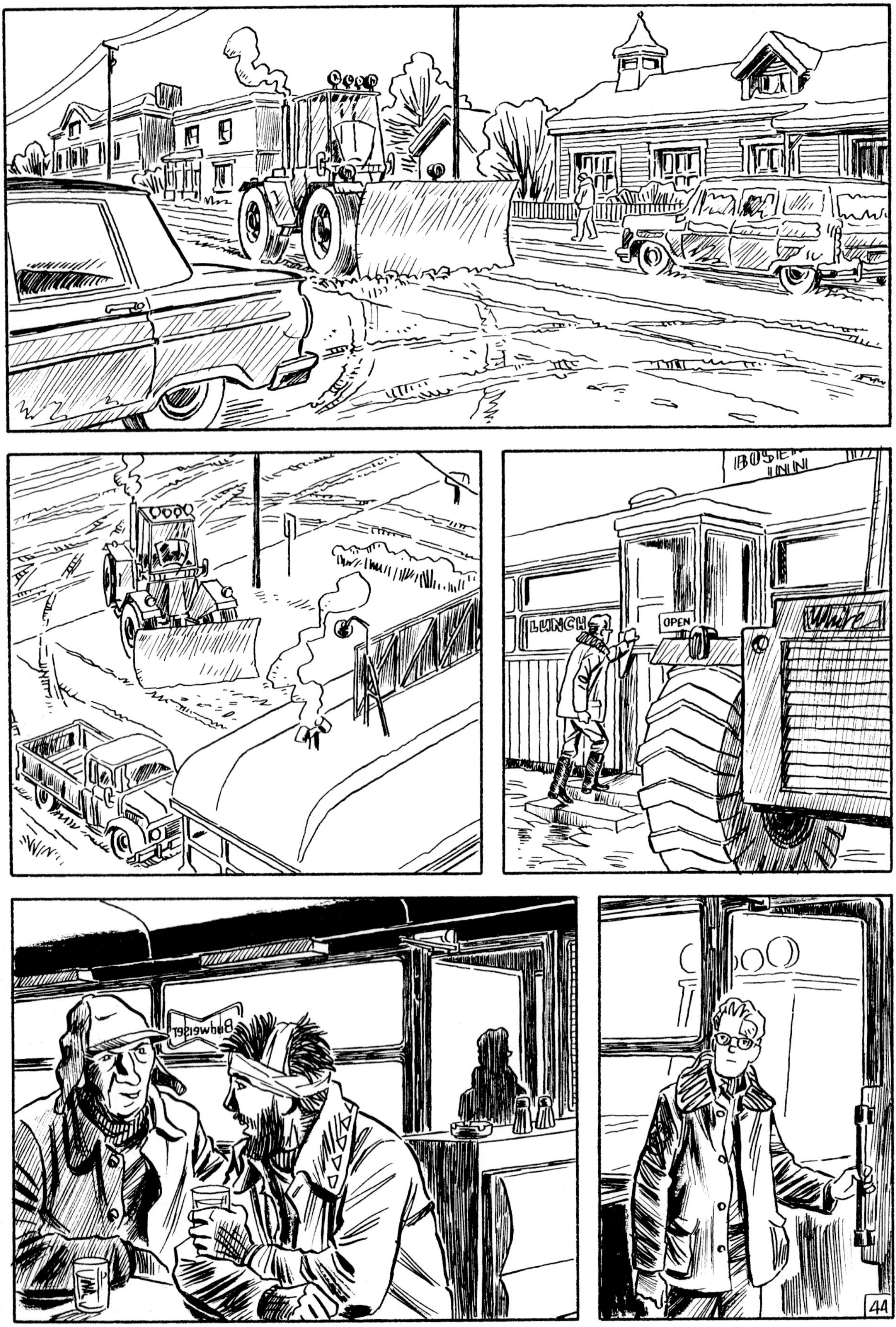
LUNCH
OPEN
Budweiser

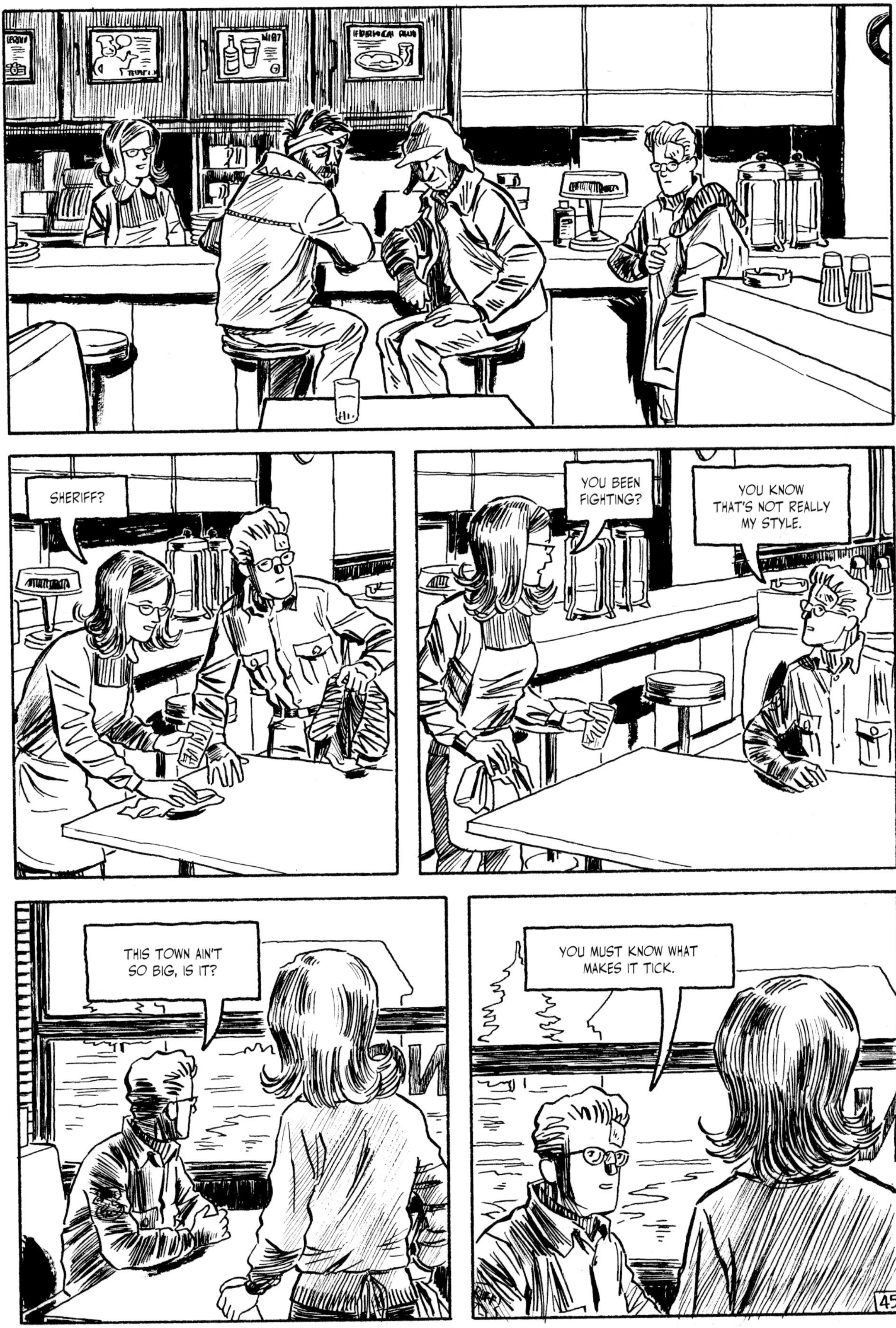
SHERIFF?
YOU BEEN FIGHTING?
YOU KNOW THAT'S NOT REALLY MY STYLE.
THIS TOWN AIN'T SO BIG, IS IT?
YOU MUST KNOW WHAT MAKES IT TICK.

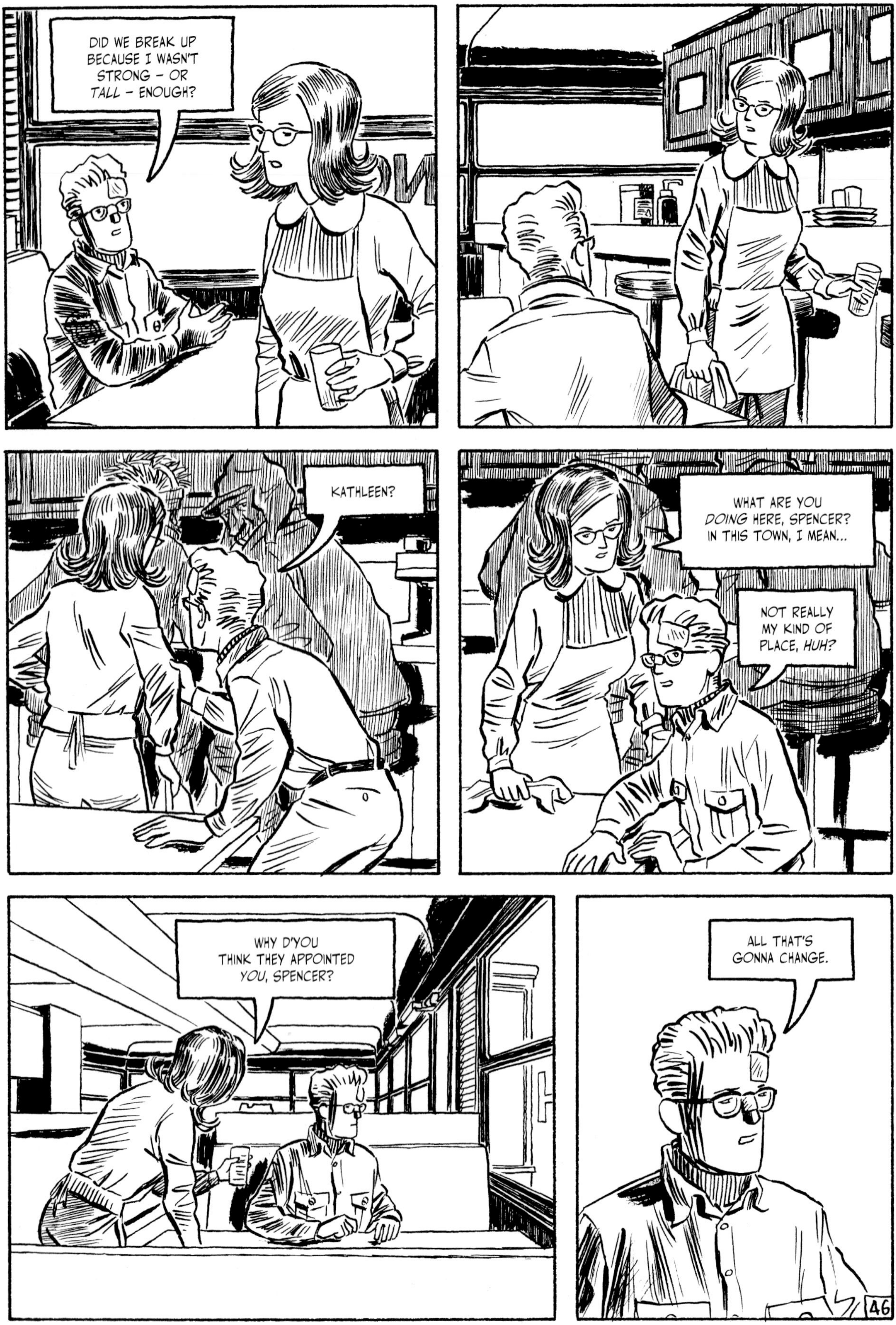
DID WE BREAK UP BECAUSE I WASN'T STRONG – OR *TALL* – ENOUGH?
KATHLEEN?
WHAT ARE YOU *DOING* HERE, SPENCER? IN THIS TOWN, I MEAN...
NOT REALLY MY KIND OF PLACE, *HUH?*
WHY D'YOU THINK THEY APPOINTED *YOU*, SPENCER?
ALL THAT'S GONNA CHANGE.
46

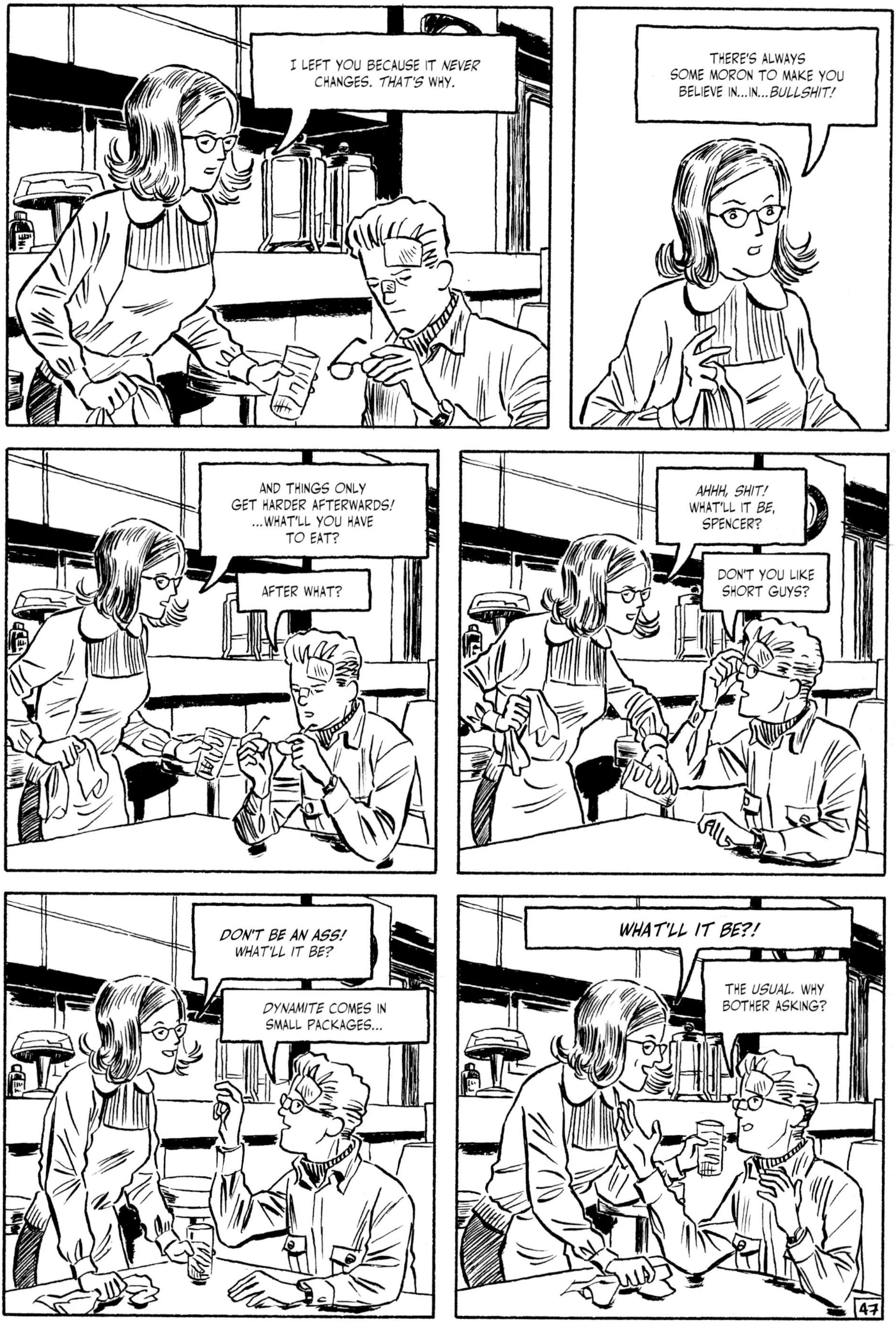
I LEFT YOU BECAUSE IT *NEVER* CHANGES. *THAT'S* WHY.
THERE'S ALWAYS SOME MORON TO MAKE YOU BELIEVE IN...IN...*BULLSHIT!*
AND THINGS ONLY GET HARDER AFTERWARDS! ...WHAT'LL YOU HAVE TO EAT?
AFTER WHAT?
AHHH, SHIT! WHAT'LL IT BE, SPENCER?
DON'T YOU LIKE SHORT GUYS?
DON'T BE AN ASS! WHAT'LL IT BE?
DYNAMITE COMES IN SMALL PACKAGES...
WHAT'LL IT BE?!
THE *USUAL*. WHY BOTHER ASKING?

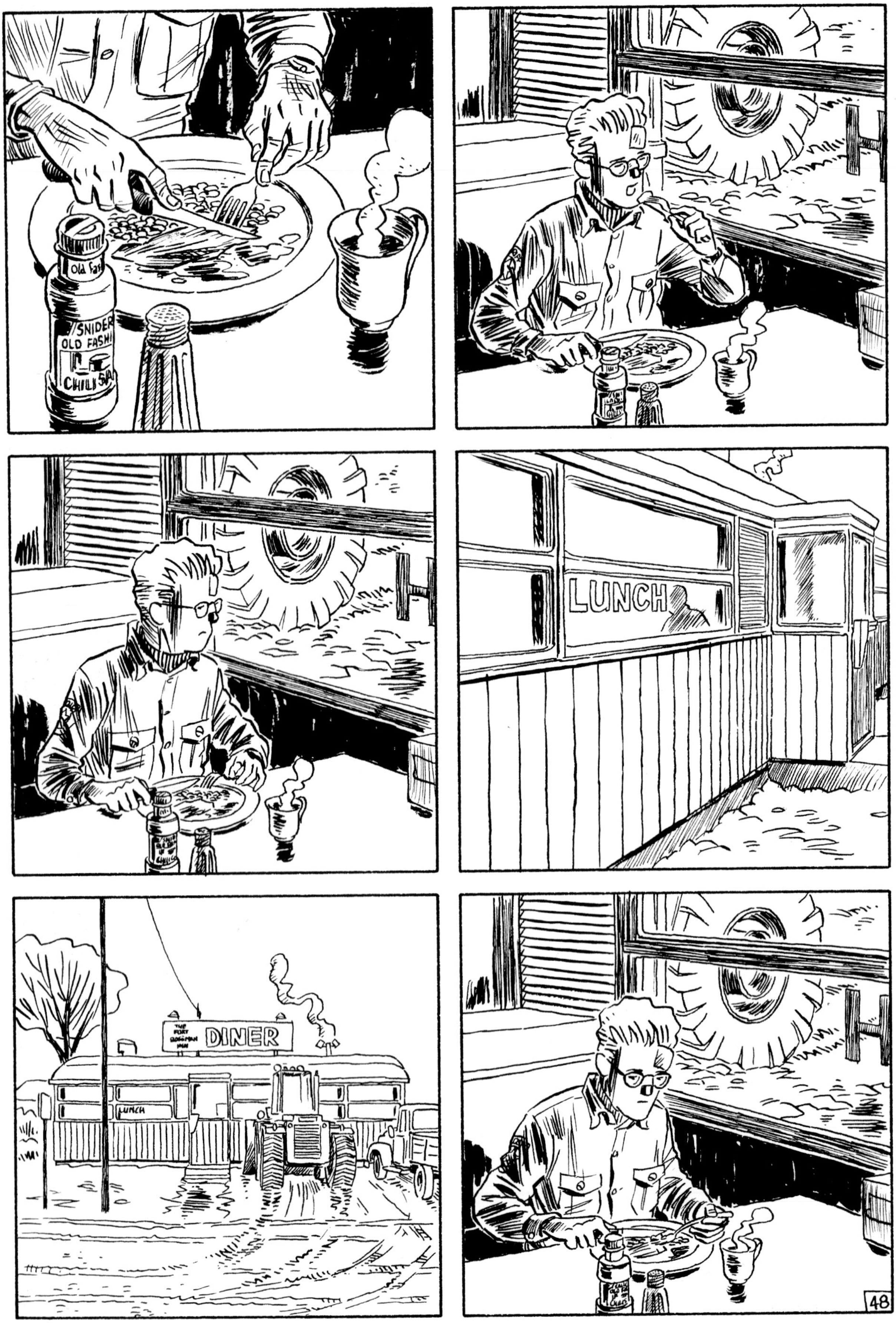
LUNCH
DINER

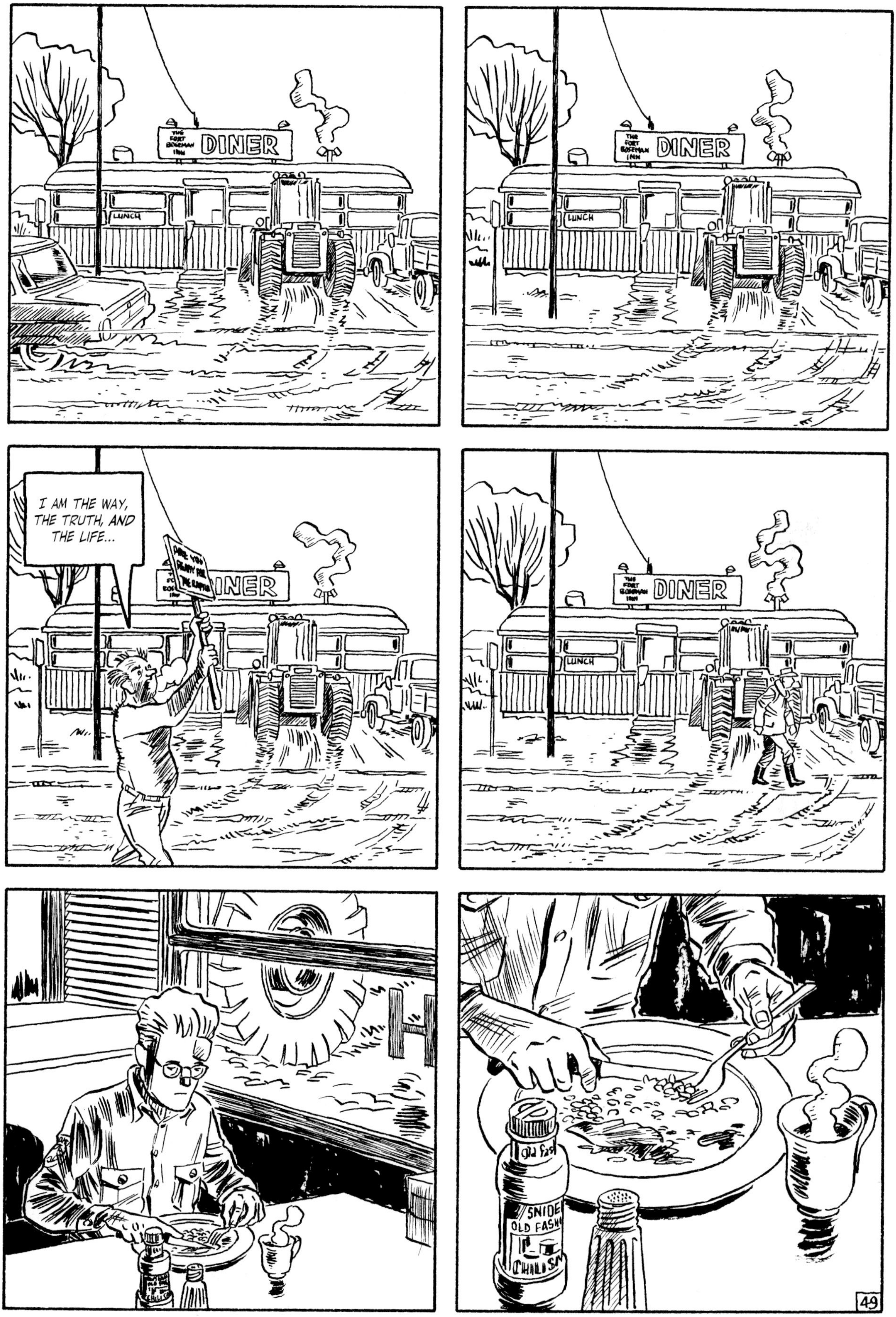
THE FORT BOZEMAN INN
DINER
LUNCH
I AM THE WAY, THE TRUTH, AND THE LIFE...

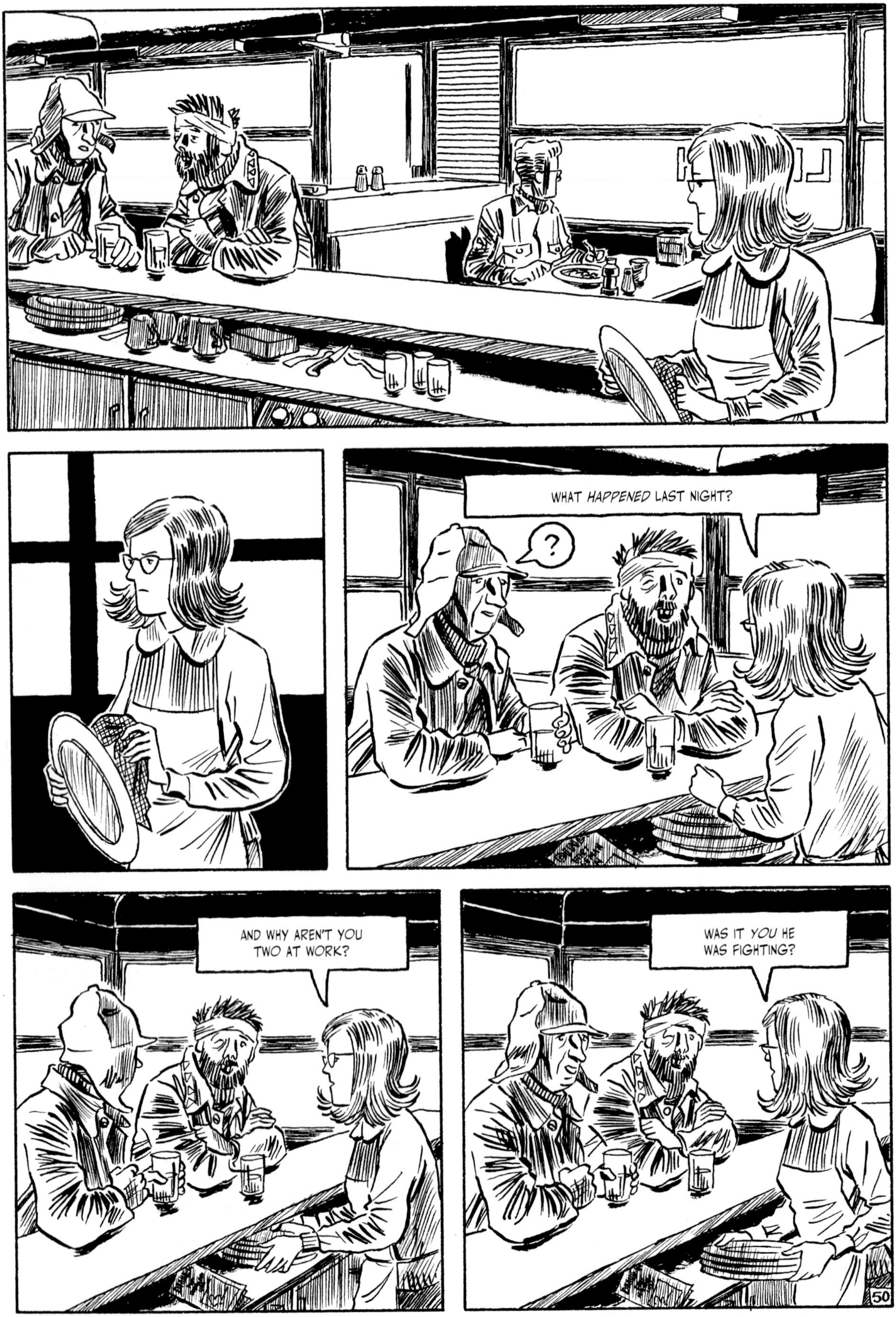
WHAT *HAPPENED* LAST NIGHT?
?
AND WHY AREN'T YOU TWO AT WORK?
WAS IT *YOU* HE WAS FIGHTING?

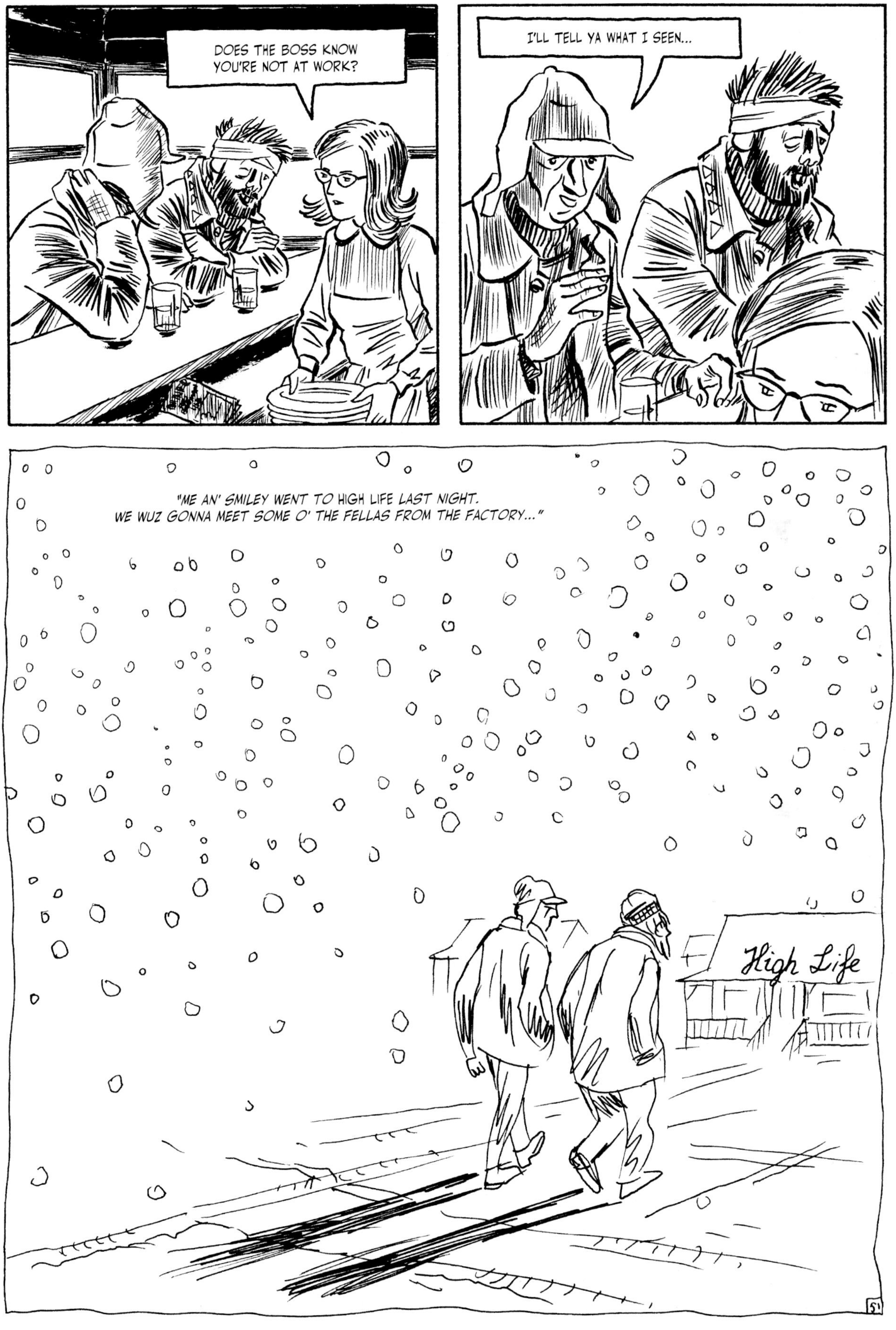
DOES THE BOSS KNOW YOU'RE NOT AT WORK?
I'LL TELL YA WHAT I SEEN...
"ME AN' SMILEY WENT TO HIGH LIFE LAST NIGHT. WE WUZ GONNA MEET SOME O' THE FELLAS FROM THE FACTORY..."
High Life

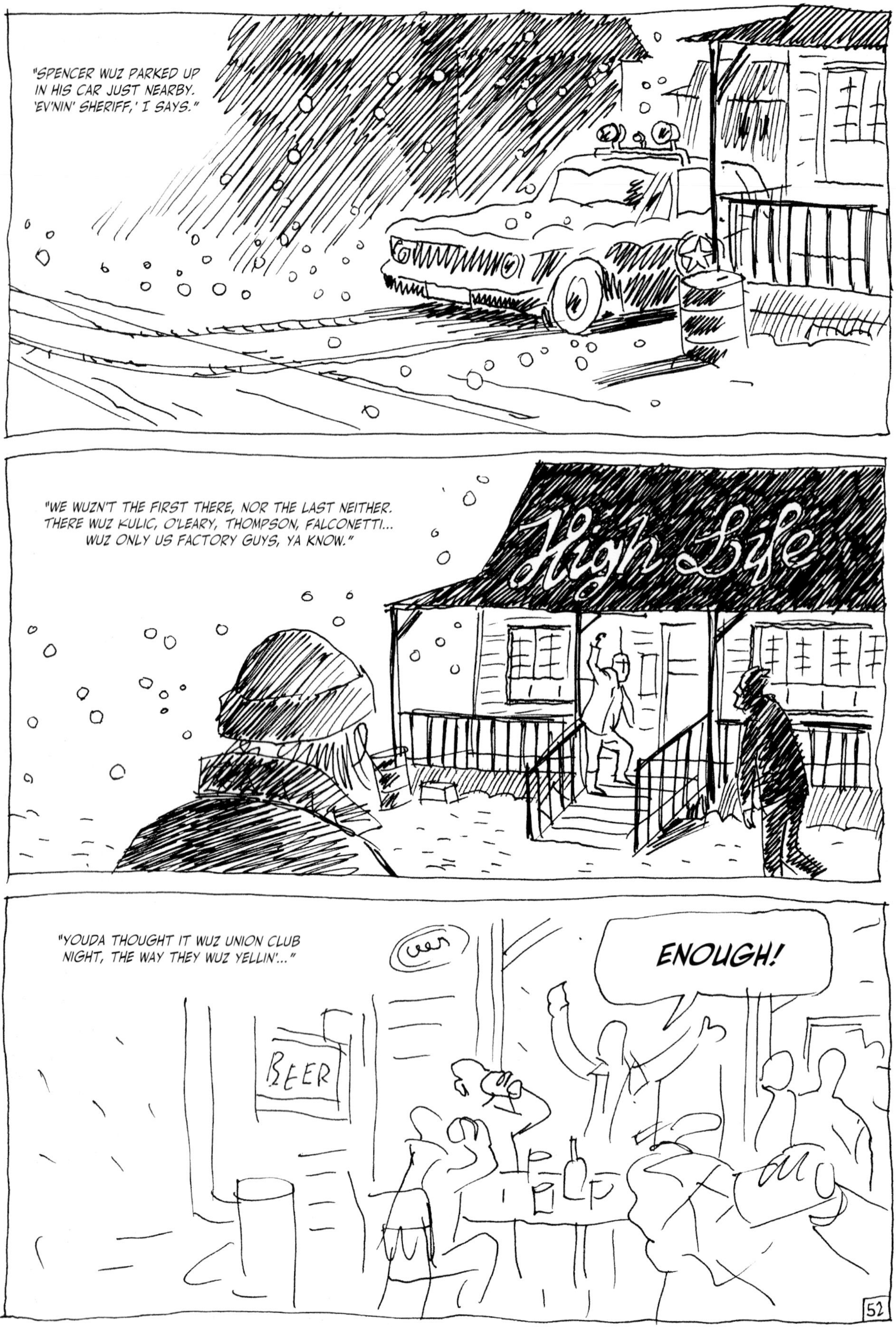
"SPENCER WUZ PARKED UP IN HIS CAR JUST NEARBY. 'EV'NIN' SHERIFF,' I SAYS."
"WE WUZN'T THE FIRST THERE, NOR THE LAST NEITHER. THERE WUZ KULIC, O'LEARY, THOMPSON, FALCONETTI... WUZ ONLY US FACTORY GUYS, YA KNOW."
High Life
"YOUDA THOUGHT IT WUZ UNION CLUB NIGHT, THE WAY THEY WUZ YELLIN'..."
ENOUGH!
BEER

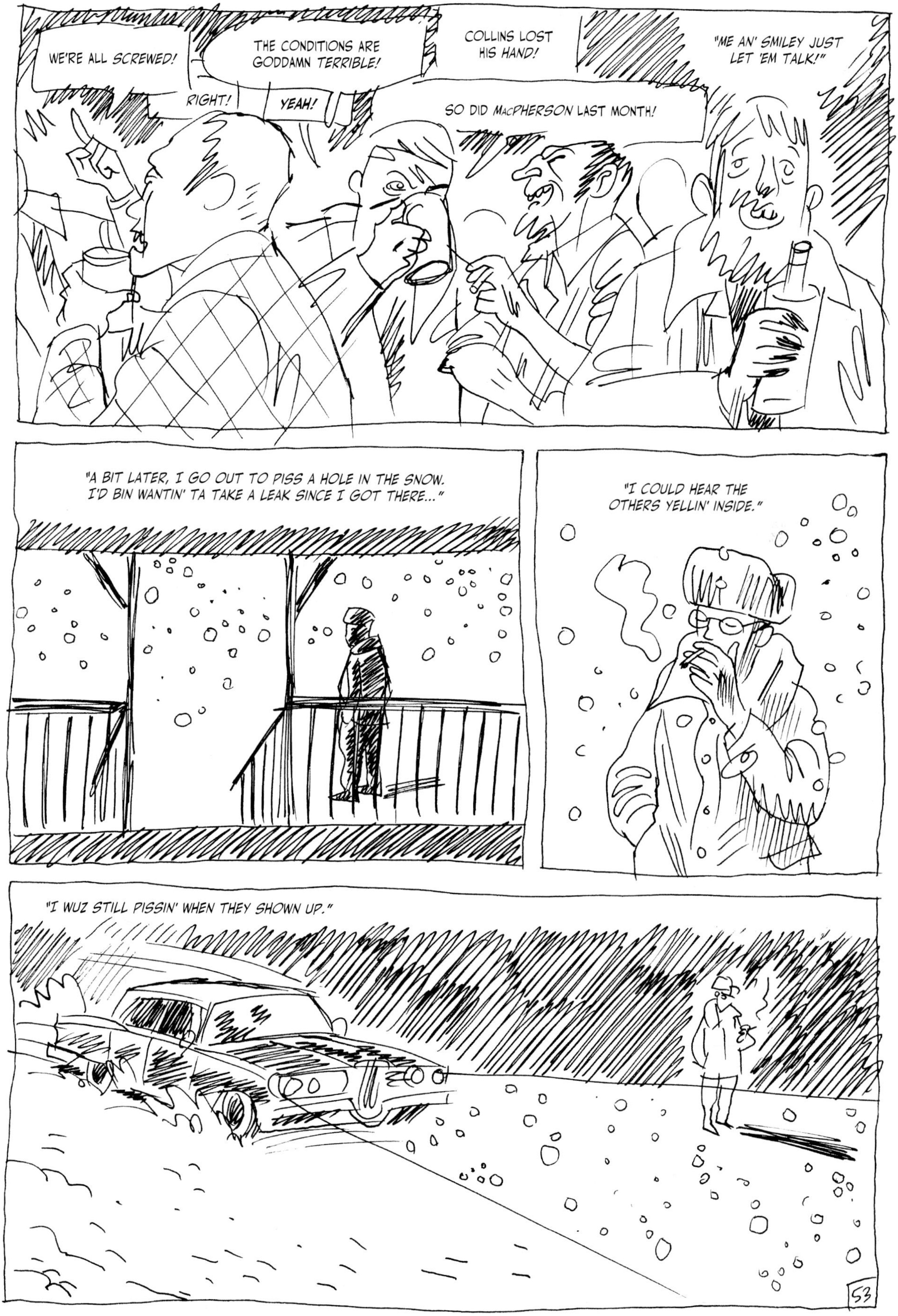
WE'RE ALL SCREWED!
THE CONDITIONS ARE GODDAMN TERRIBLE!
COLLINS LOST HIS HAND!
"ME AN' SMILEY JUST LET 'EM TALK!"
RIGHT!
YEAH!
SO DID MACPHERSON LAST MONTH!
"A BIT LATER, I GO OUT TO PISS A HOLE IN THE SNOW. I'D BIN WANTIN' TA TAKE A LEAK SINCE I GOT THERE..."
"I COULD HEAR THE OTHERS YELLIN' INSIDE."
"I WUZ STILL PISSIN' WHEN THEY SHOWN UP."

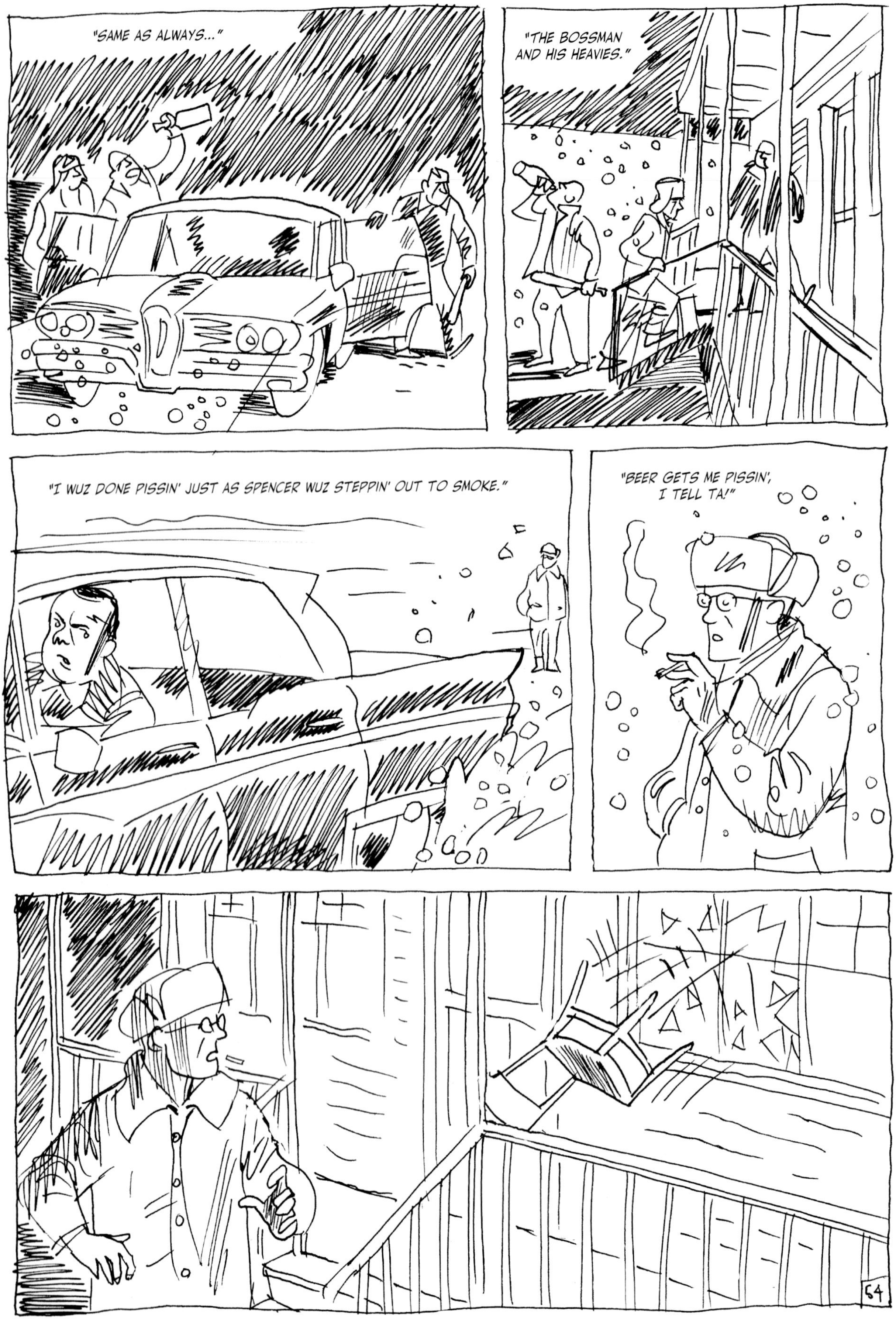
"SAME AS ALWAYS..."
"THE BOSSMAN AND HIS HEAVIES."
"I WUZ DONE PISSIN' JUST AS SPENCER WUZ STEPPIN' OUT TO SMOKE."
"BEER GETS ME PISSIN', I TELL TA!"

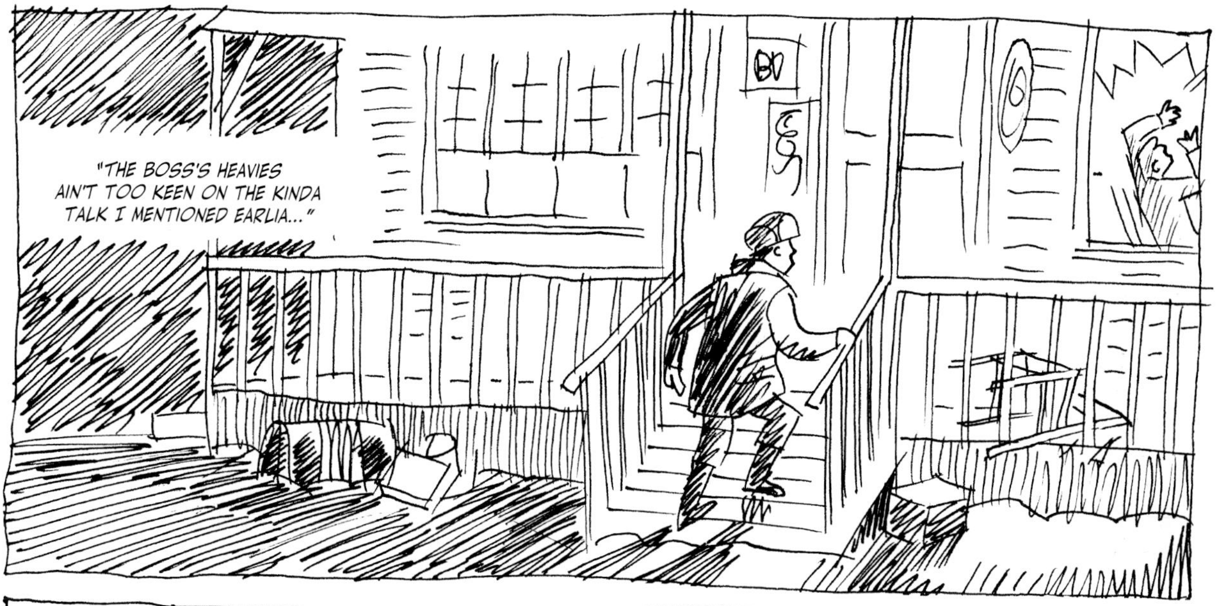
"THE BOSS'S HEAVIES
AIN'T TOO KEEN ON THE KINDA
TALK I MENTIONED EARLIA..."

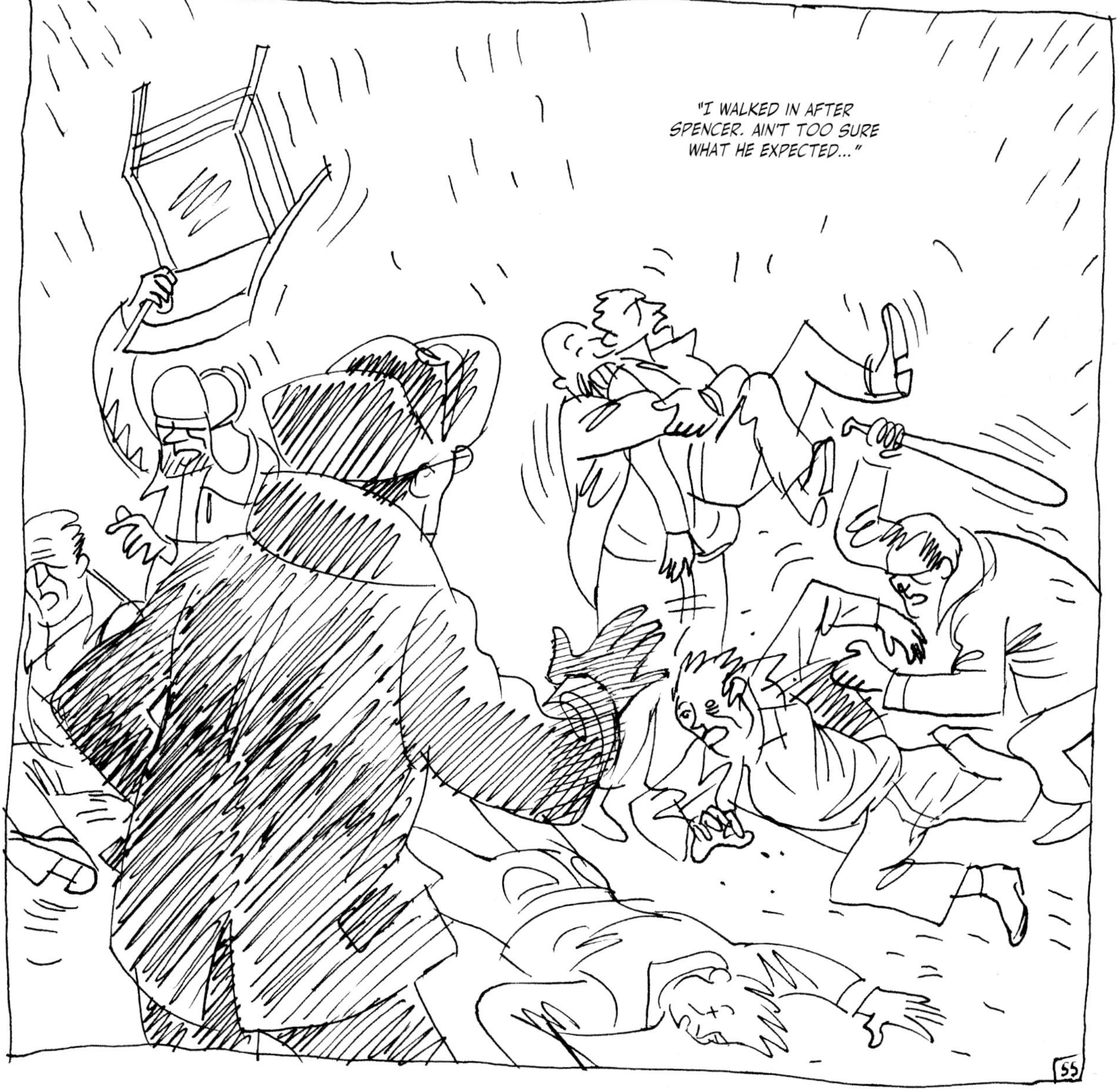
"I WALKED IN AFTER
SPENCER. AIN'T TOO SURE
WHAT HE EXPECTED..."

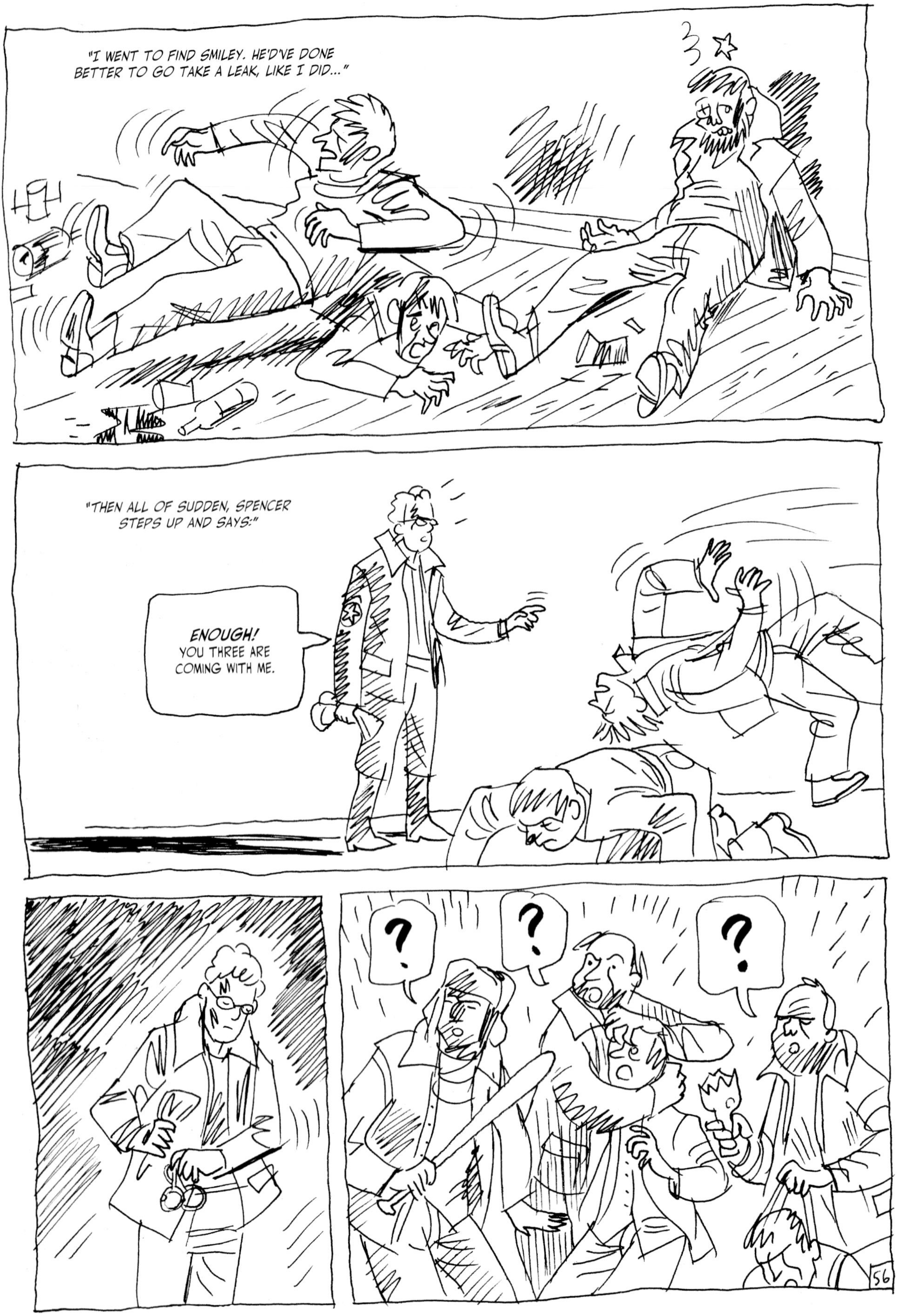
"I WENT TO FIND SMILEY. HE'D'VE DONE BETTER TO GO TAKE A LEAK, LIKE I DID..."
"THEN ALL OF SUDDEN, SPENCER STEPS UP AND SAYS:"
ENOUGH! YOU THREE ARE COMING WITH ME.
?
?
?

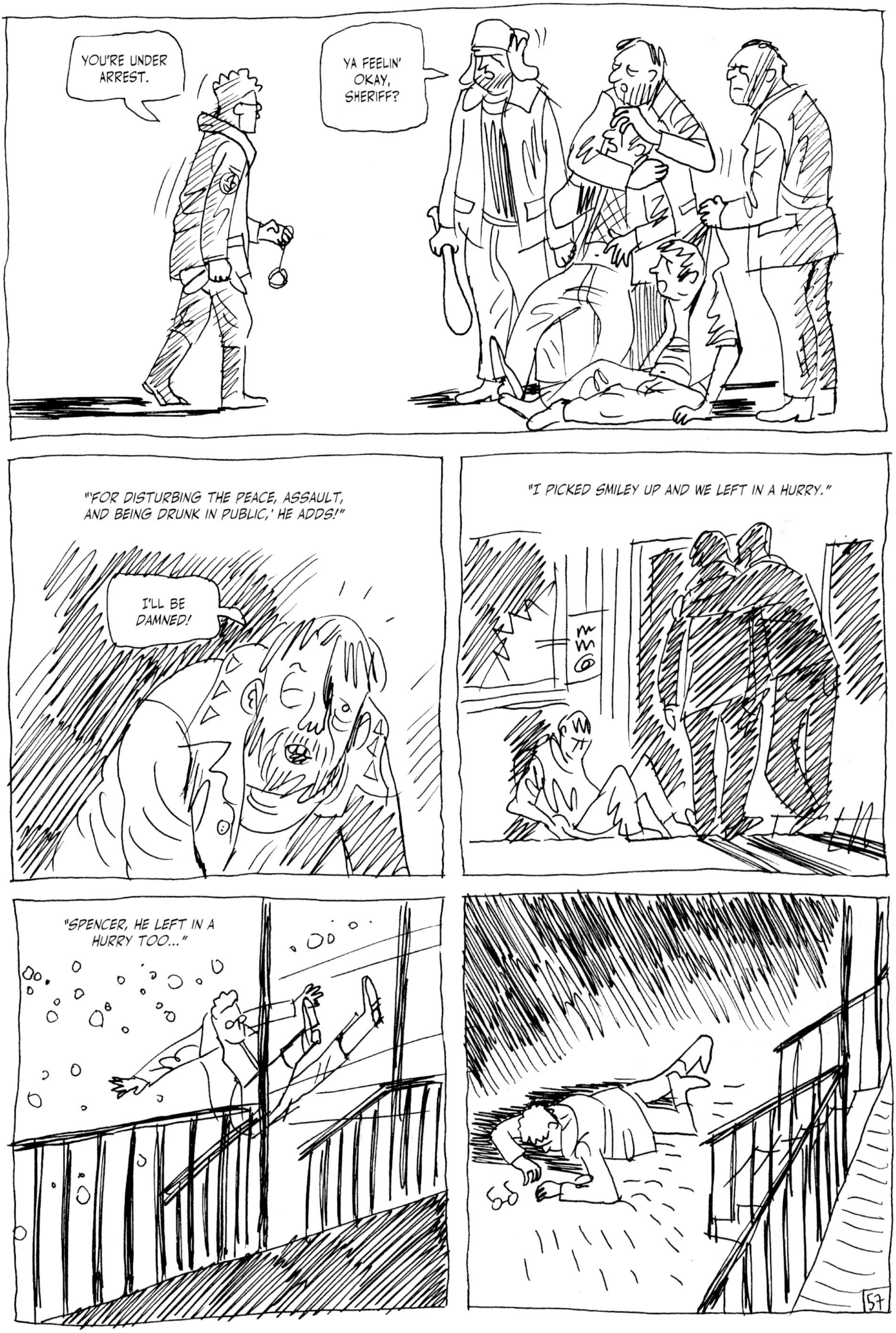
YOU'RE UNDER ARREST.
YA FEELIN' OKAY, SHERIFF?
"FOR DISTURBING THE PEACE, ASSAULT, AND BEING DRUNK IN PUBLIC,' HE ADDS!"
I'LL BE DAMNED!
"I PICKED SMILEY UP AND WE LEFT IN A HURRY."
"SPENCER, HE LEFT IN A HURRY TOO..."

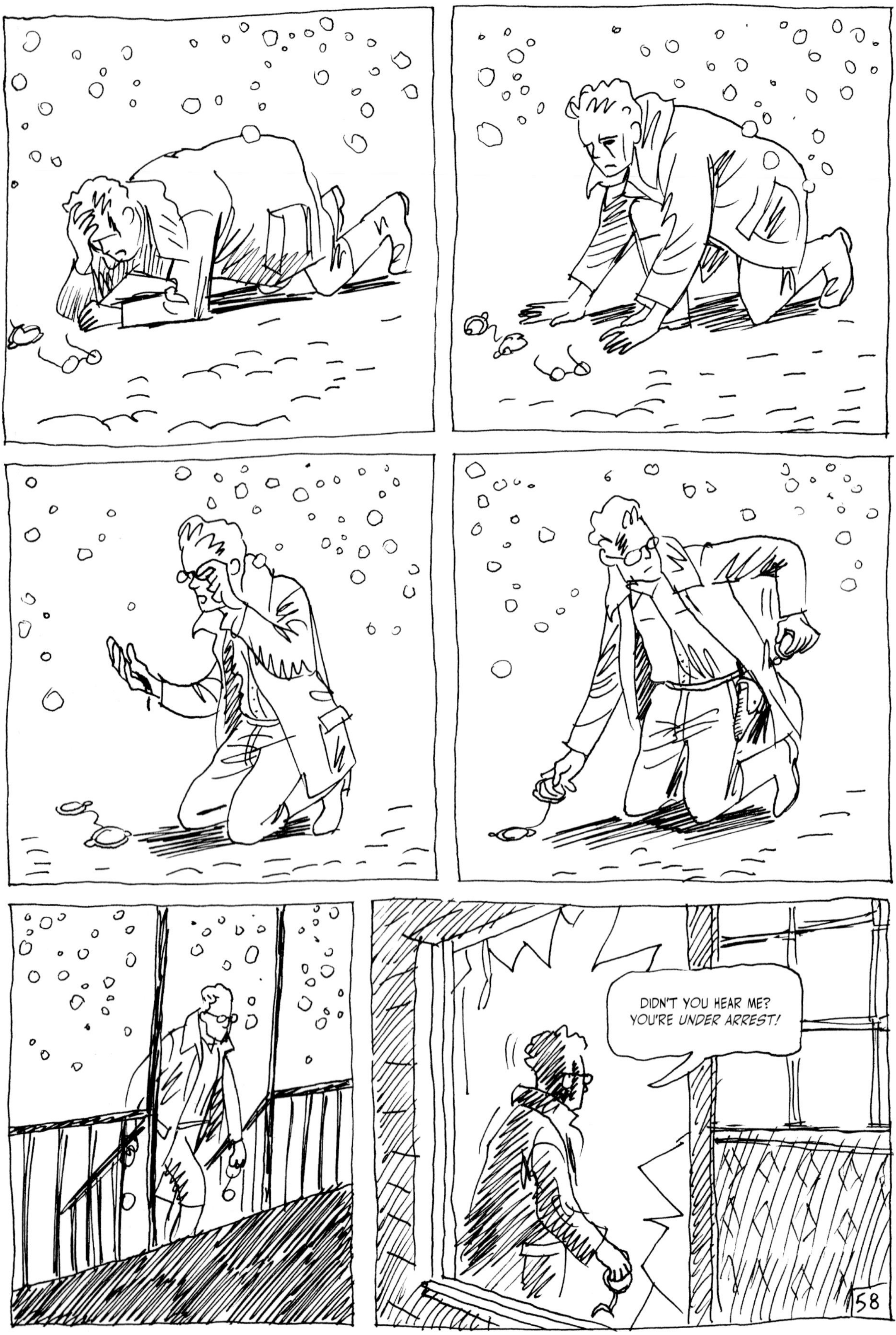
DIDN'T YOU HEAR ME? YOU'RE *UNDER ARREST!*

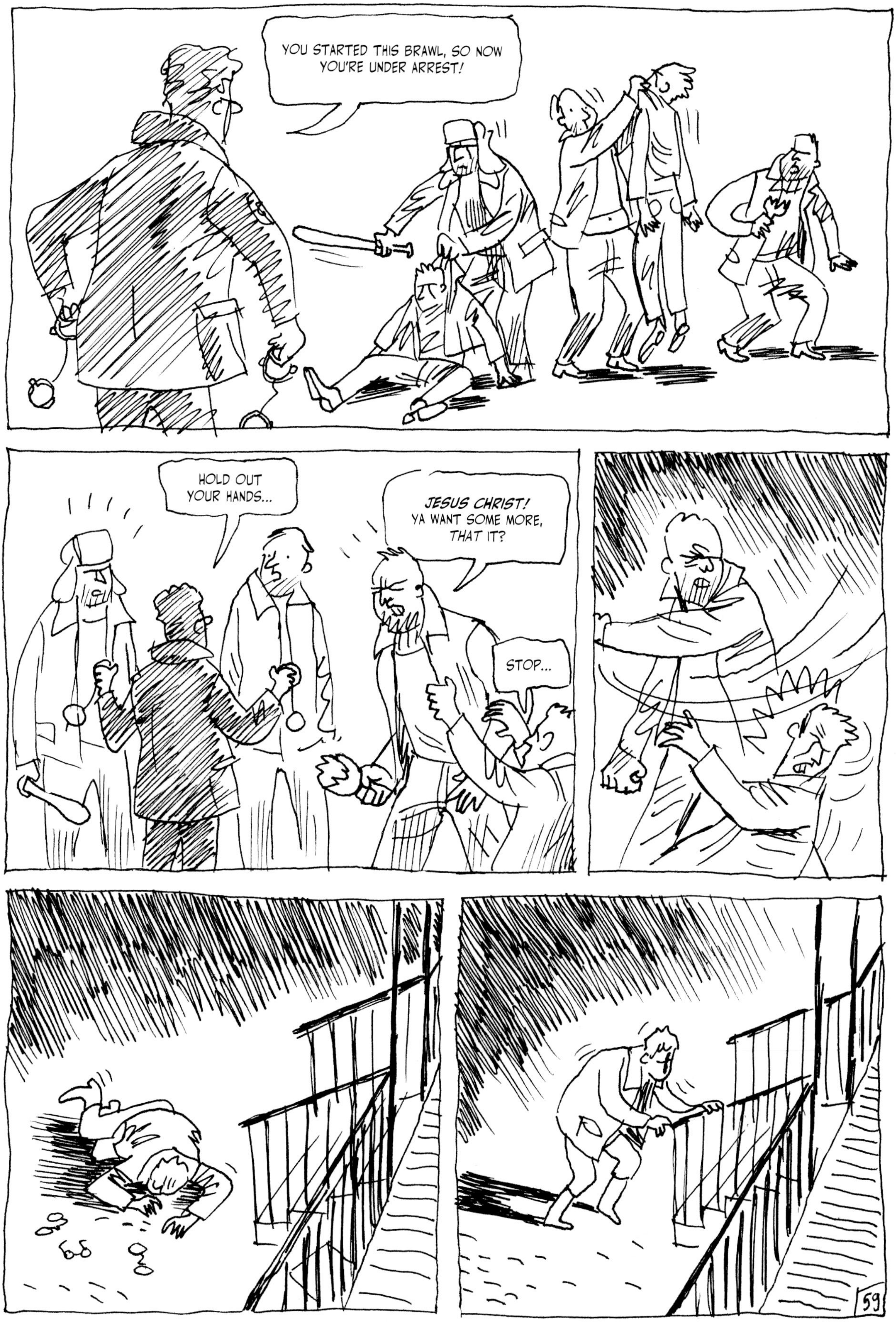

YOU STARTED THIS BRAWL, SO NOW YOU'RE UNDER ARREST!
HOLD OUT YOUR HANDS...
JESUS CHRIST! YA WANT SOME MORE, THAT IT?
STOP...

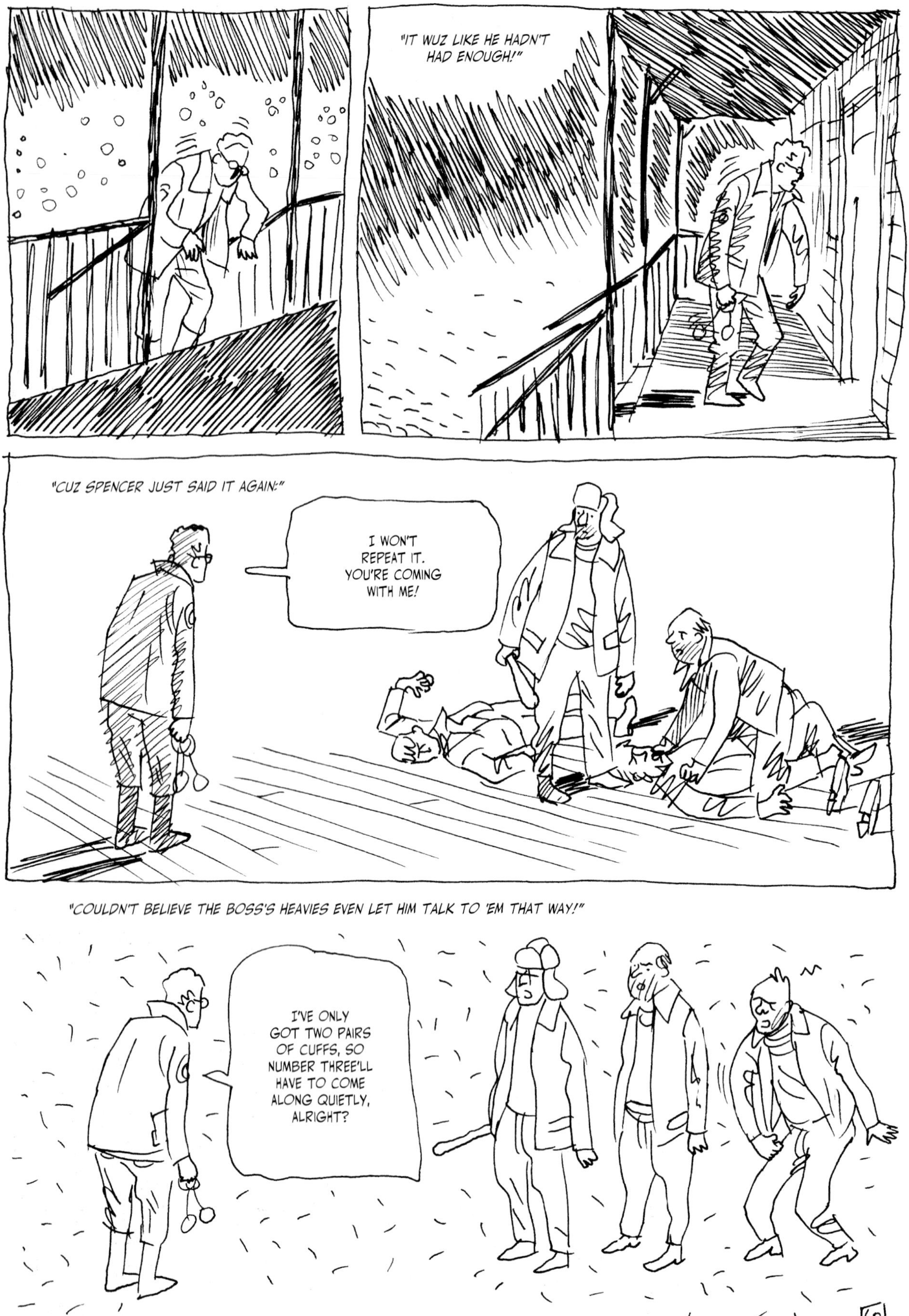
"IT WUZ LIKE HE HADN'T HAD ENOUGH!"
"CUZ SPENCER JUST SAID IT AGAIN:"
I WON'T REPEAT IT. YOU'RE COMING WITH ME!
"COULDN'T BELIEVE THE BOSS'S HEAVIES EVEN LET HIM TALK TO 'EM THAT WAY!"
I'VE ONLY GOT TWO PAIRS OF CUFFS, SO NUMBER THREE'LL HAVE TO COME ALONG QUIETLY, ALRIGHT?

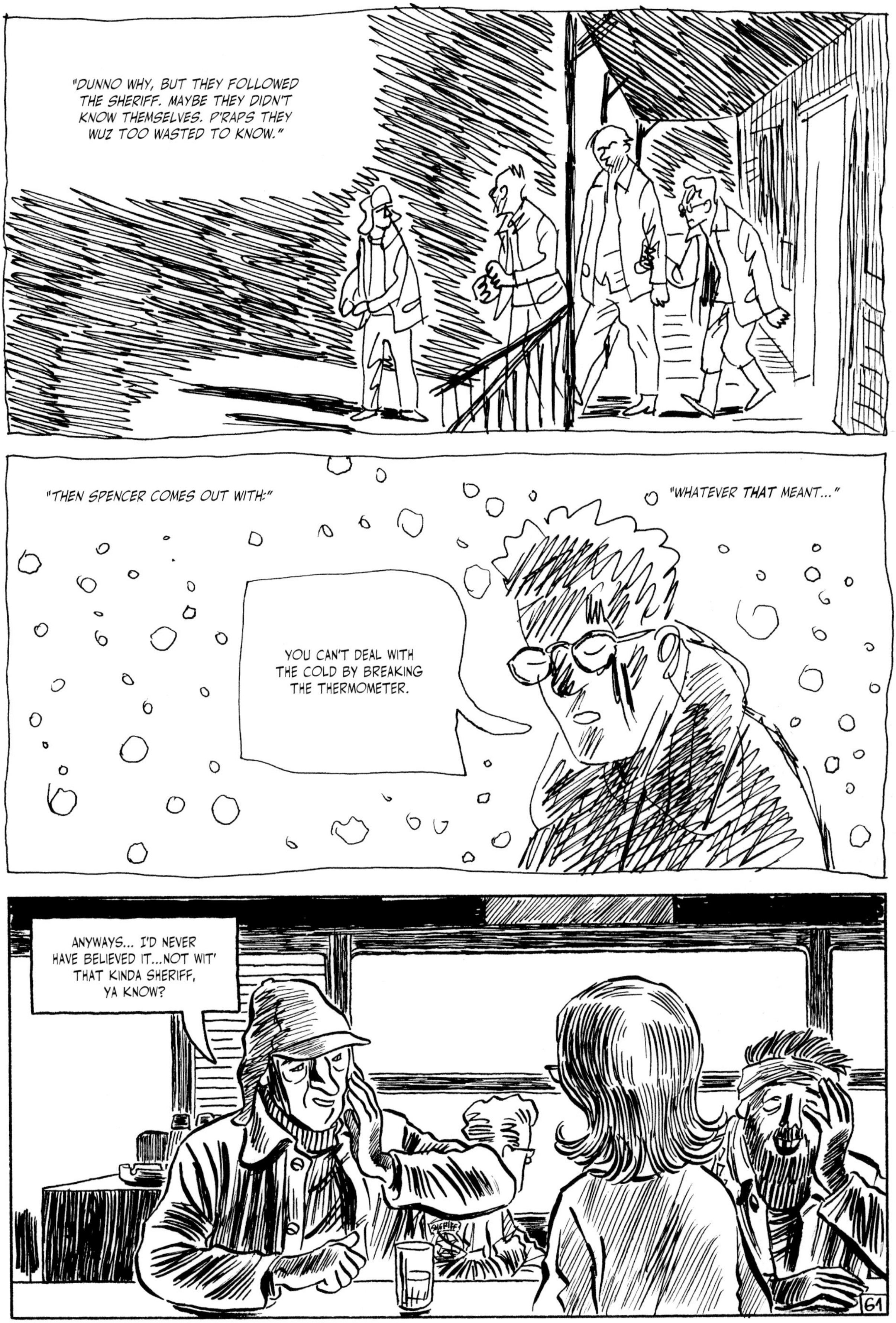
"DUNNO WHY, BUT THEY FOLLOWED THE SHERIFF. MAYBE THEY DIDN'T KNOW THEMSELVES. P'RAPS THEY WUZ TOO WASTED TO KNOW."
"THEN SPENCER COMES OUT WITH:"
YOU CAN'T DEAL WITH THE COLD BY BREAKING THE THERMOMETER.
"WHATEVER *THAT* MEANT..."
ANYWAYS... I'D NEVER HAVE BELIEVED IT...NOT WIT' THAT KINDA SHERIFF, YA KNOW?
SHERIFF
61

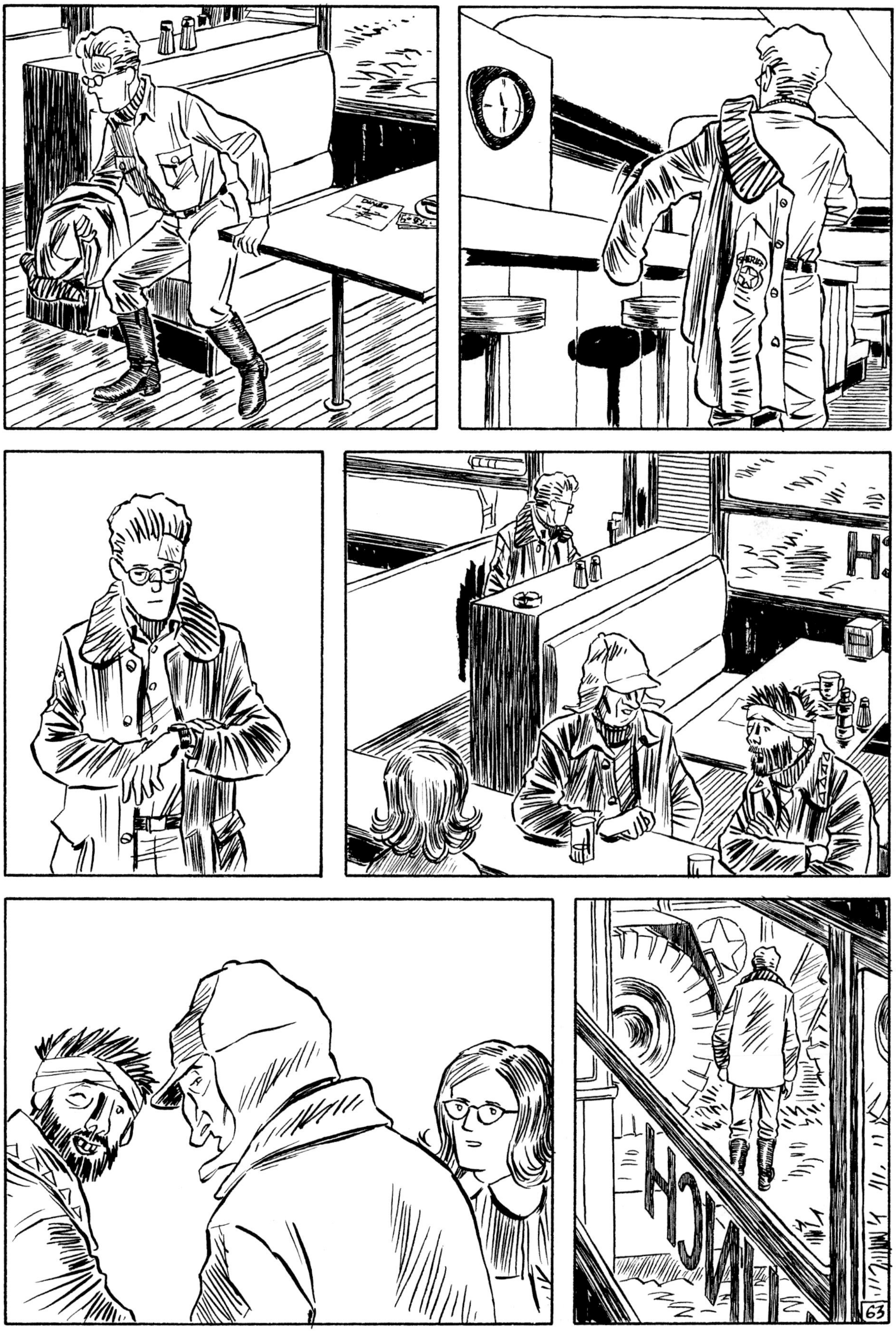

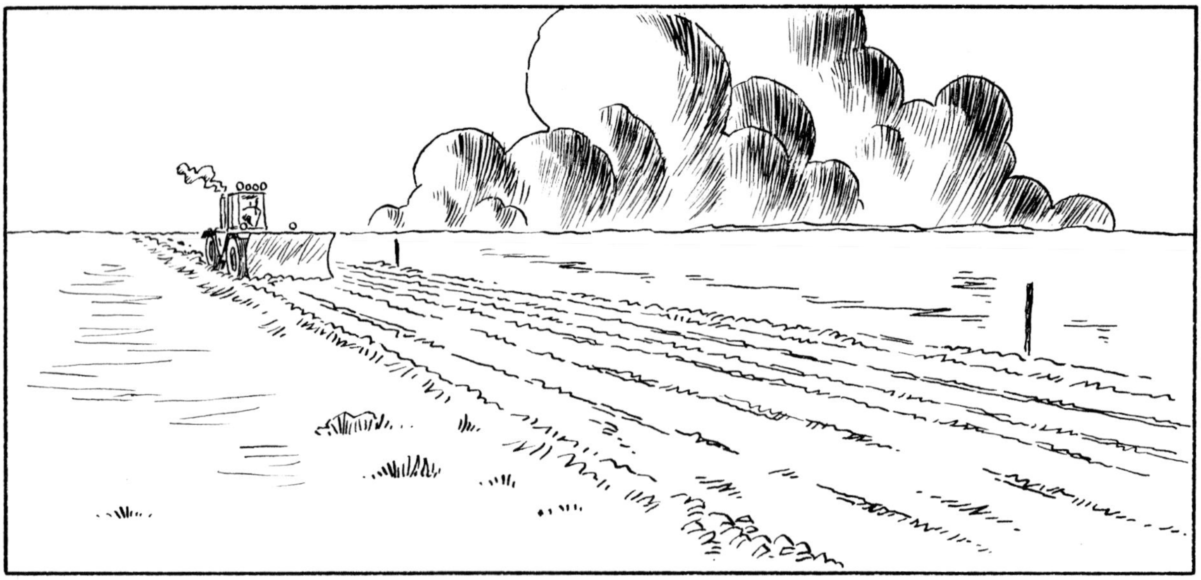
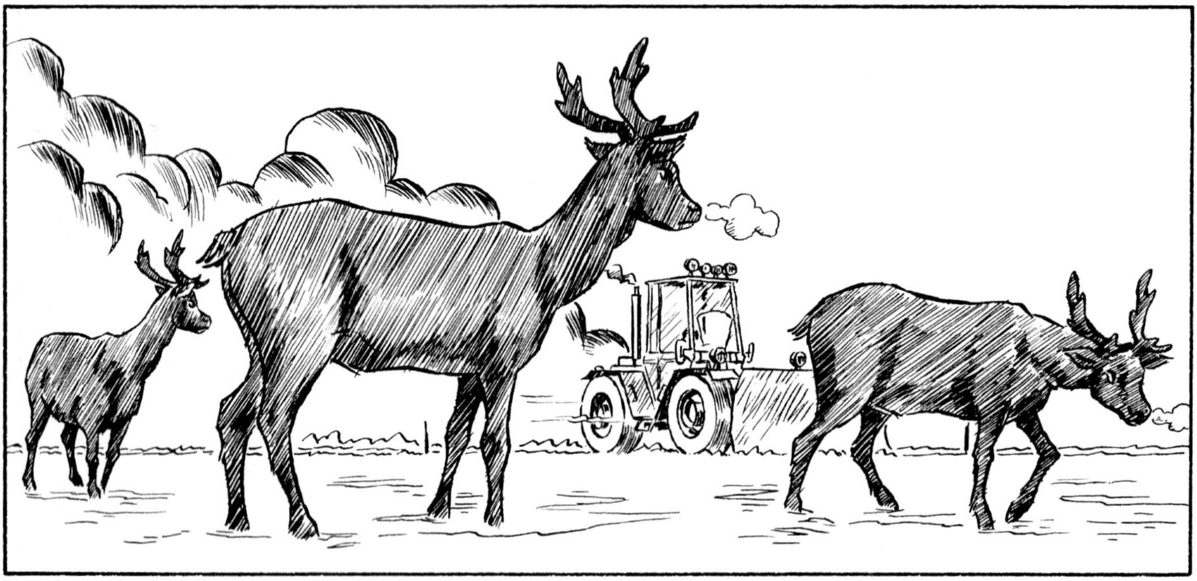
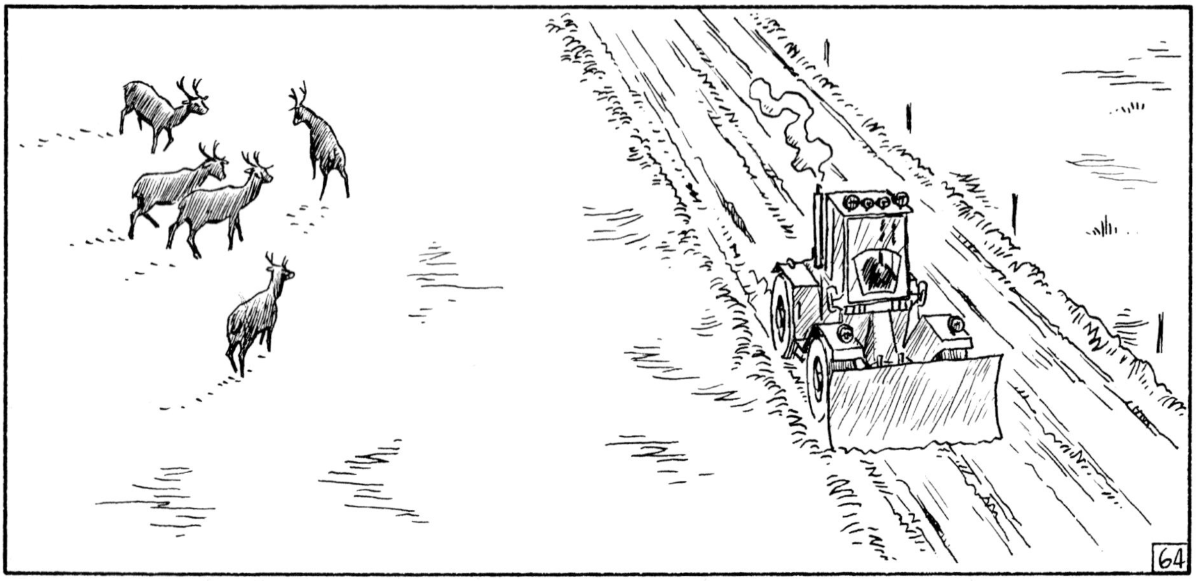

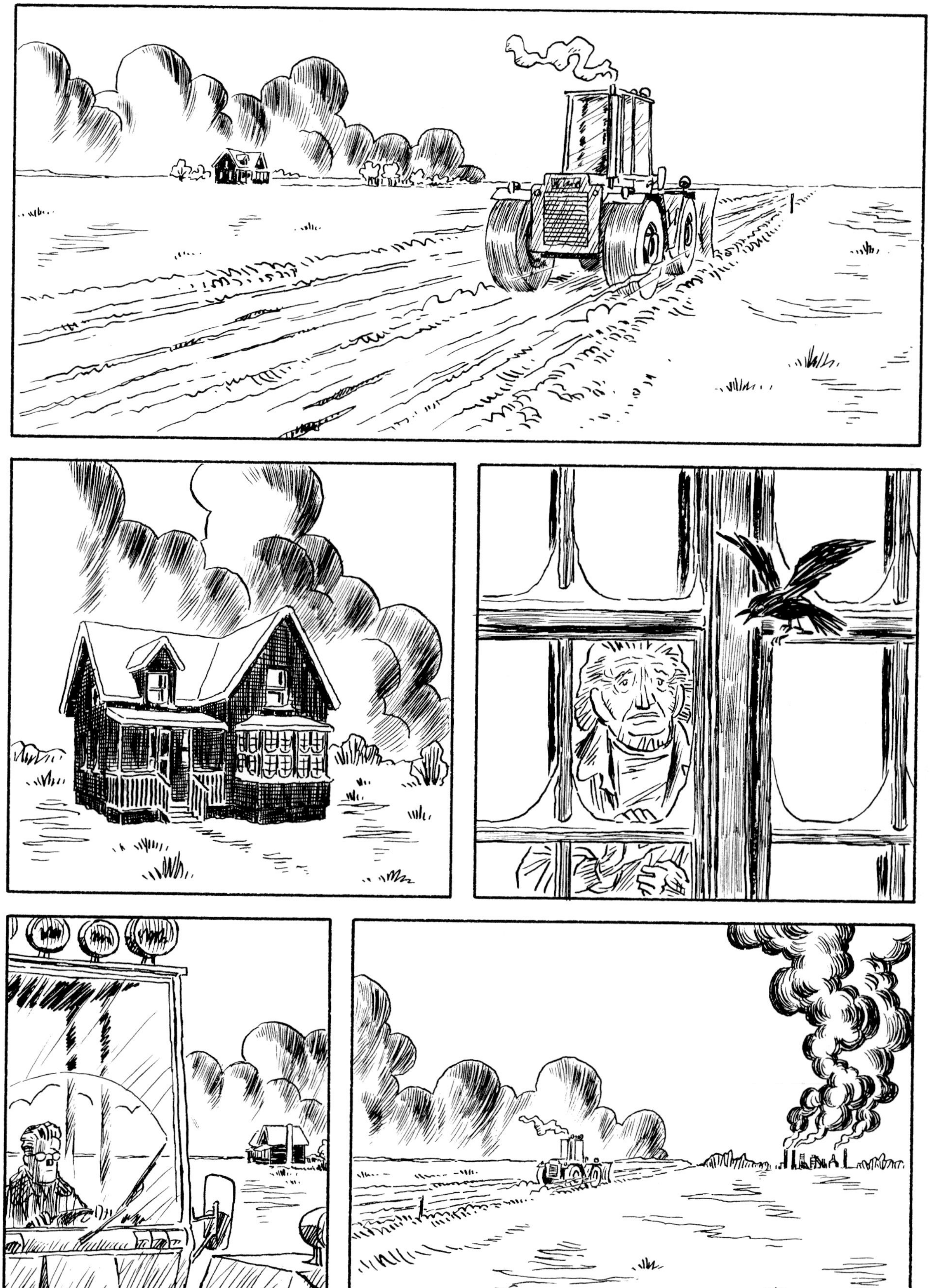

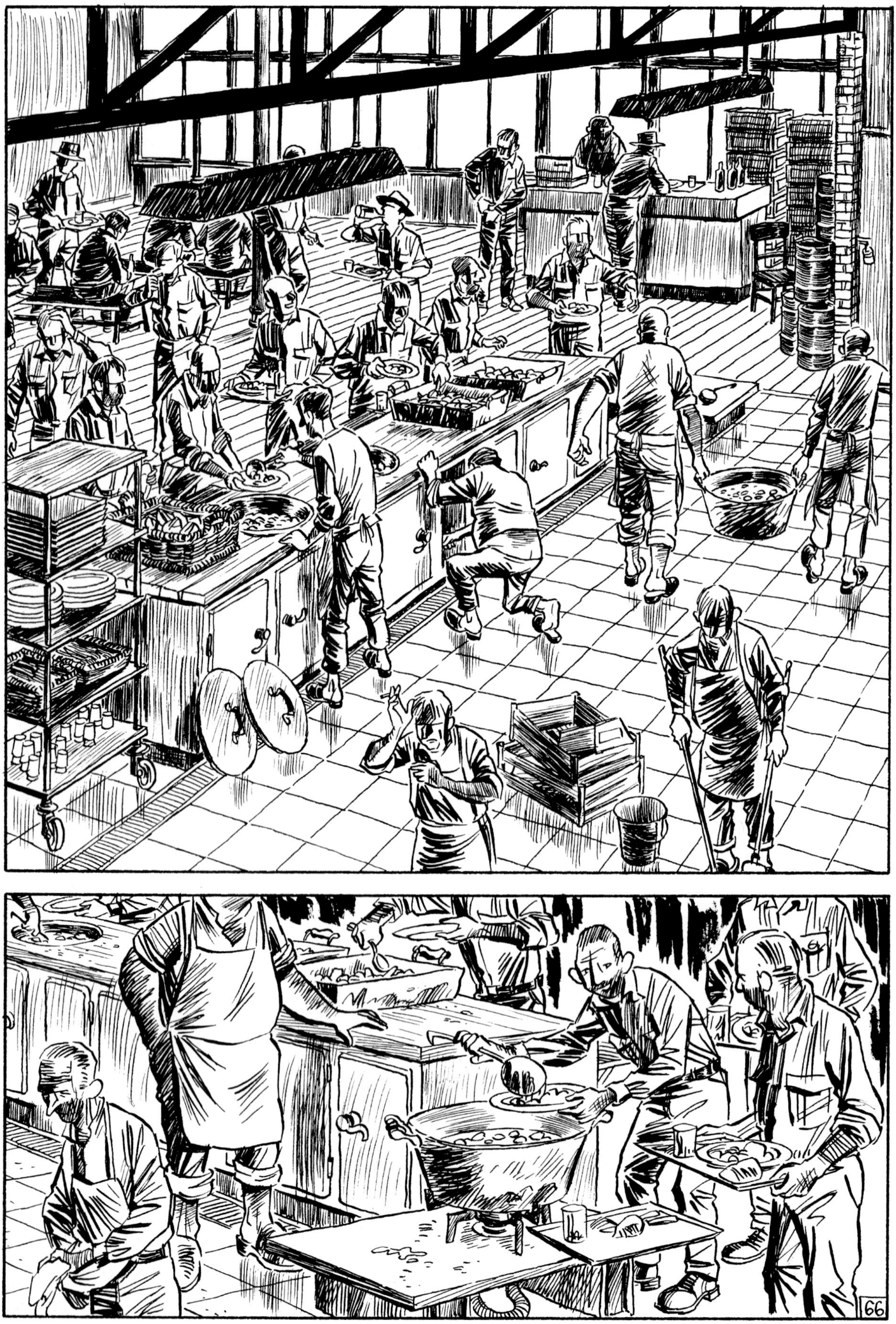

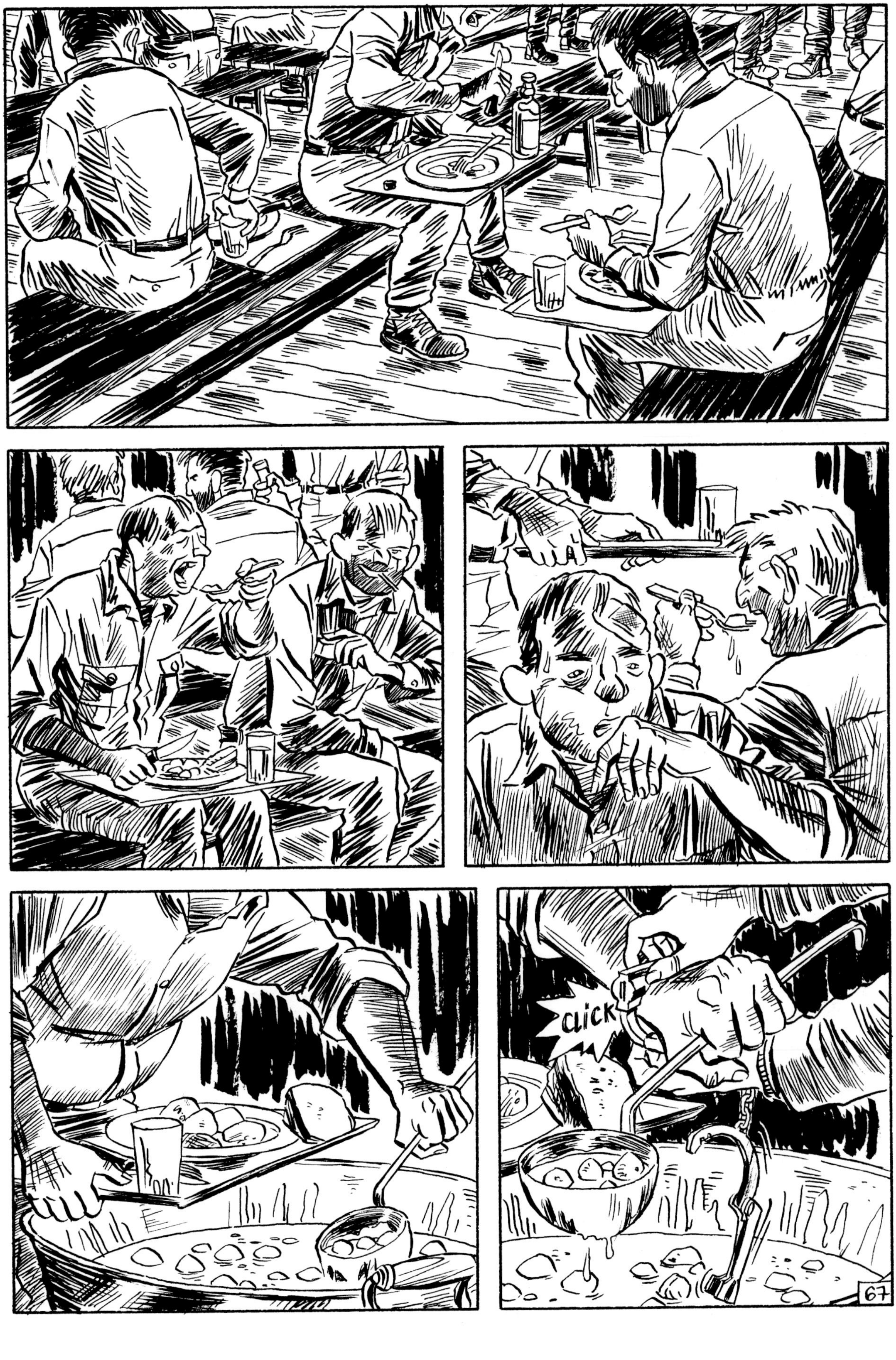
CLICK
67

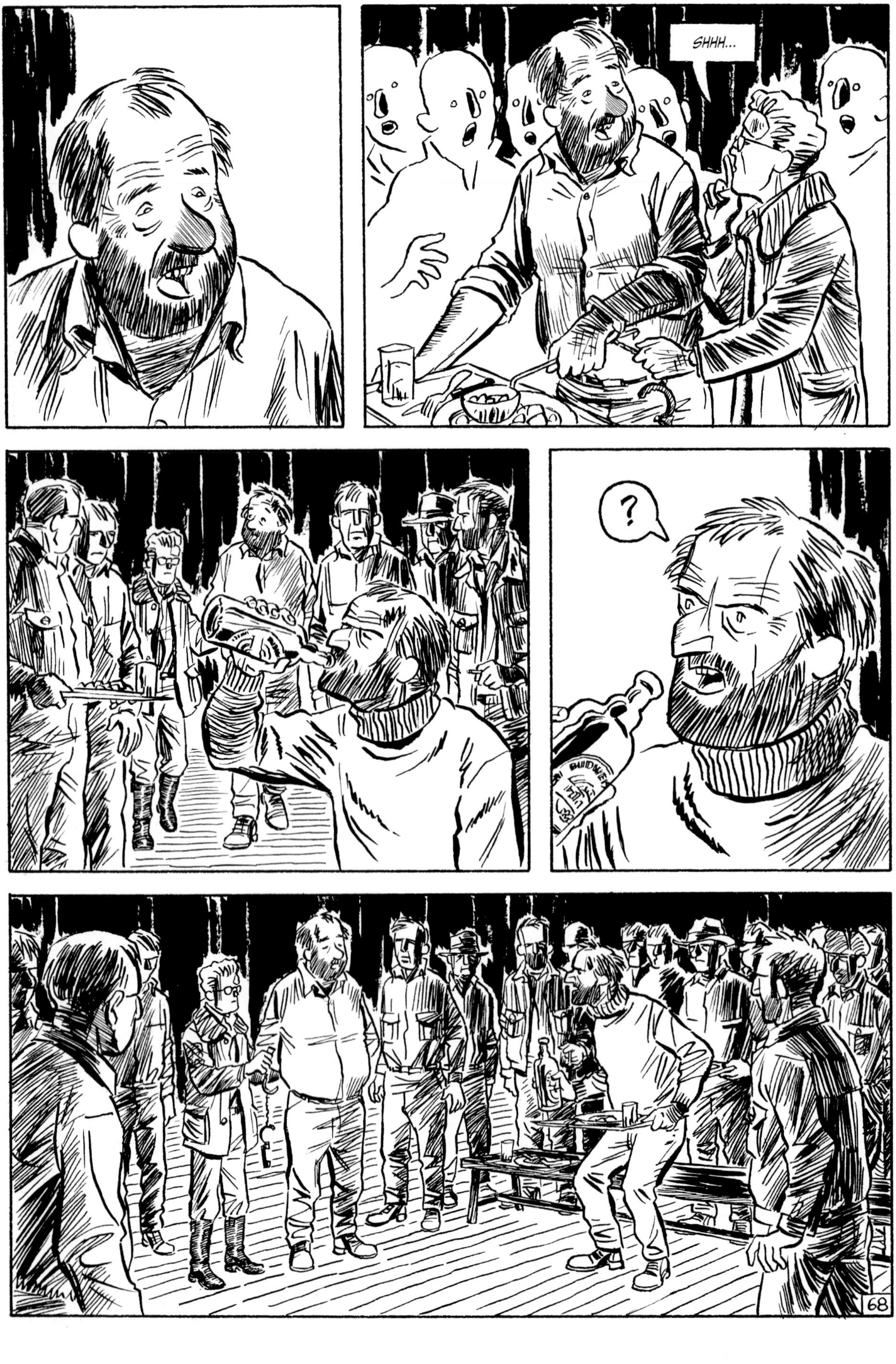
SHHH...
?

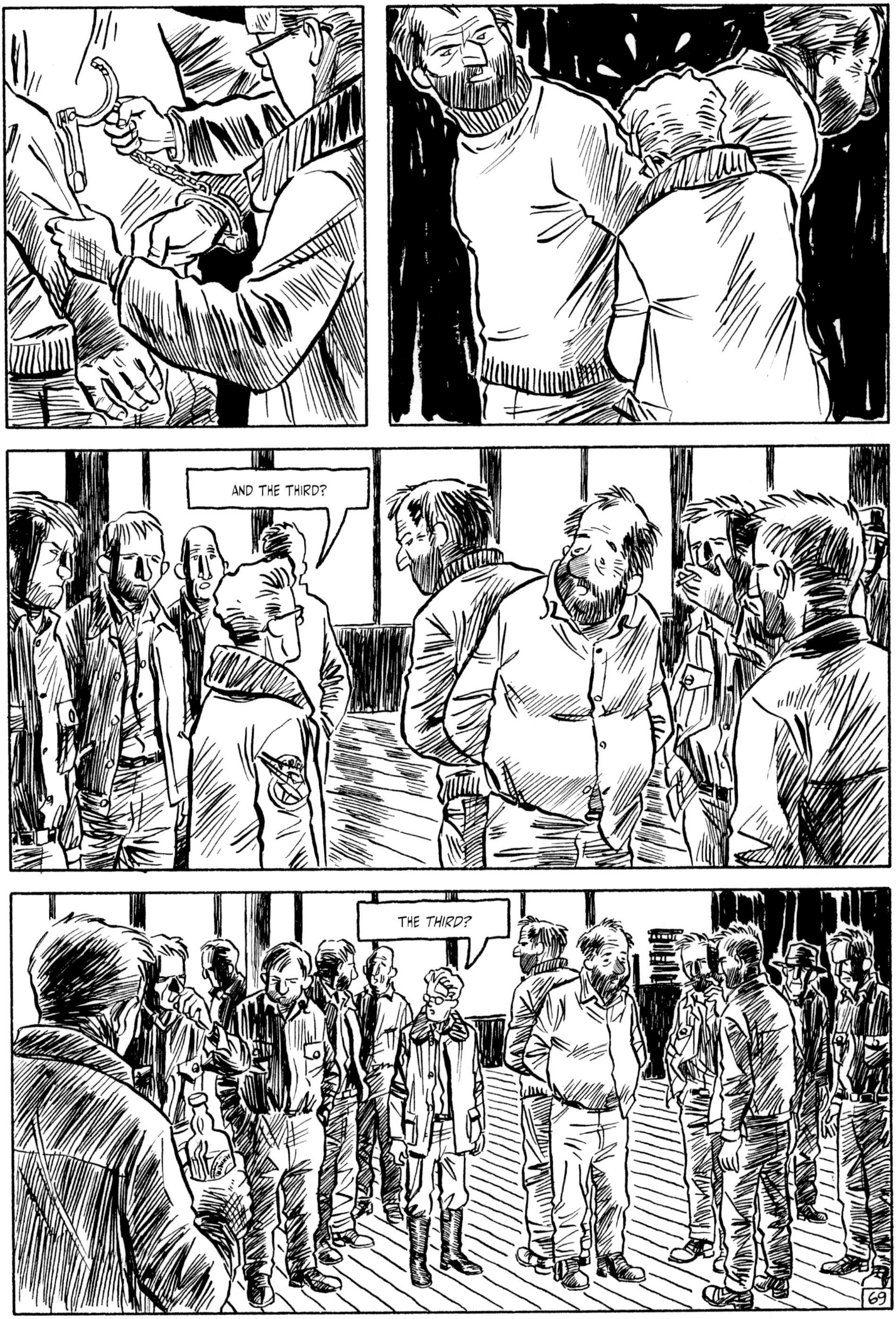
AND THE THIRD?
THE THIRD?

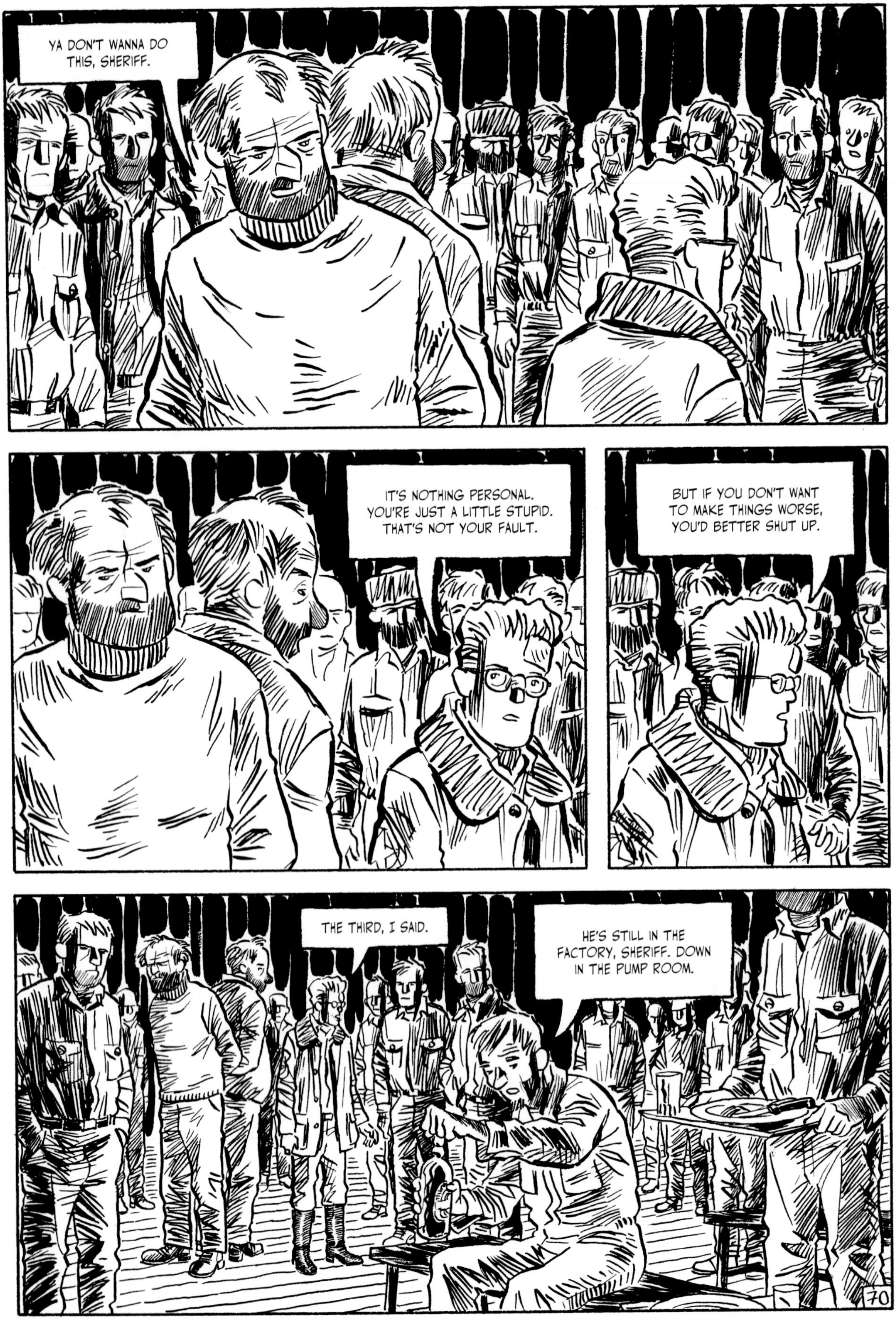
YA DON'T WANNA DO THIS, SHERIFF.
IT'S NOTHING PERSONAL. YOU'RE JUST A LITTLE STUPID. THAT'S NOT YOUR FAULT.
BUT IF YOU DON'T WANT TO MAKE THINGS WORSE, YOU'D BETTER SHUT UP.
THE THIRD, I SAID.
HE'S STILL IN THE FACTORY, SHERIFF. DOWN IN THE PUMP ROOM.
70

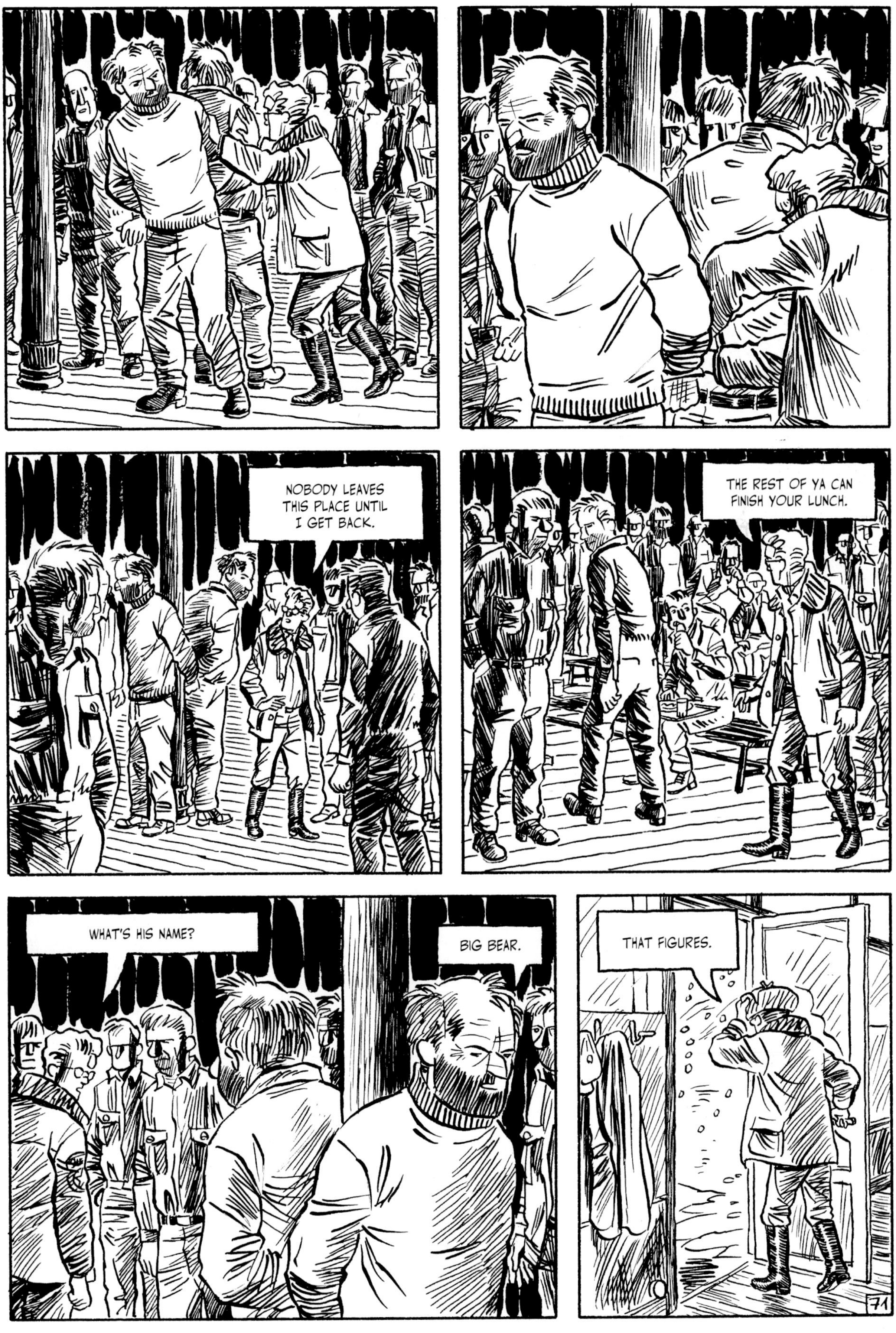

NOBODY LEAVES THIS PLACE UNTIL I GET BACK.
THE REST OF YA CAN FINISH YOUR LUNCH.
WHAT'S HIS NAME?
BIG BEAR.
THAT FIGURES.

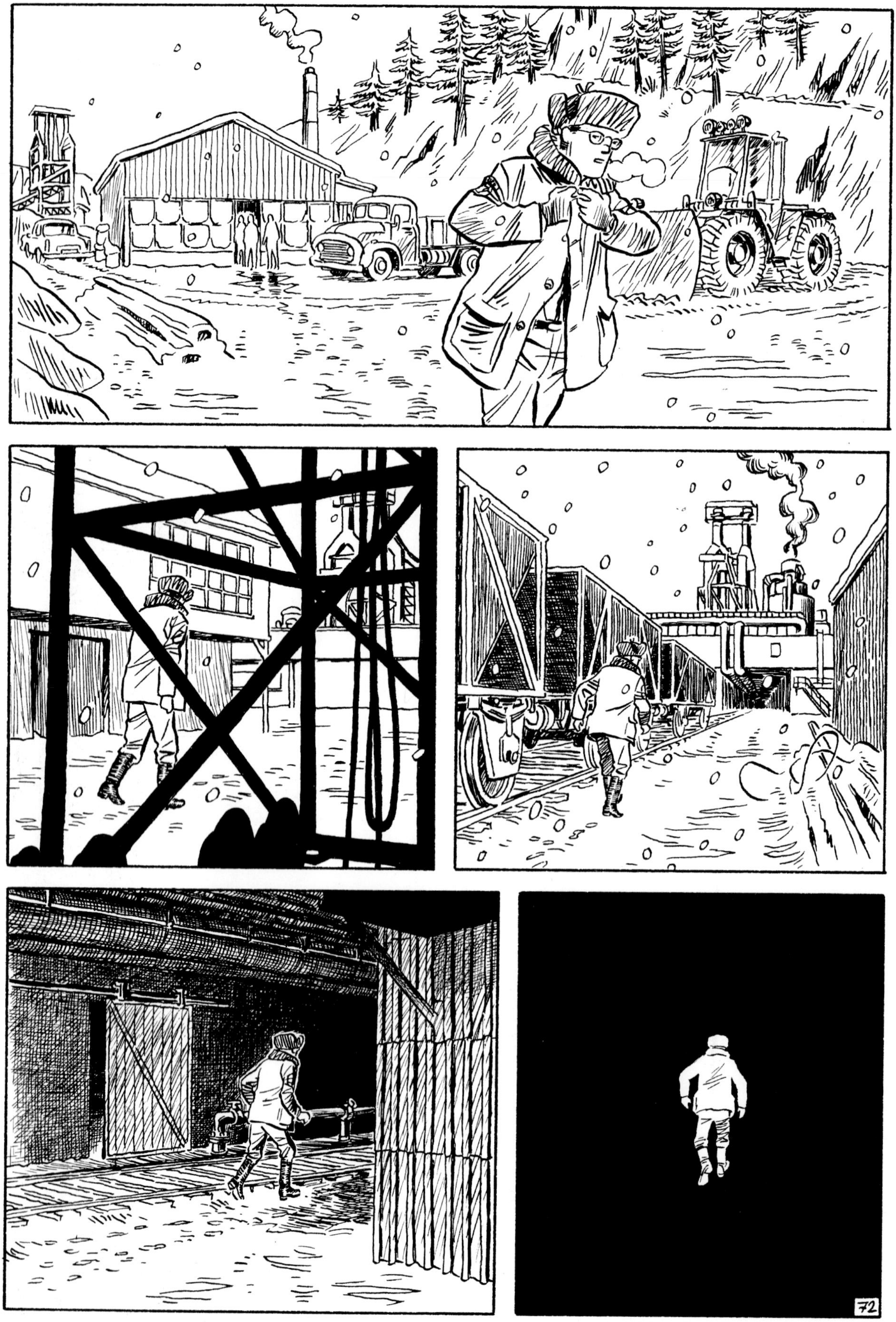

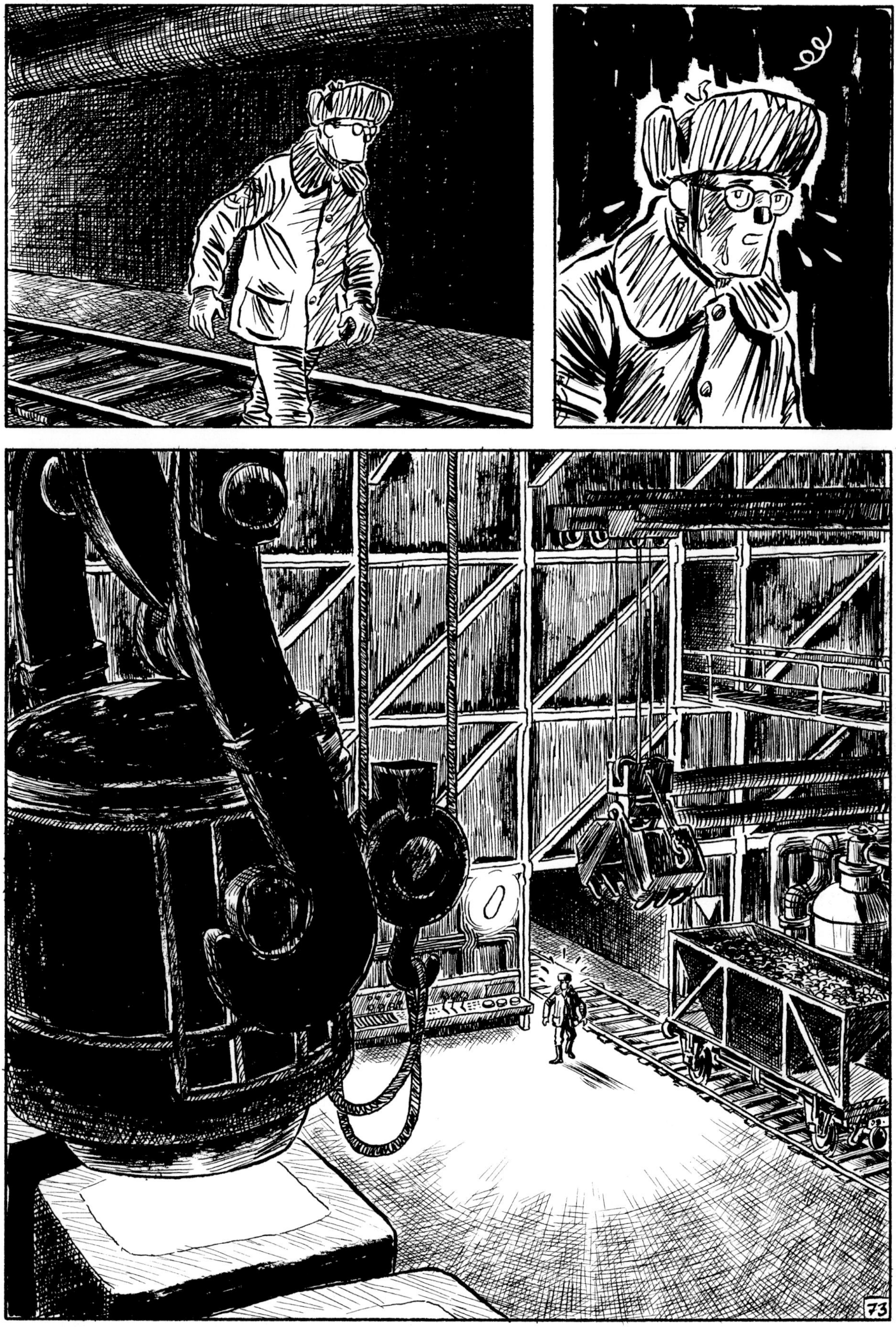

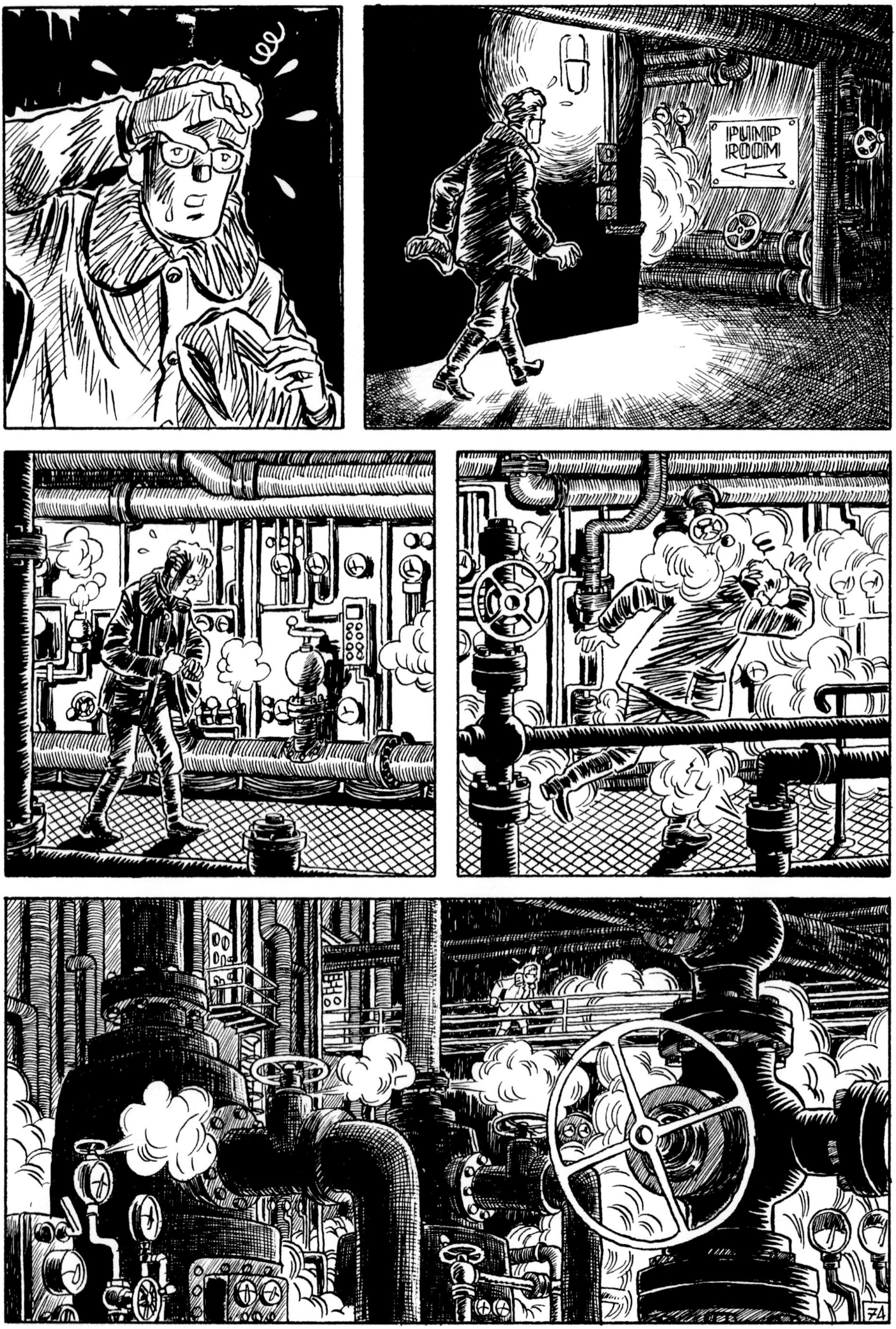
PUMP ROOM
74

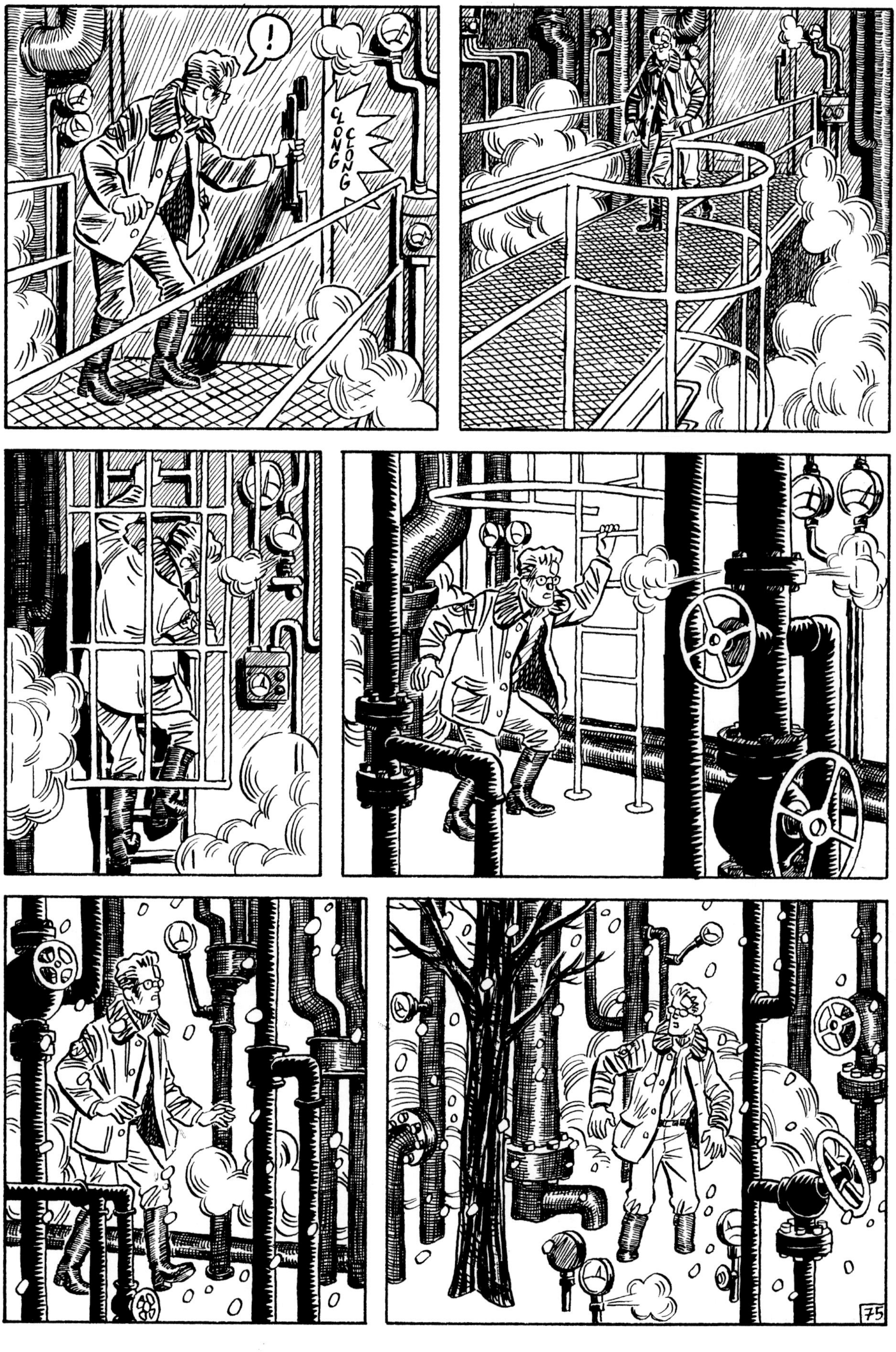
!
CLONG CLONG

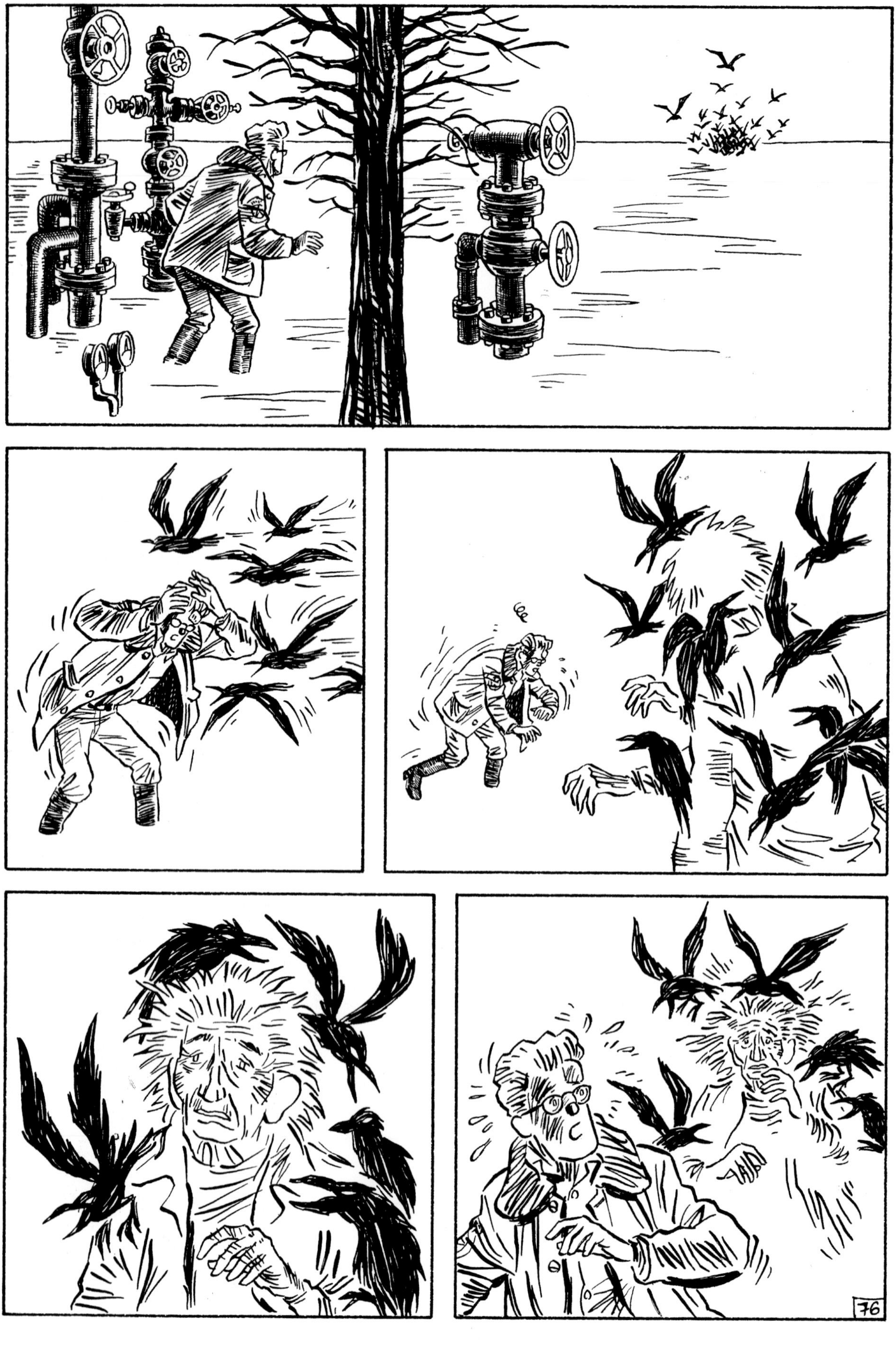

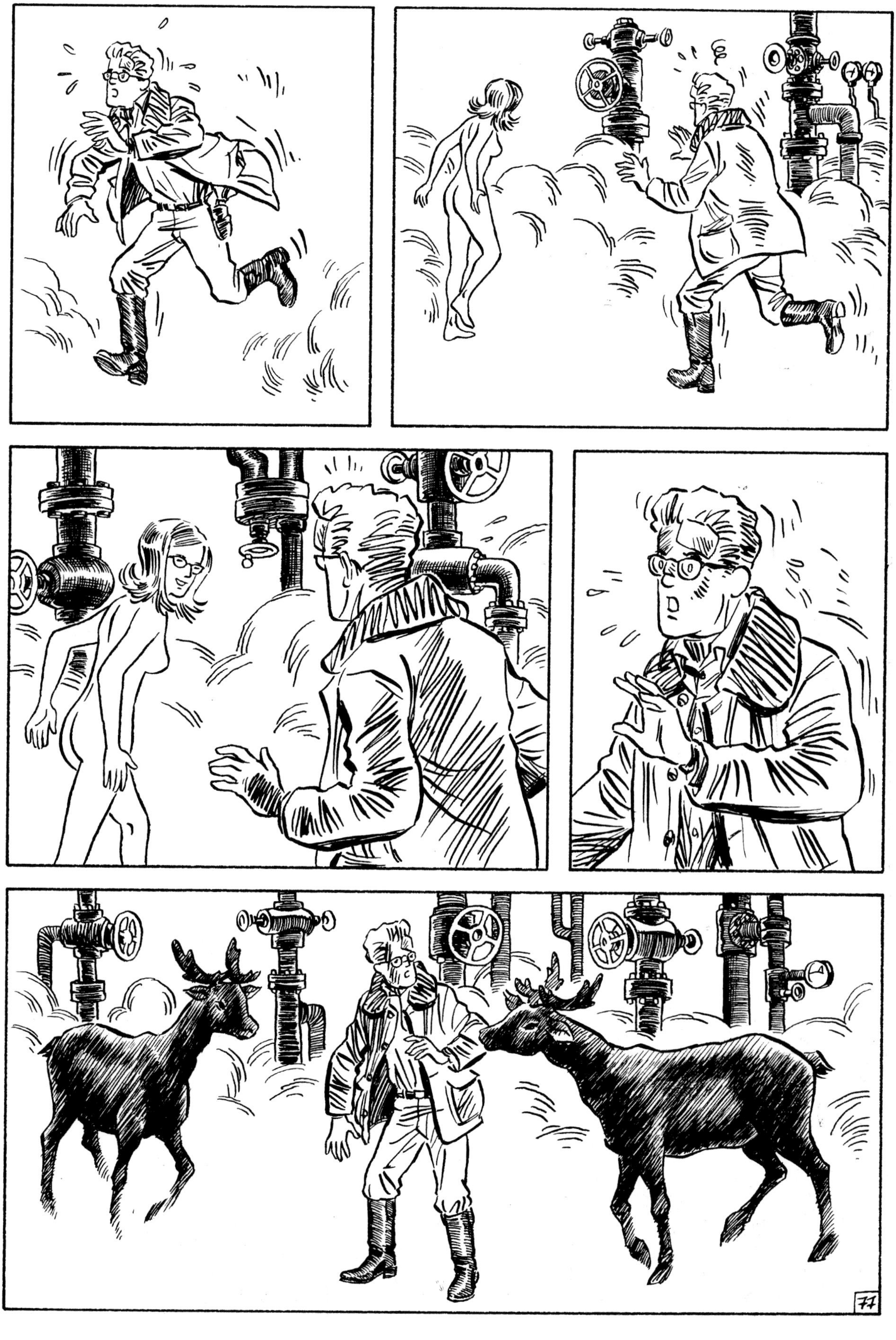

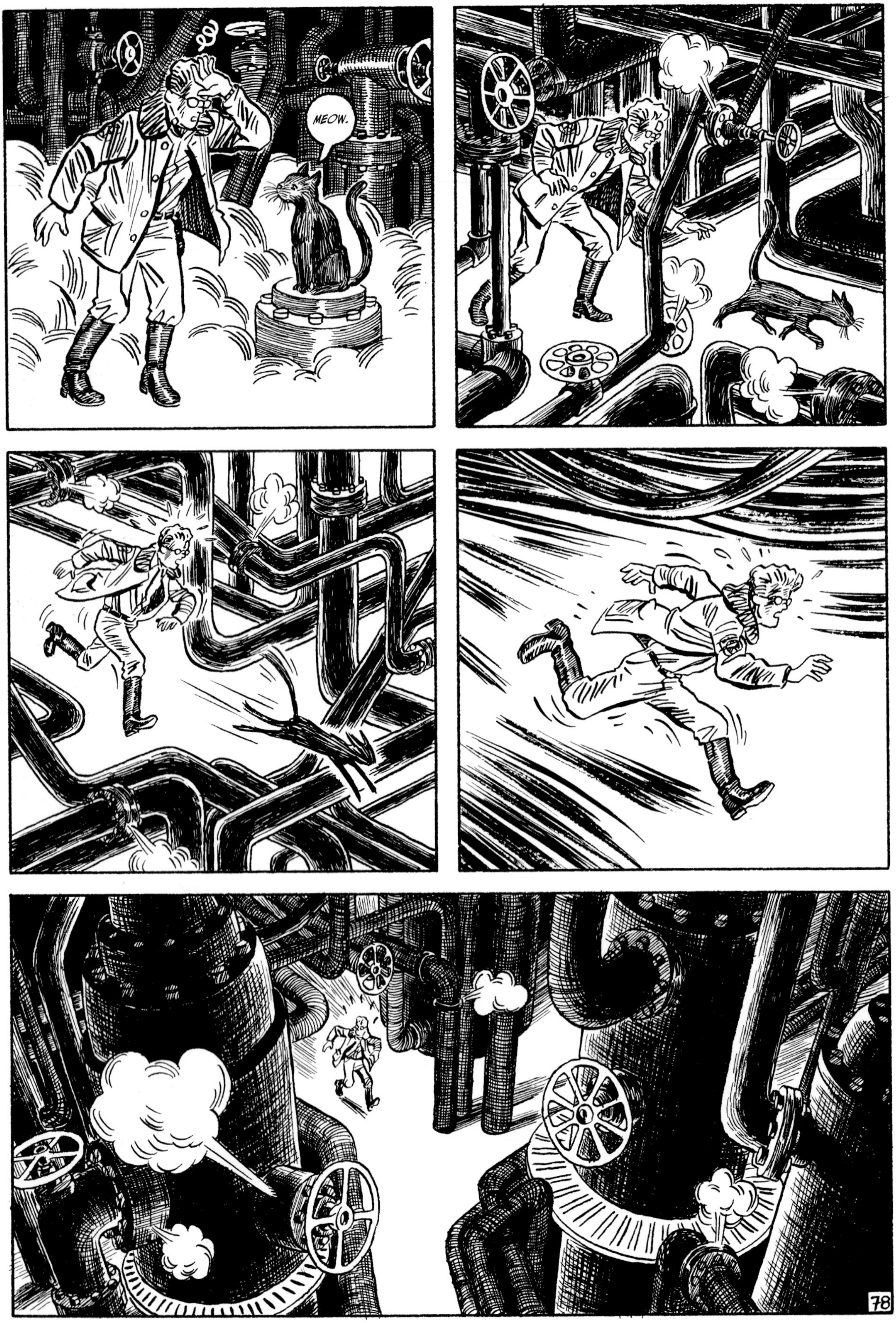
MEOW.

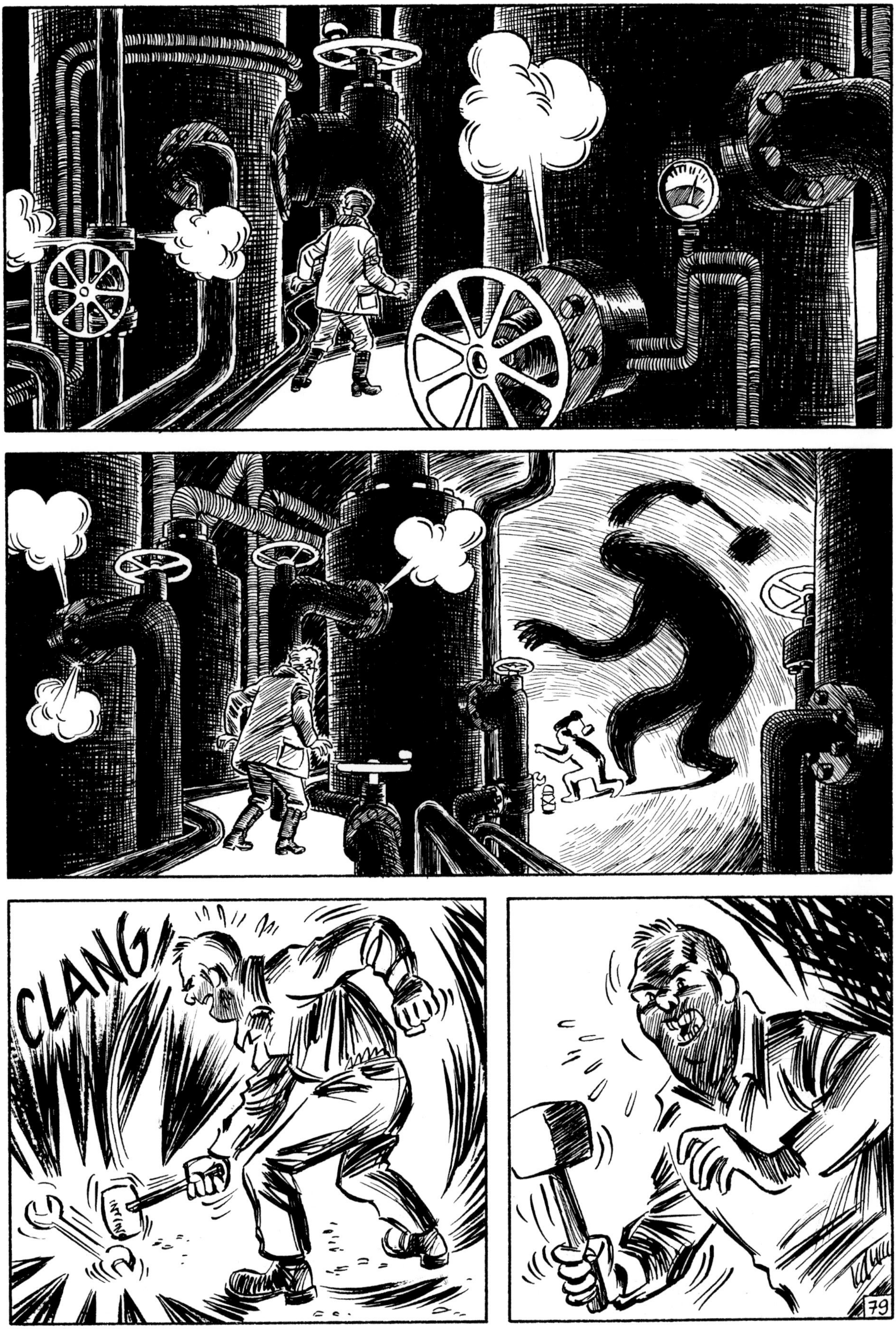
CLANG!

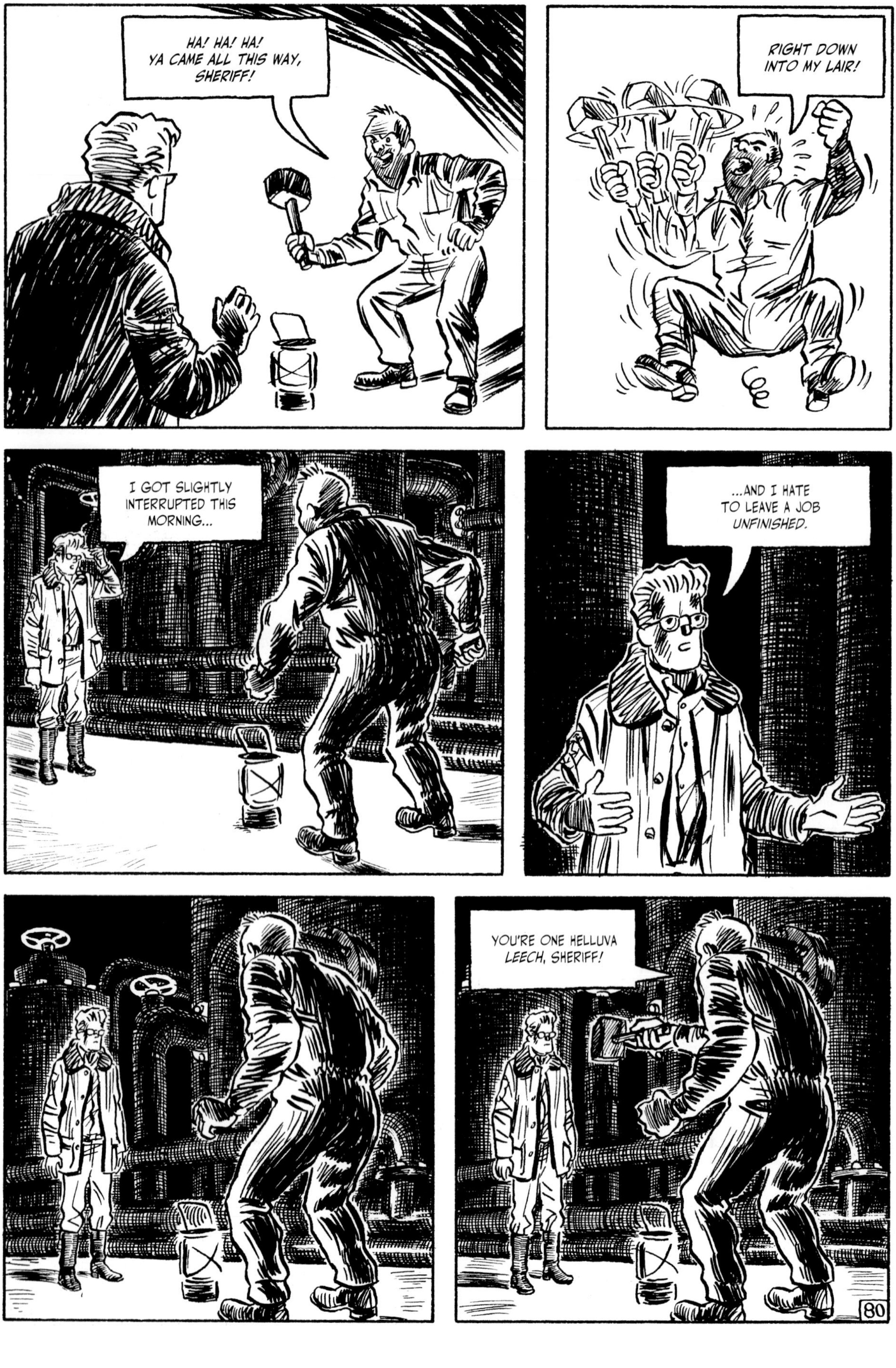
HA! HA! HA!
YA CAME ALL THIS WAY, SHERIFF!
RIGHT DOWN INTO MY LAIR!
I GOT SLIGHTLY INTERRUPTED THIS MORNING...
...AND I HATE TO LEAVE A JOB UNFINISHED.
YOU'RE ONE HELLUVA LEECH, SHERIFF!

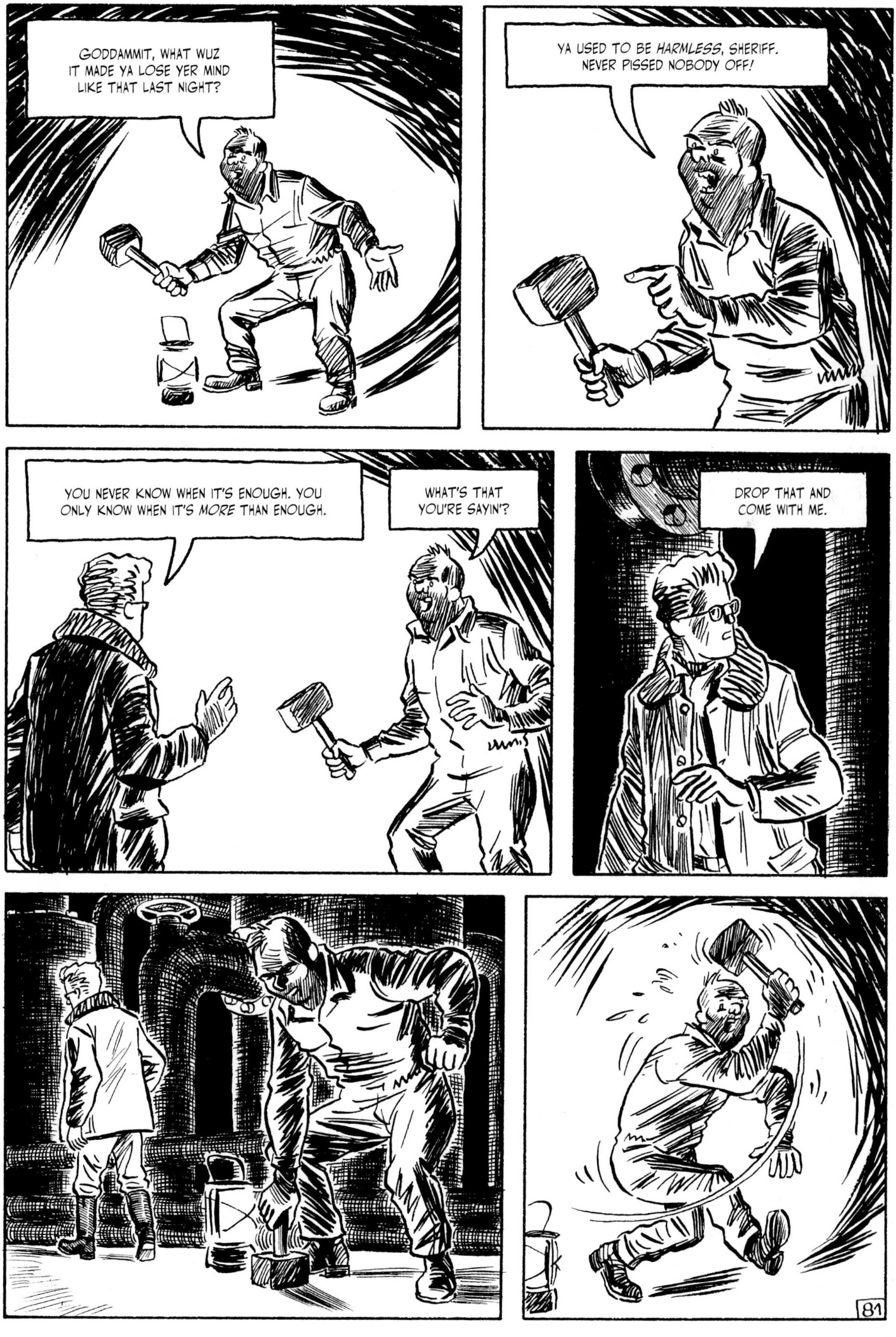
GODDAMMIT, WHAT WUZ IT MADE YA LOSE YER MIND LIKE THAT LAST NIGHT?
YA USED TO BE *HARMLESS*, SHERIFF. NEVER PISSED NOBODY OFF!
YOU NEVER KNOW WHEN IT'S ENOUGH. YOU ONLY KNOW WHEN IT'S *MORE* THAN ENOUGH.
WHAT'S THAT YOU'RE SAYIN'?
DROP THAT AND COME WITH ME.
81

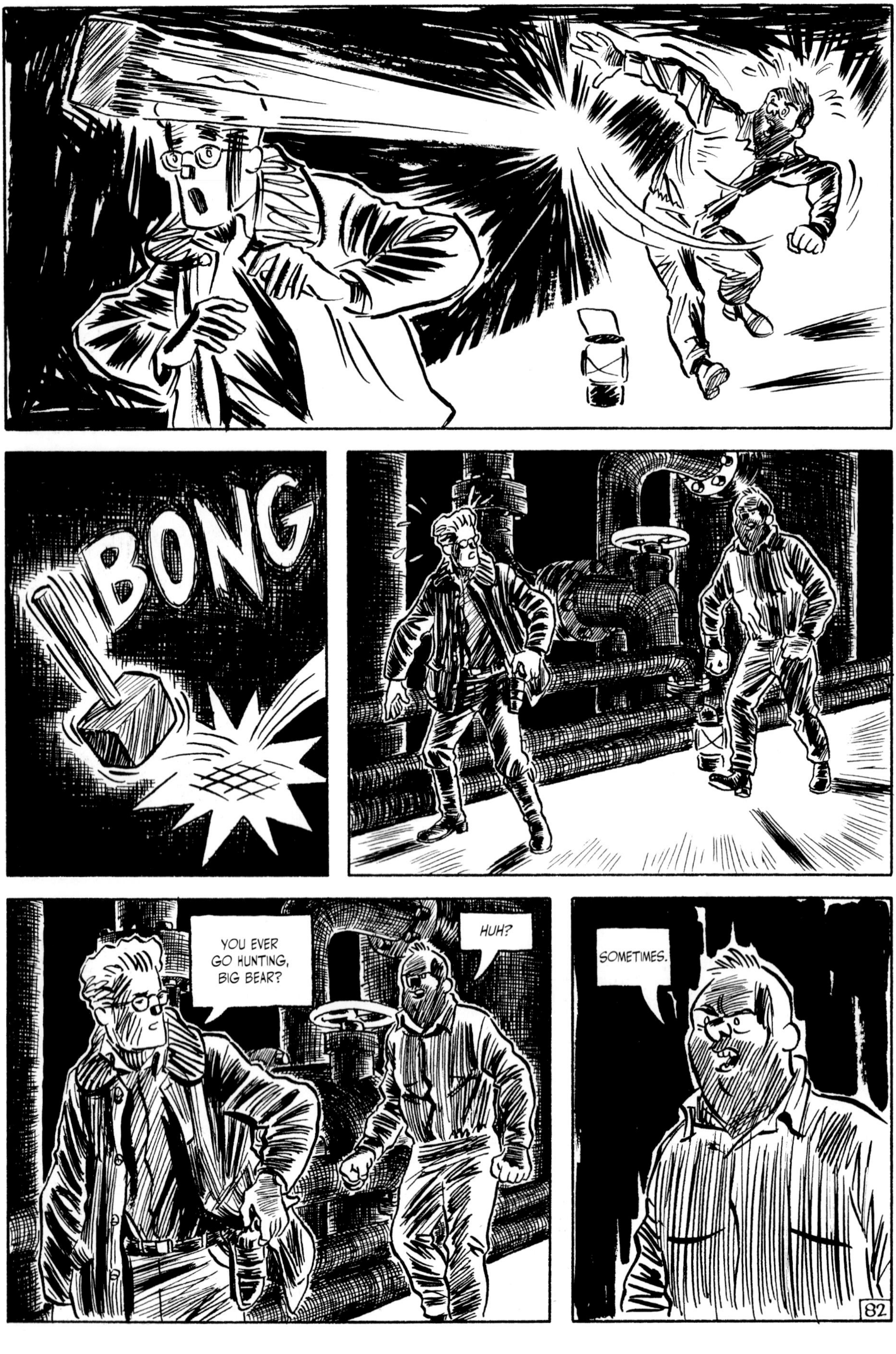
BONG
YOU EVER GO HUNTING, BIG BEAR?
HUH?
SOMETIMES.

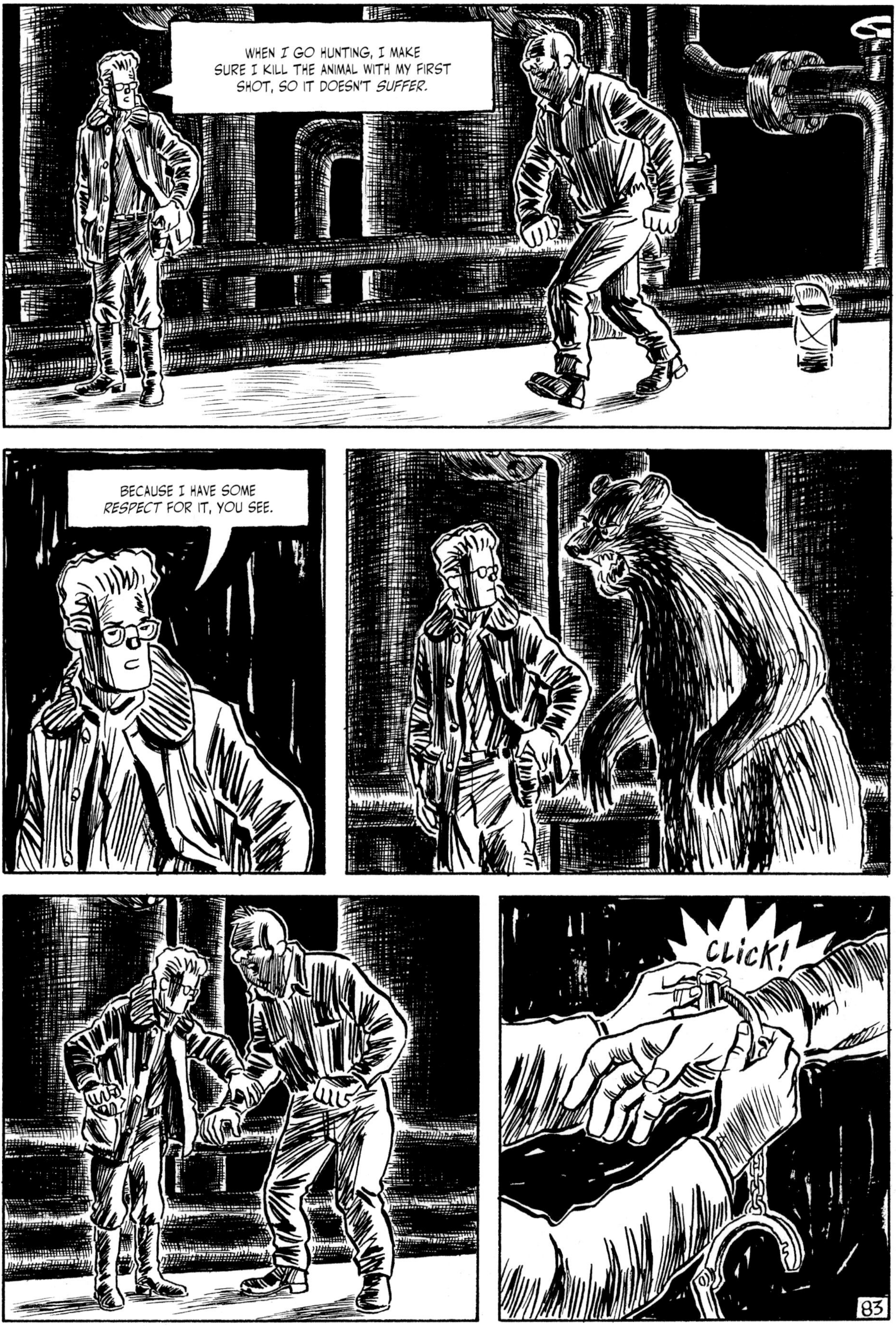
WHEN *I* GO HUNTING, I MAKE SURE I KILL THE ANIMAL WITH MY FIRST SHOT, SO IT DOESN'T *SUFFER*.
BECAUSE I HAVE SOME *RESPECT* FOR IT, YOU SEE.
CLICK!

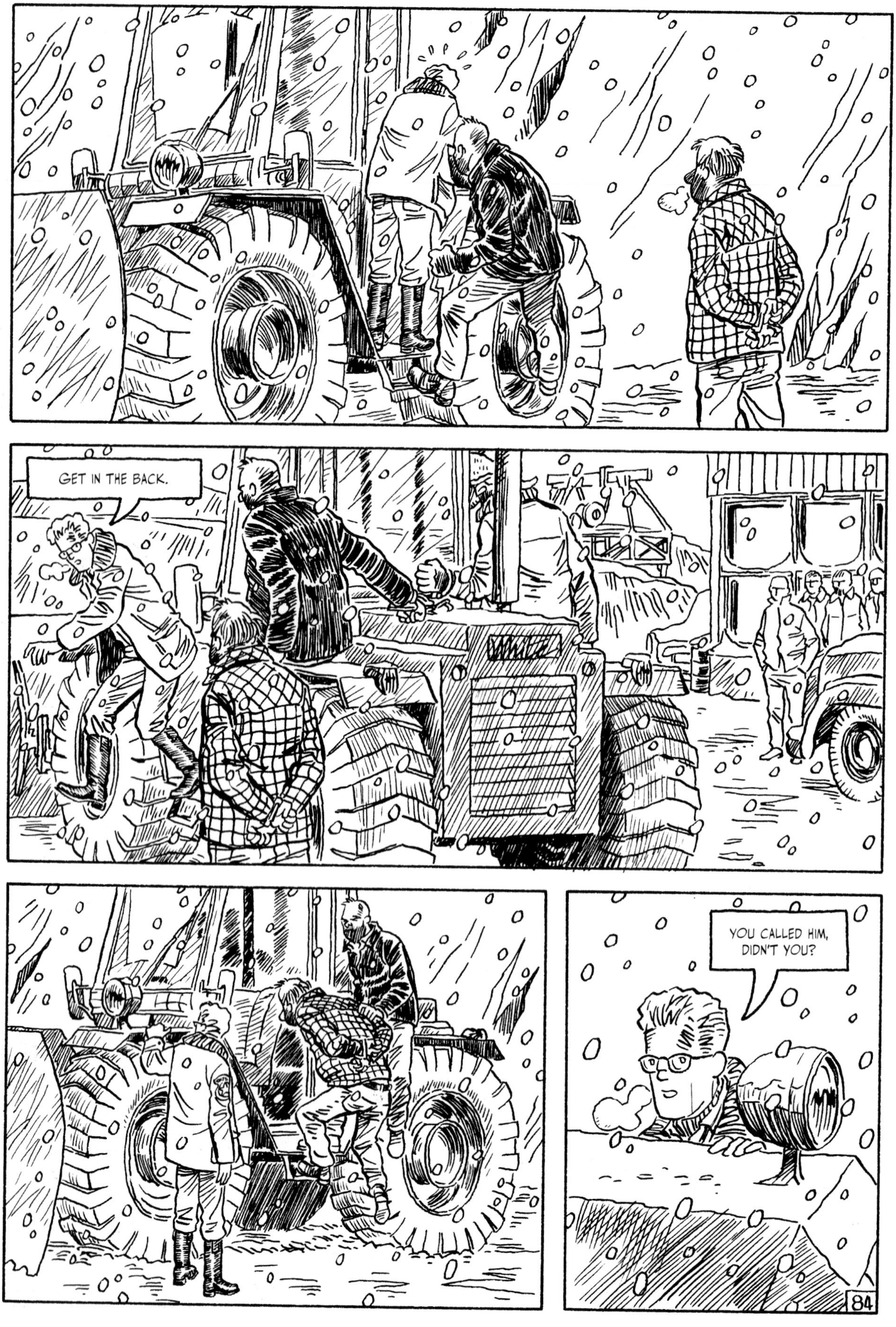
GET IN THE BACK.
YOU CALLED HIM, DIDN'T YOU?

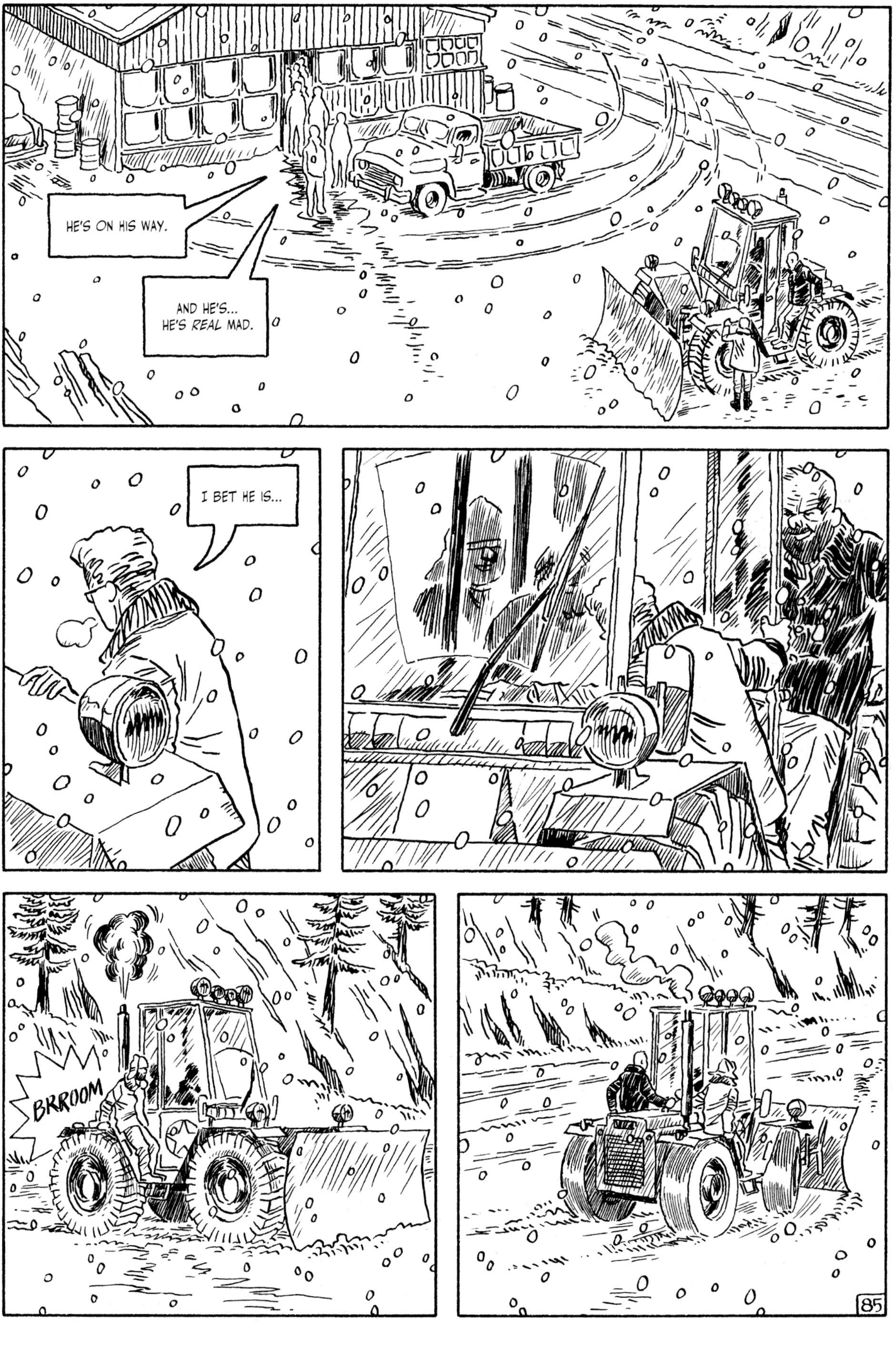
HE'S ON HIS WAY.
AND HE'S... HE'S *REAL* MAD.
I BET HE IS...
BRROOM

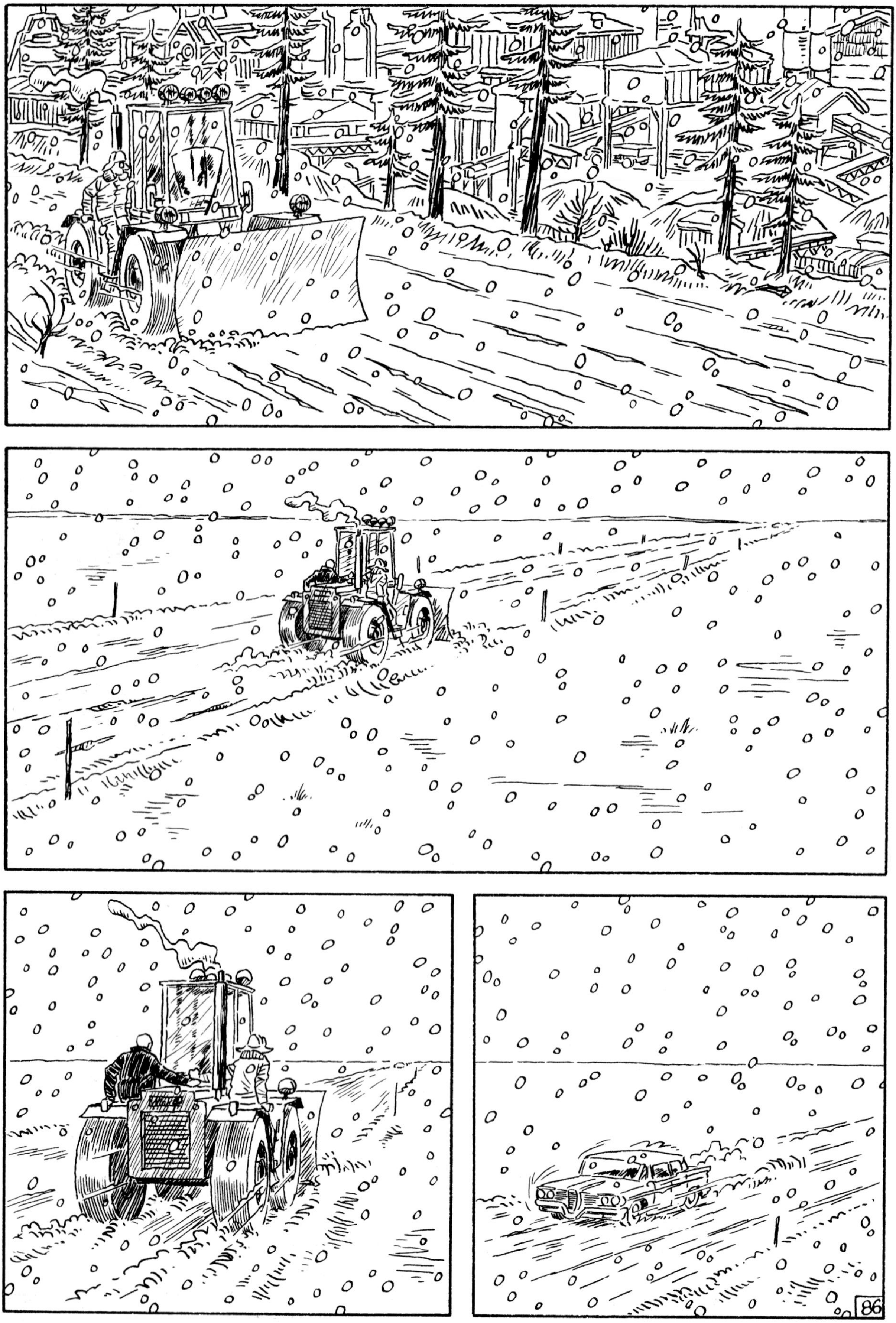

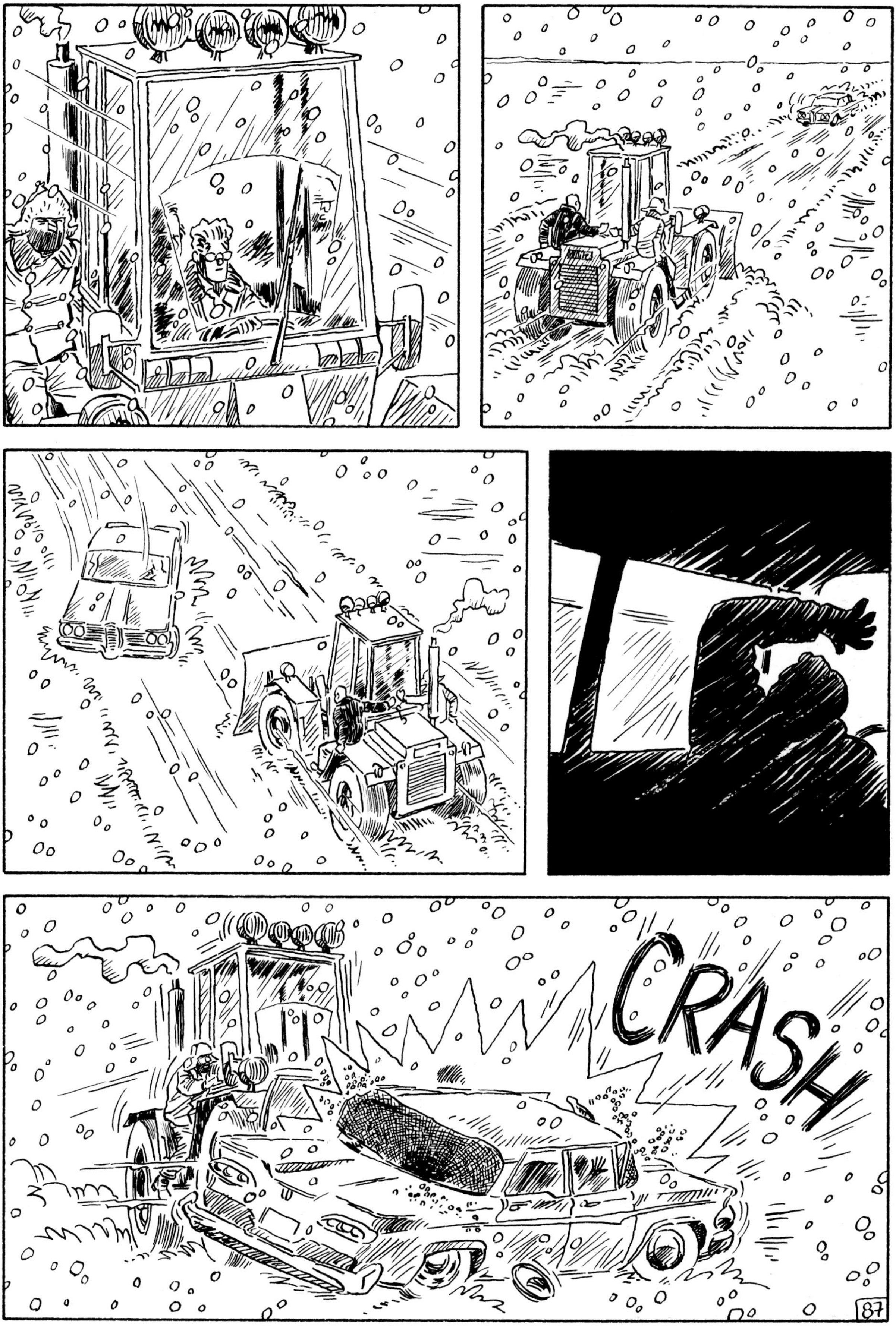

CRASH

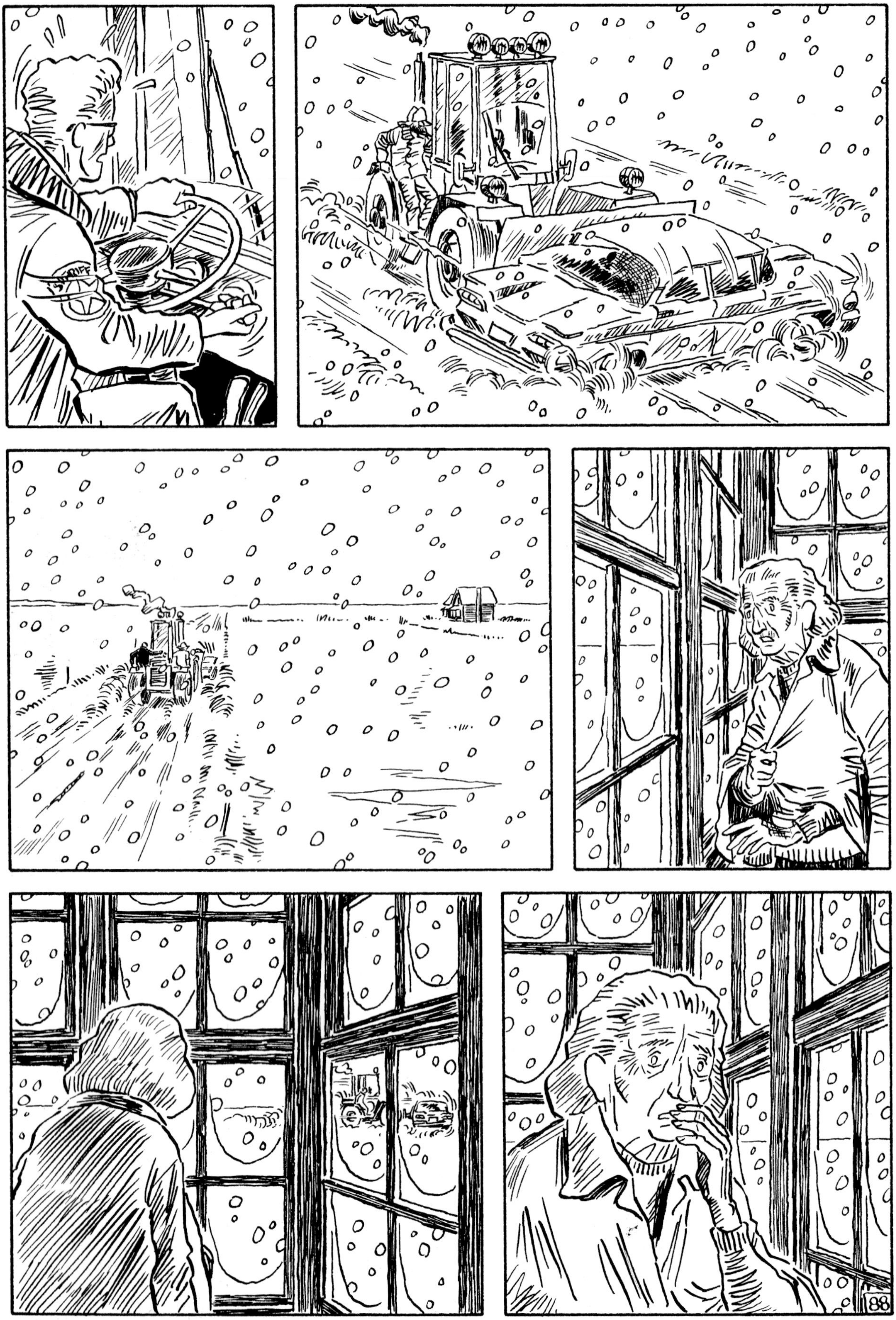

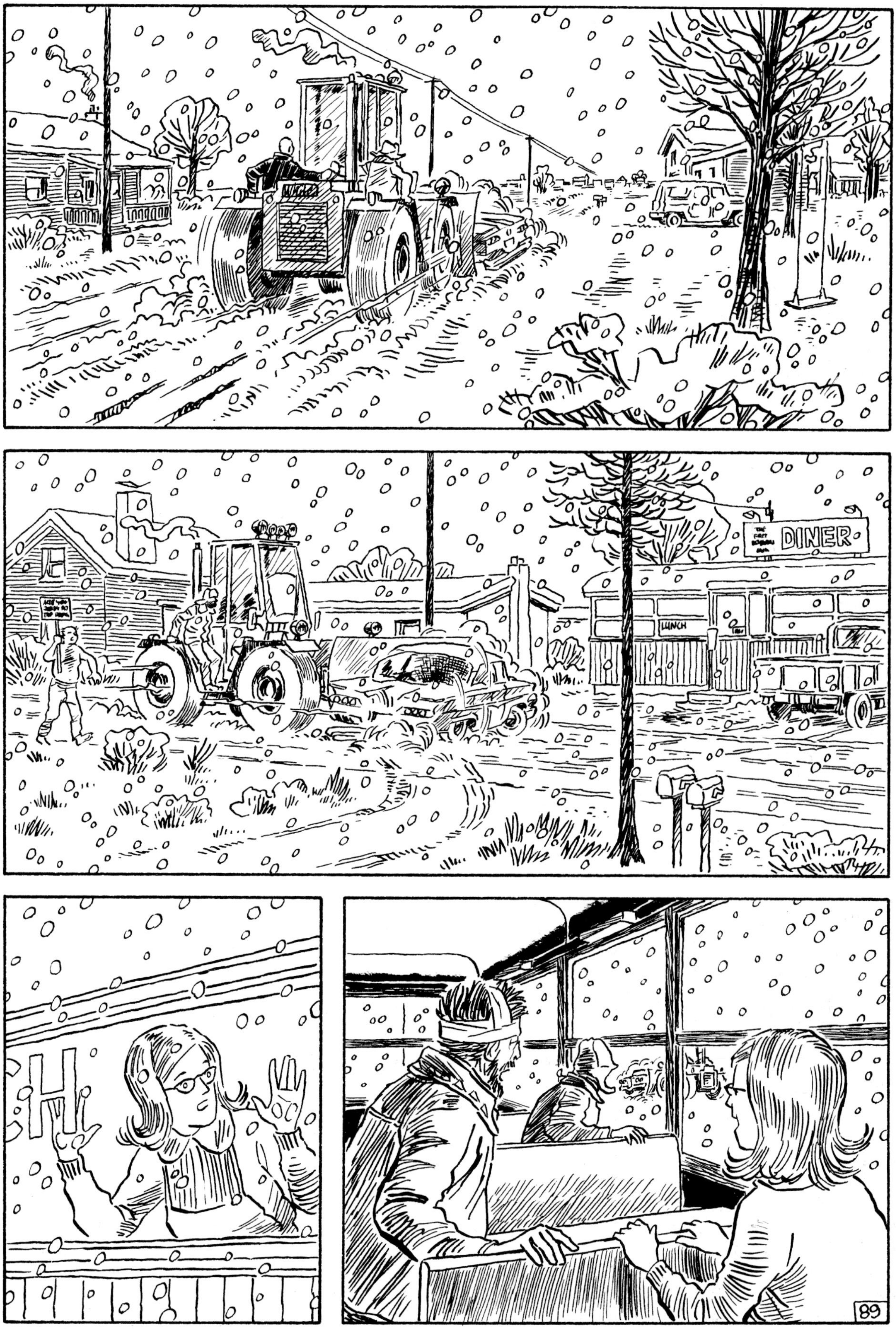
DINER
LUNCH

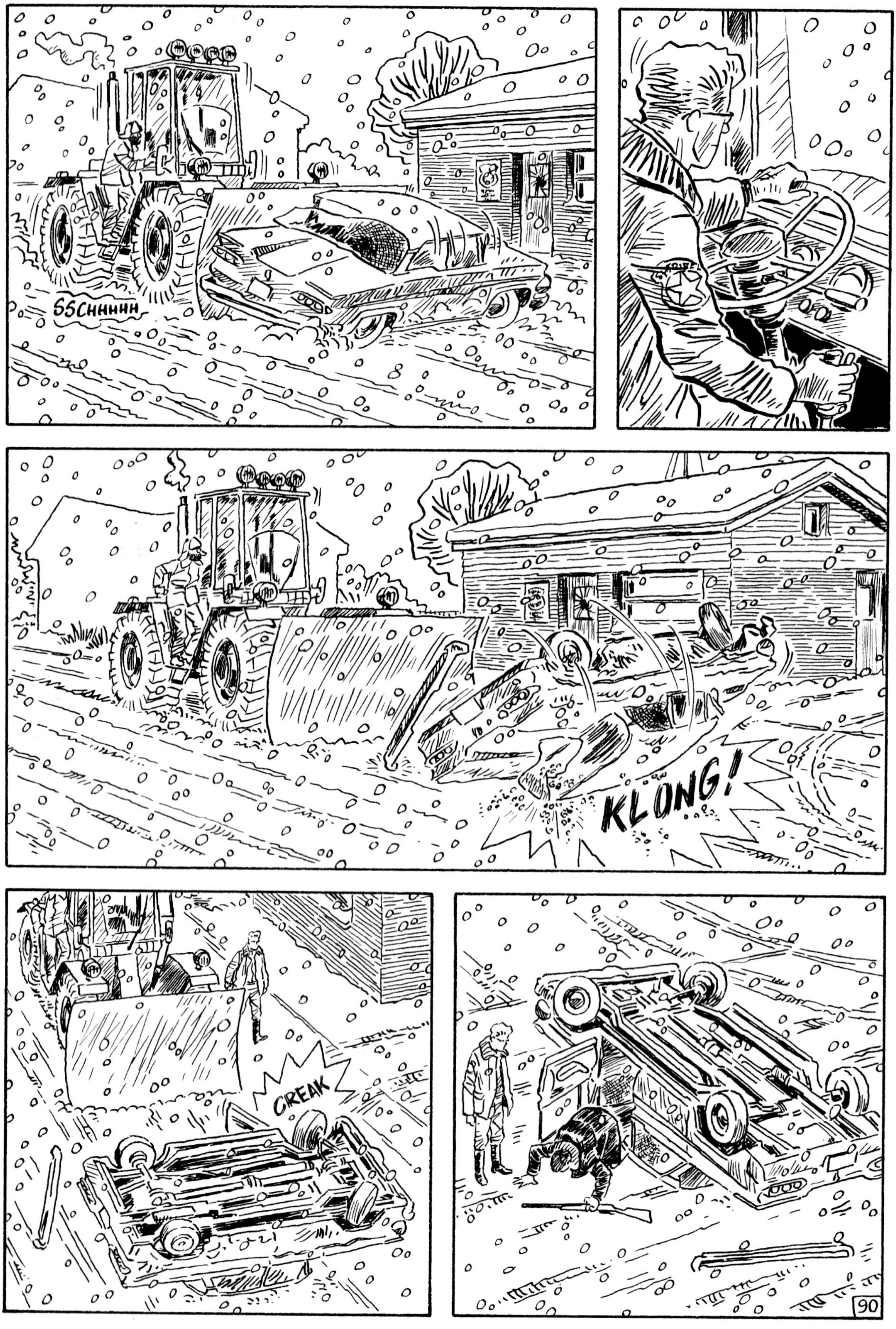
SSCHHHHH
KLONG!
CREAK

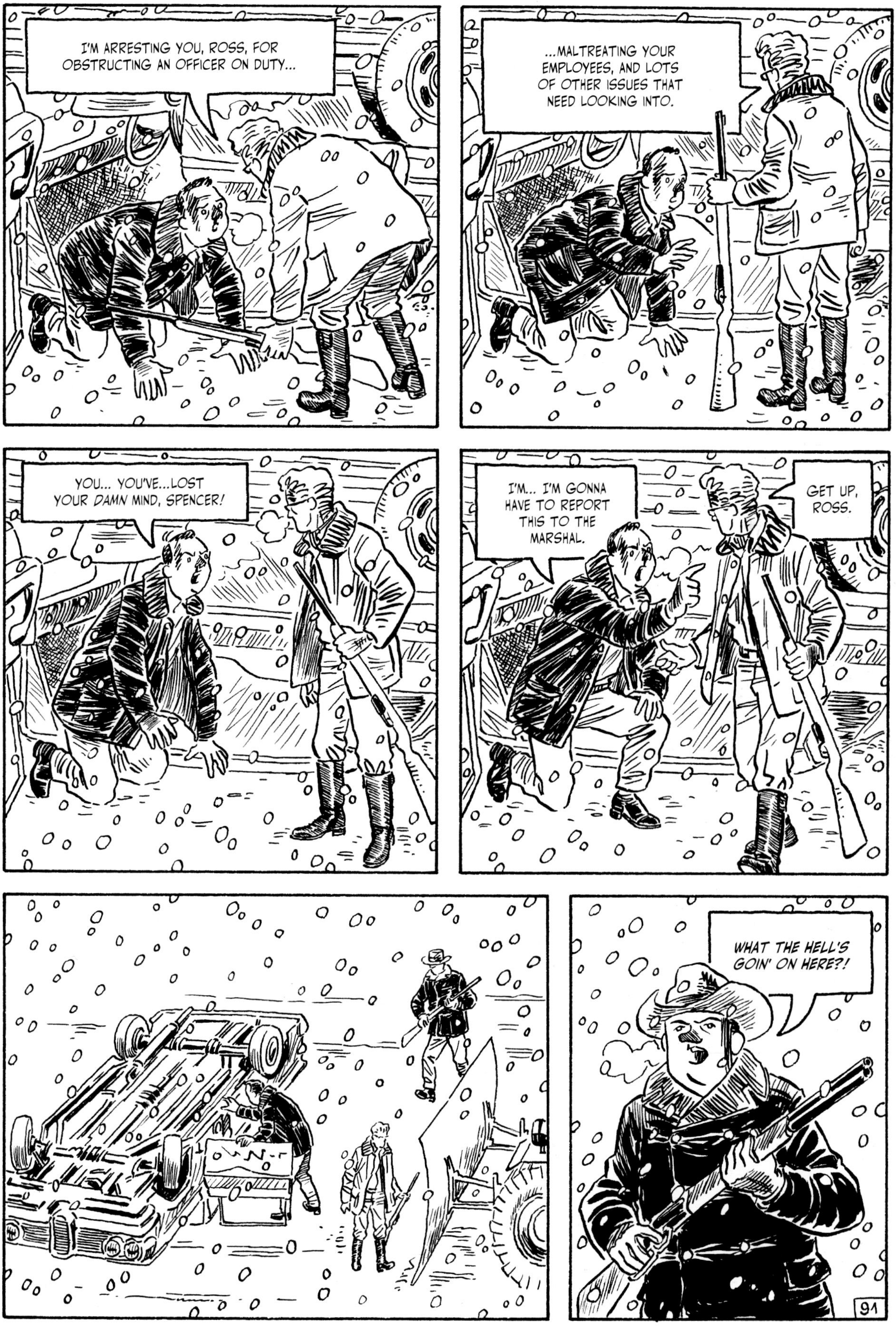
I'M ARRESTING YOU, ROSS, FOR OBSTRUCTING AN OFFICER ON DUTY...
...MALTREATING YOUR EMPLOYEES, AND LOTS OF OTHER ISSUES THAT NEED LOOKING INTO.
YOU... YOU'VE...LOST YOUR *DAMN* MIND, SPENCER!
I'M... I'M GONNA HAVE TO REPORT THIS TO THE MARSHAL.
GET UP, ROSS.
WHAT THE HELL'S GOIN' ON HERE?!
91

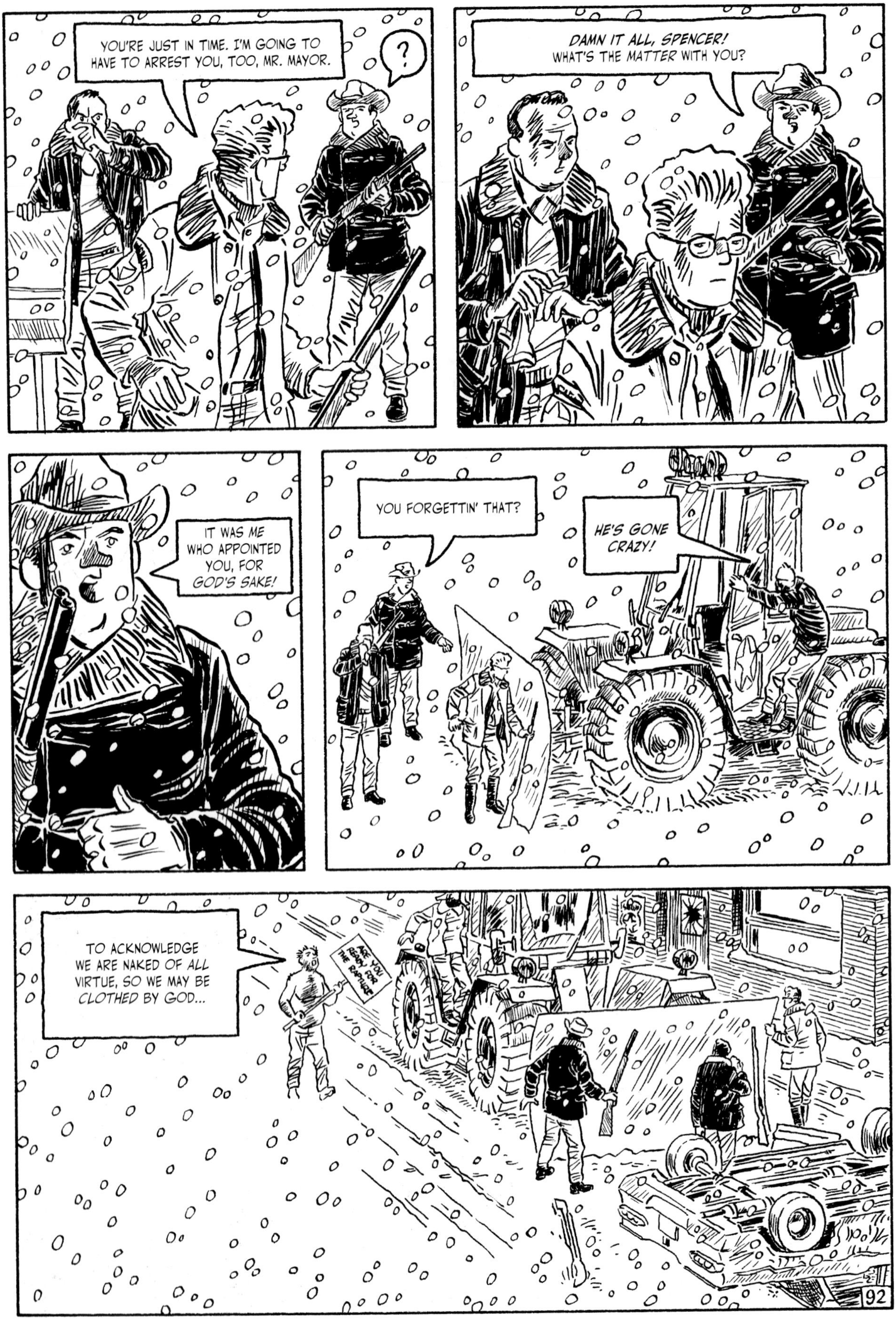
YOU'RE JUST IN TIME. I'M GOING TO HAVE TO ARREST YOU, TOO, MR. MAYOR.
?
DAMN IT ALL, SPENCER! WHAT'S THE MATTER WITH YOU?
IT WAS ME WHO APPOINTED YOU, FOR GOD'S SAKE!
YOU FORGETTIN' THAT?
HE'S GONE CRAZY!
TO ACKNOWLEDGE WE ARE NAKED OF ALL VIRTUE, SO WE MAY BE CLOTHED BY GOD...
ARE YOU READY FOR THE RAPTURE

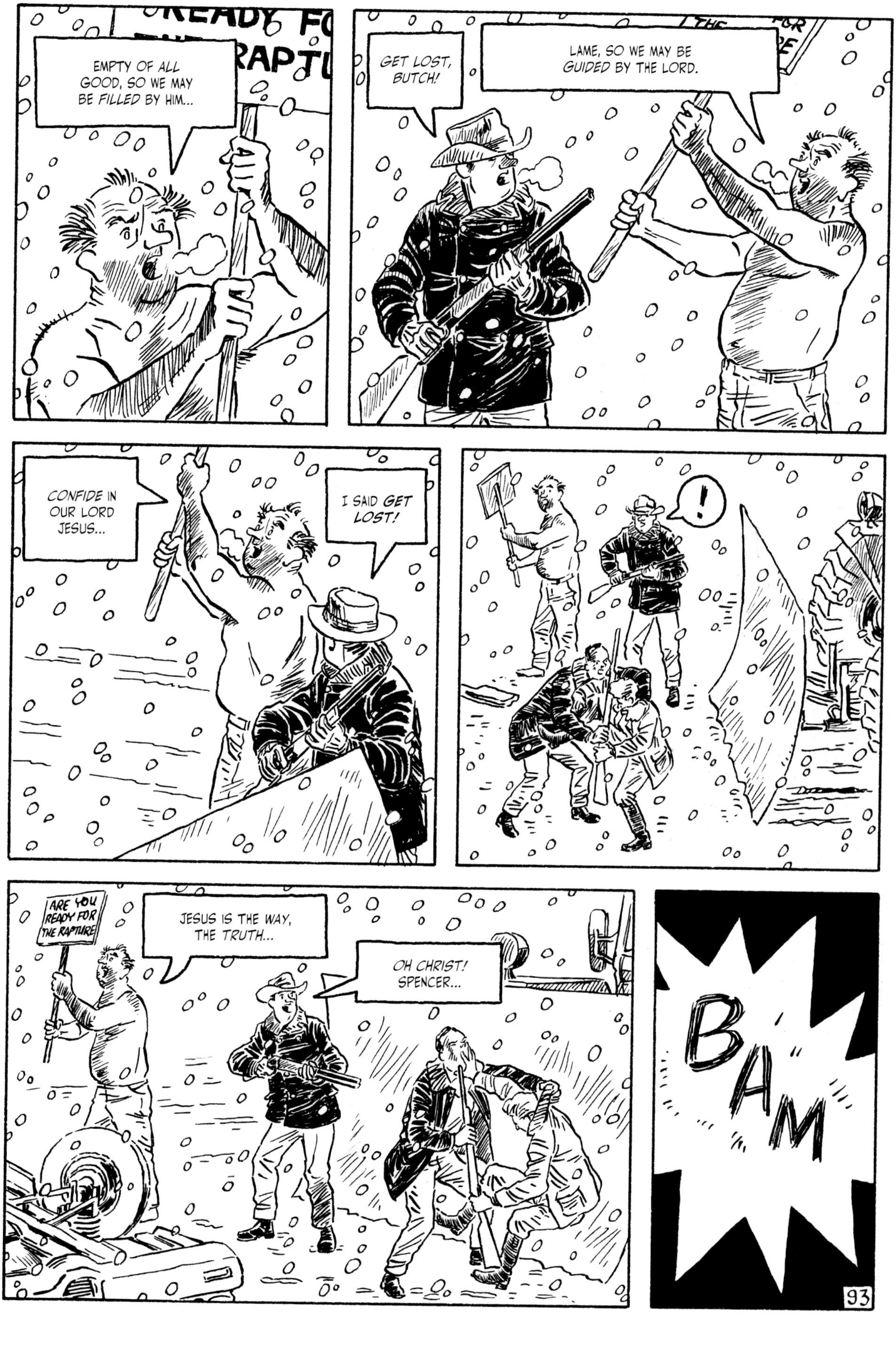
EMPTY OF ALL GOOD, SO WE MAY BE FILLED BY HIM...
GET LOST, BUTCH!
LAME, SO WE MAY BE GUIDED BY THE LORD.
CONFIDE IN OUR LORD JESUS...
I SAID GET LOST!
!
ARE YOU READY FOR THE RAPTURE
JESUS IS THE WAY, THE TRUTH...
OH CHRIST! SPENCER...
BAM

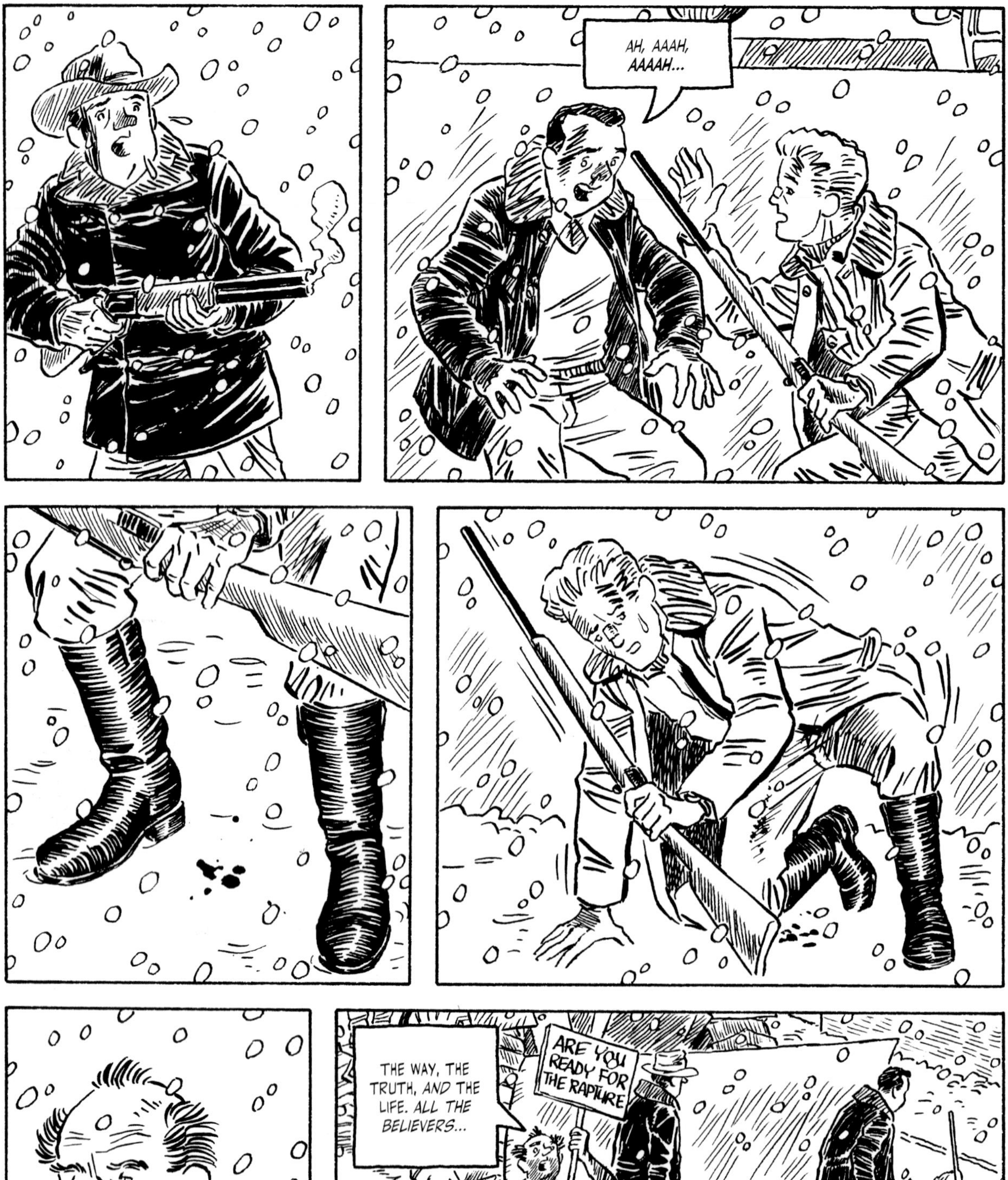
AH, AAAH, AAAAH...
THE WAY, THE TRUTH, AND THE LIFE. ALL THE BELIEVERS...
ARE YOU READY FOR THE RAPTURE

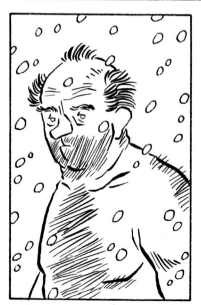

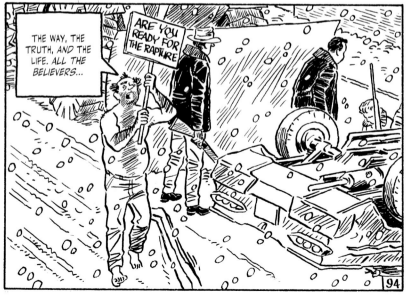

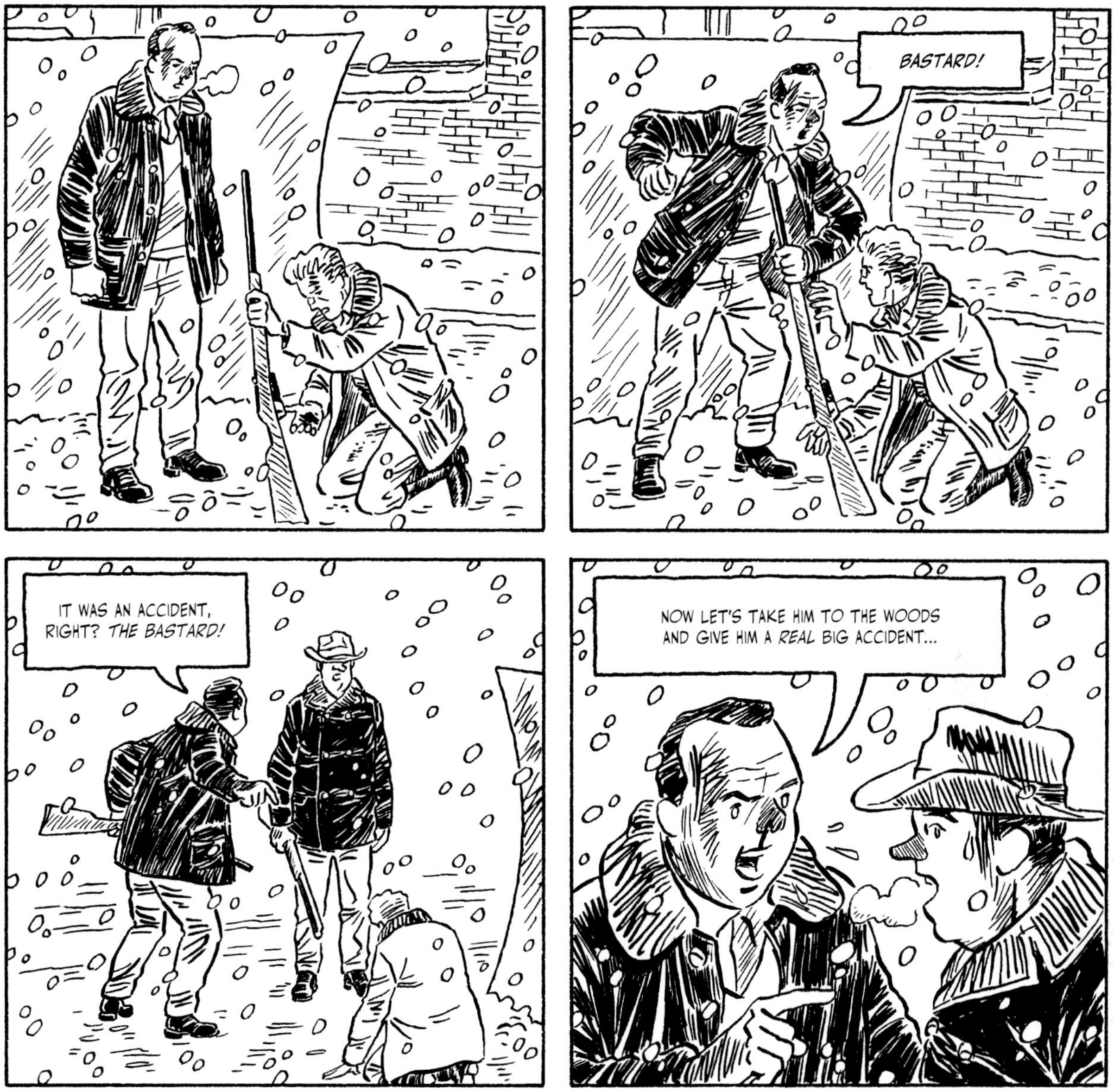
BASTARD!
IT WAS AN ACCIDENT, RIGHT? THE BASTARD!
NOW LET'S TAKE HIM TO THE WOODS AND GIVE HIM A REAL BIG ACCIDENT...
C'MON! GET UP, YOU BASTARD!
HEY! UNCUFF US, DAMMIT!

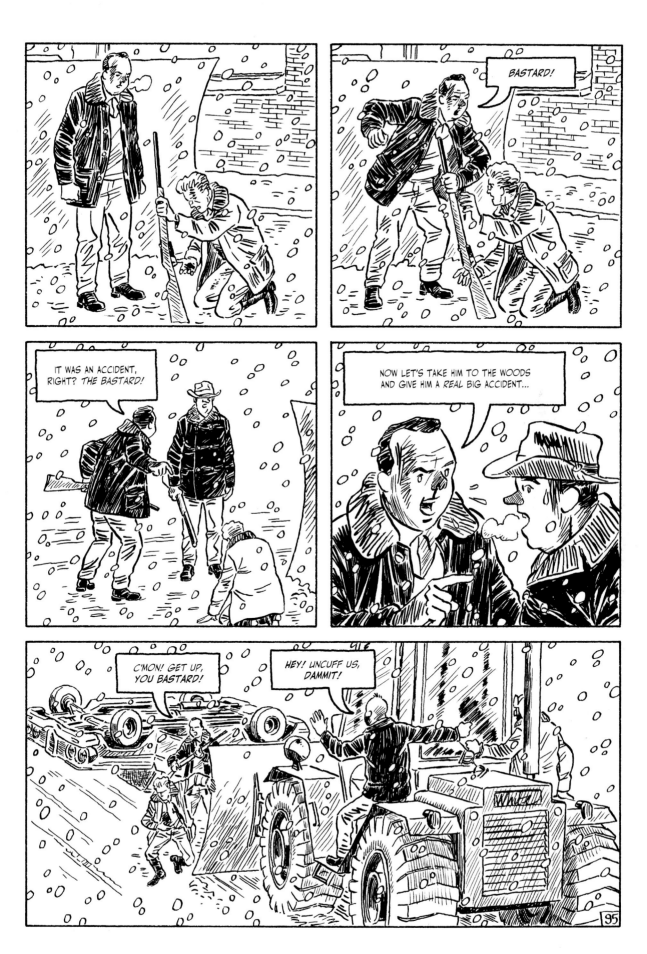

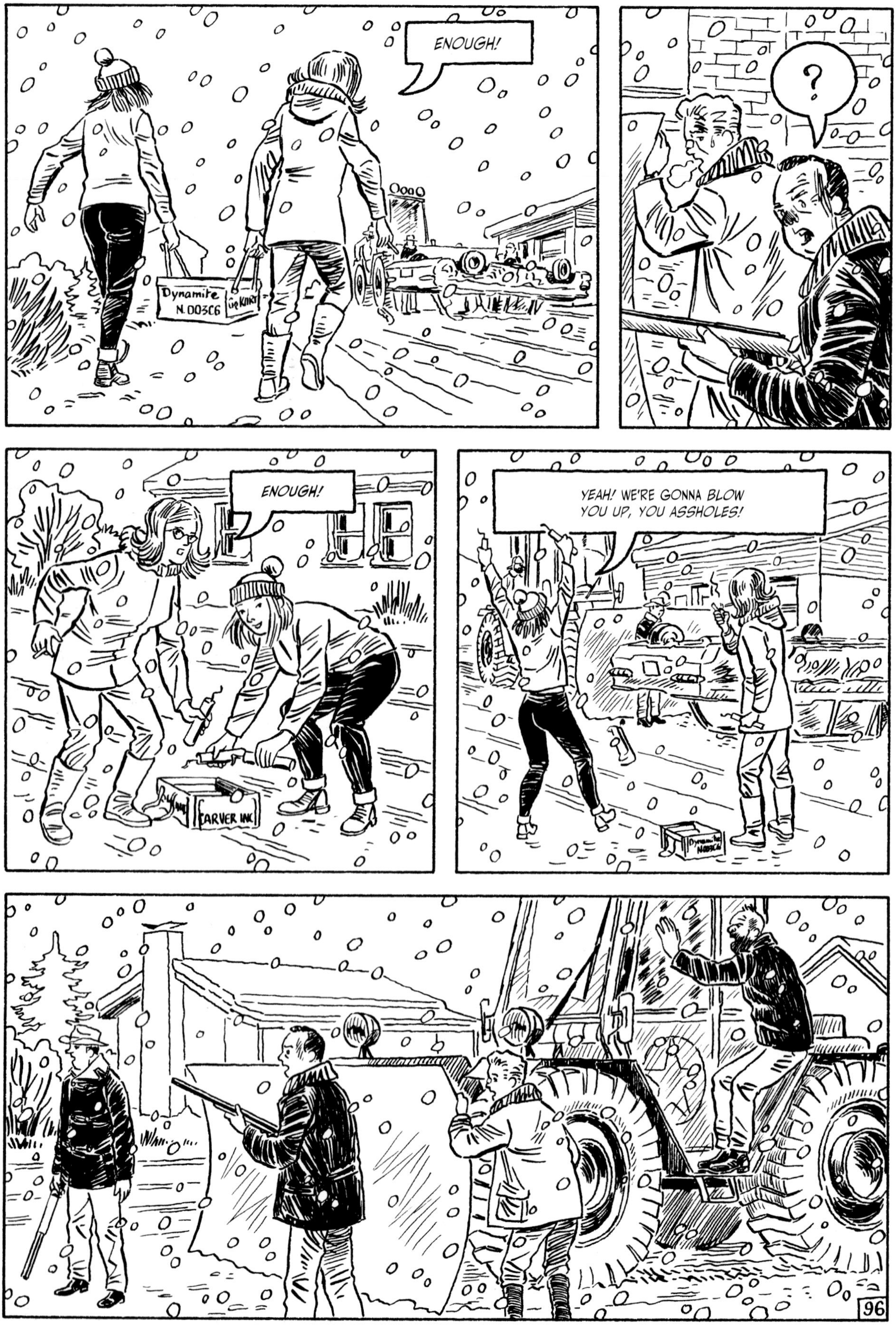
ENOUGH!
?
ENOUGH!
FARVER INC
YEAH! WE'RE GONNA BLOW YOU UP, YOU ASSHOLES!

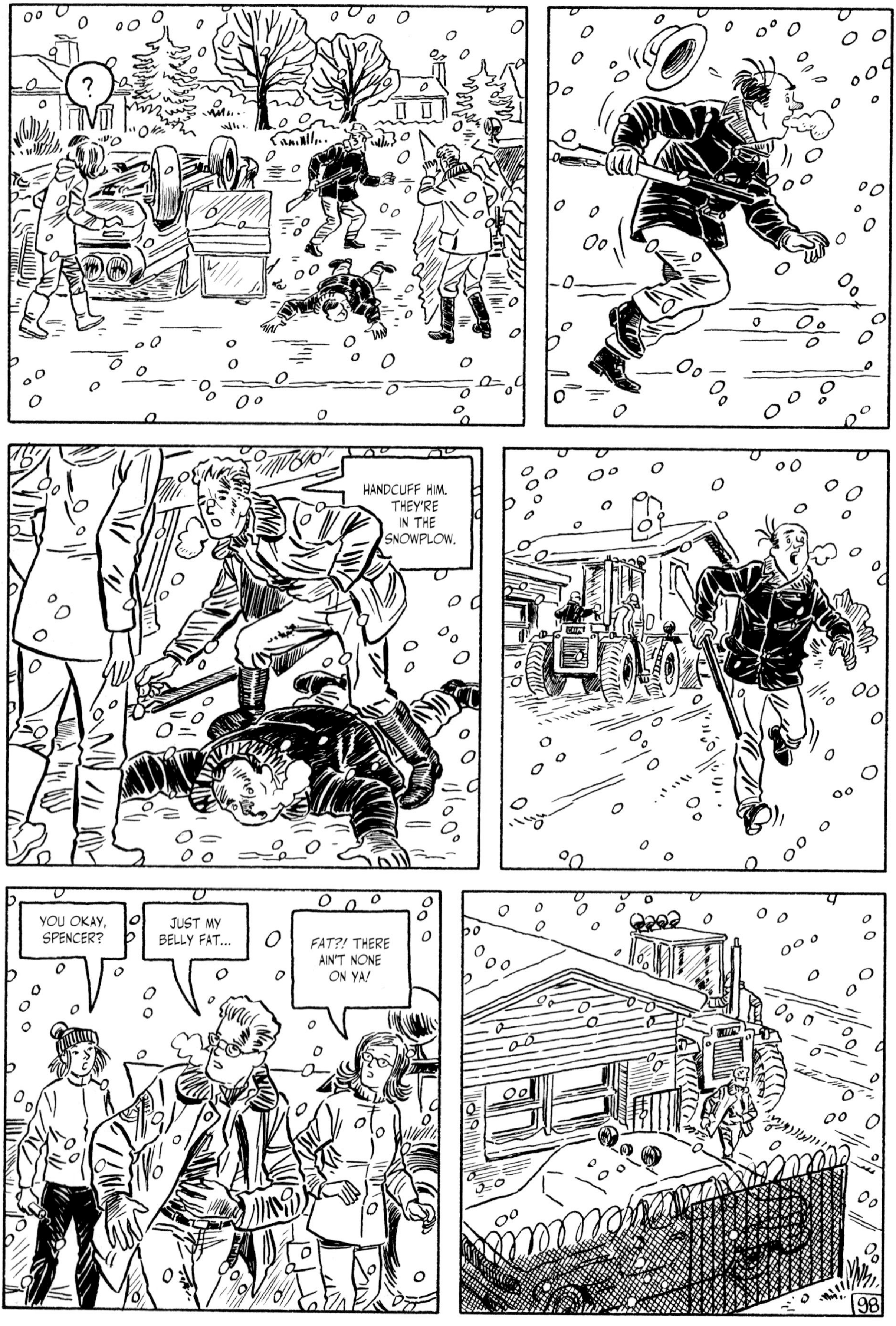
?
HANDCUFF HIM. THEY'RE IN THE SNOWPLOW.
YOU OKAY, SPENCER?
JUST MY BELLY FAT...
FAT?! THERE AIN'T NONE ON YA!

99

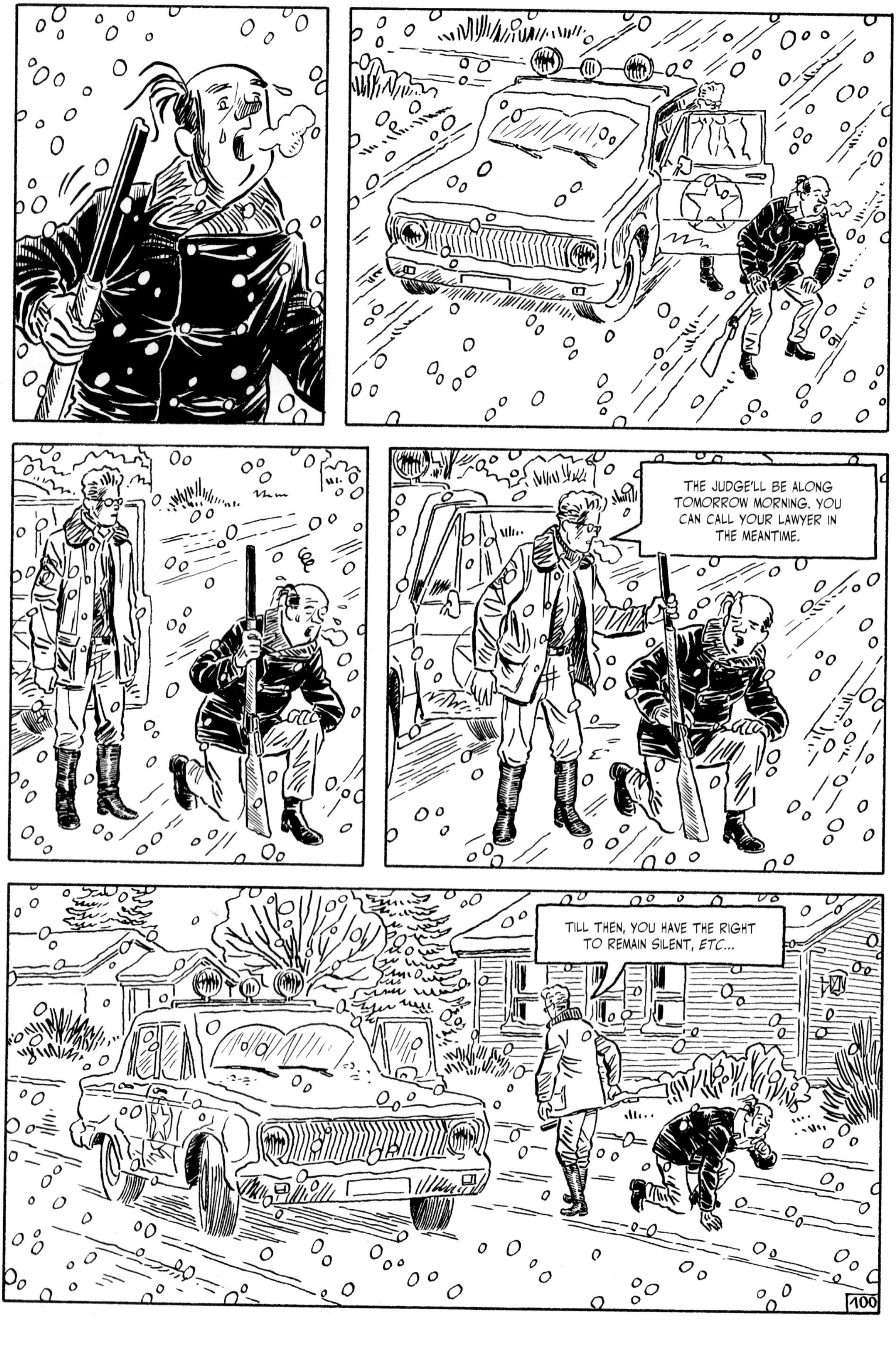
THE JUDGE'LL BE ALONG TOMORROW MORNING. YOU CAN CALL YOUR LAWYER IN THE MEANTIME.
TILL THEN, YOU HAVE THE RIGHT TO REMAIN SILENT, *ETC*...

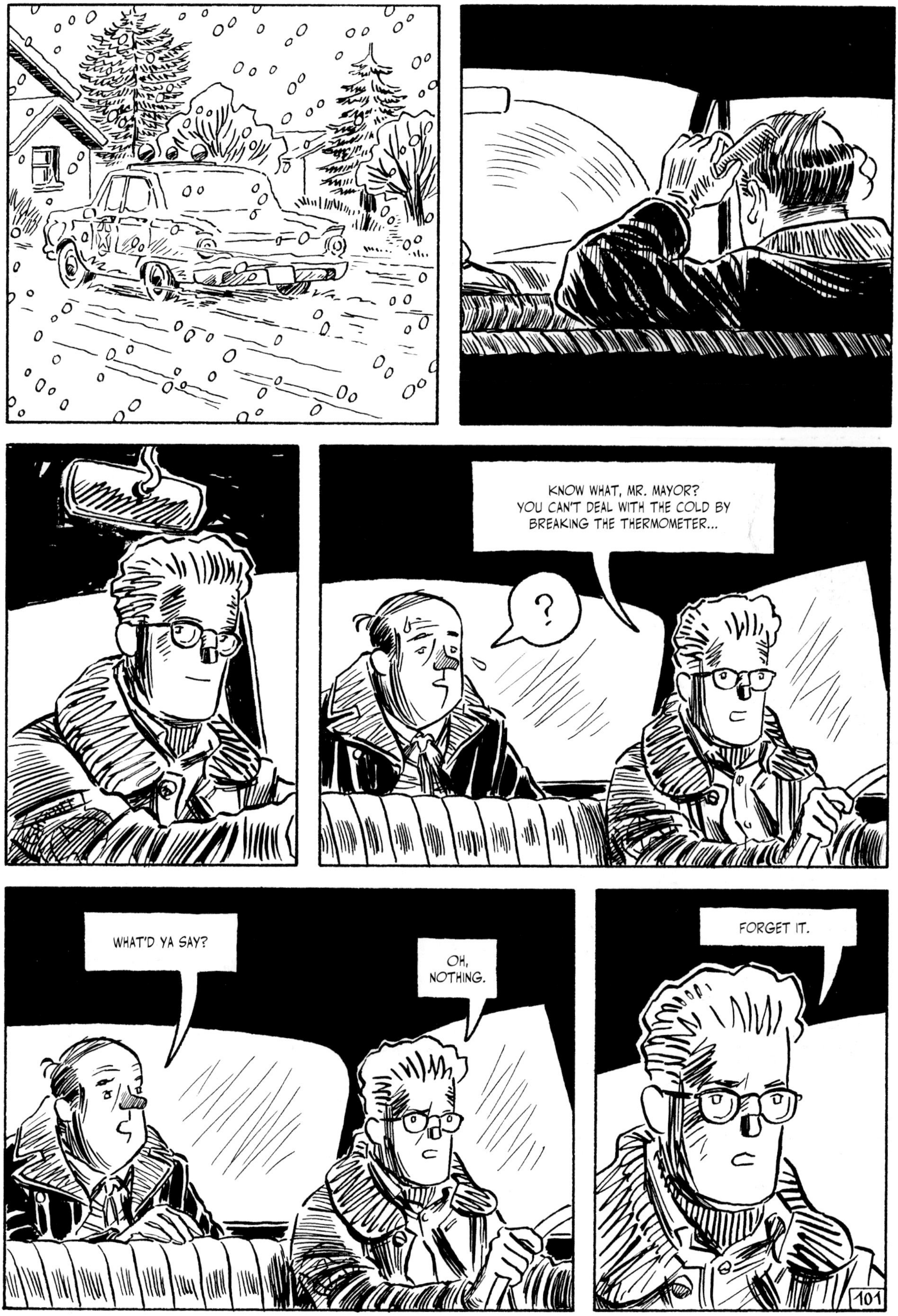
KNOW WHAT, MR. MAYOR? YOU CAN'T DEAL WITH THE COLD BY BREAKING THE THERMOMETER...
?
WHAT'D YA SAY?
OH, NOTHING.
FORGET IT.

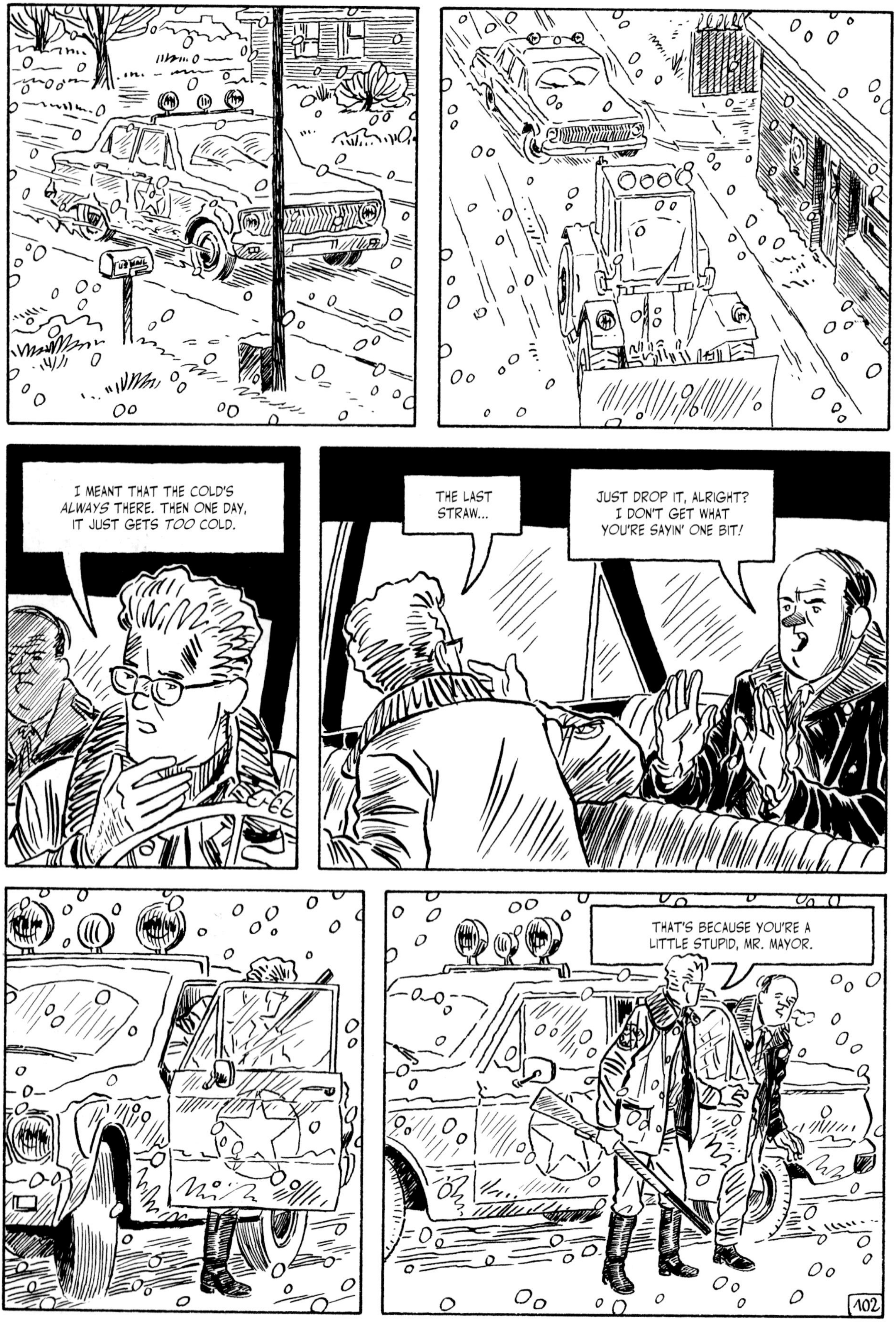
I MEANT THAT THE COLD'S *ALWAYS* THERE. THEN ONE DAY, IT JUST GETS *TOO* COLD.
THE LAST STRAW...
JUST DROP IT, ALRIGHT? I DON'T GET WHAT YOU'RE SAYIN' ONE BIT!
THAT'S BECAUSE YOU'RE A LITTLE STUPID, MR. MAYOR.
102

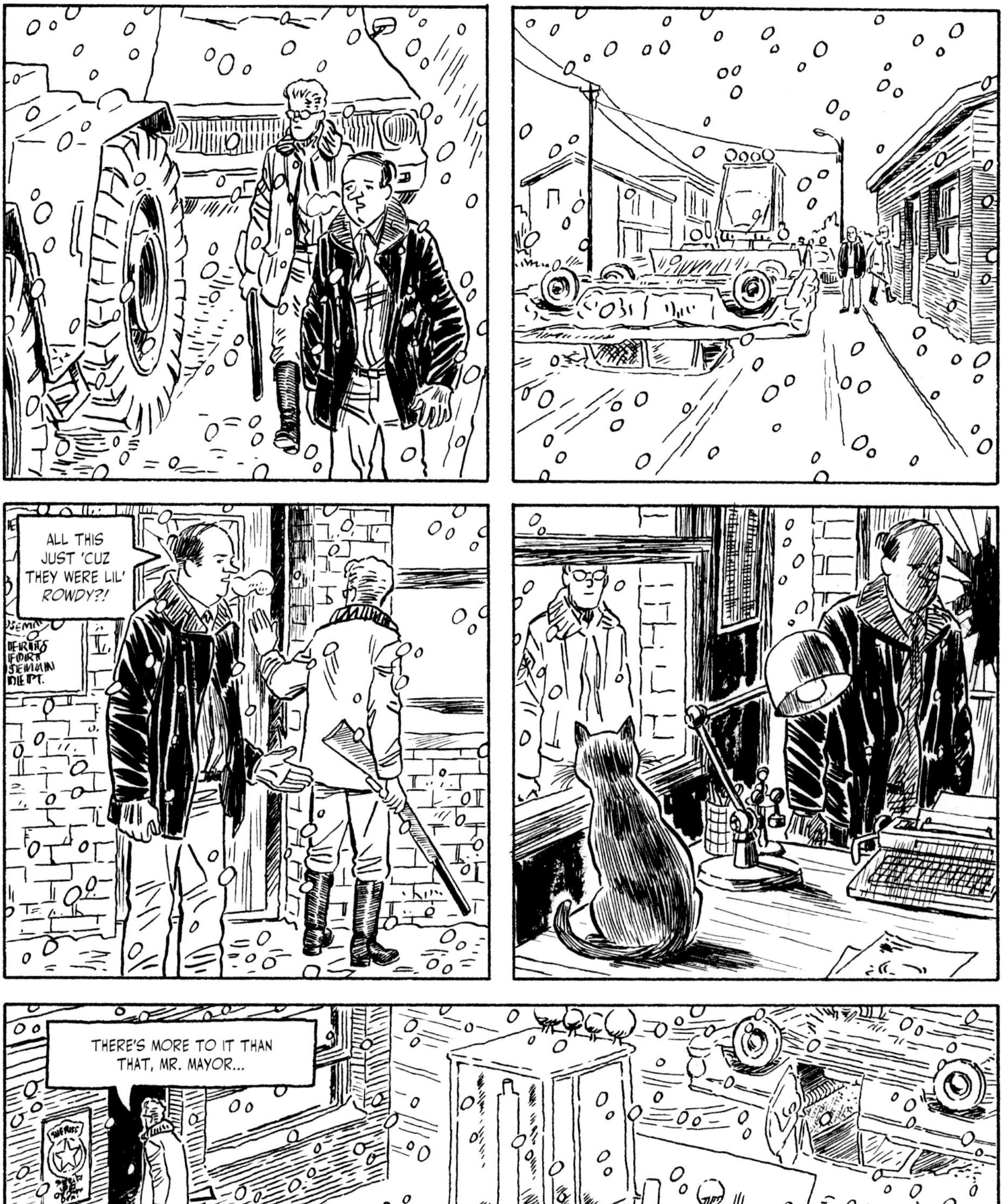
ALL THIS JUST 'CUZ THEY WERE LIL' *ROWDY?!*
THERE'S MORE TO IT THAN THAT, MR. MAYOR...

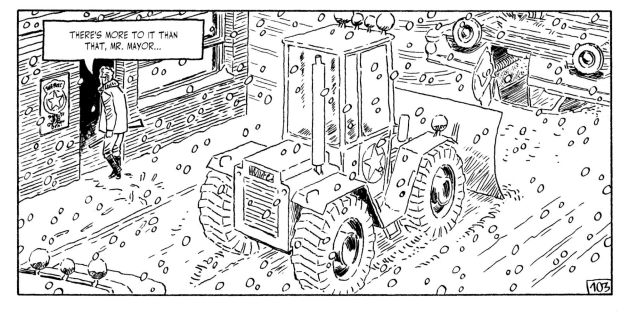

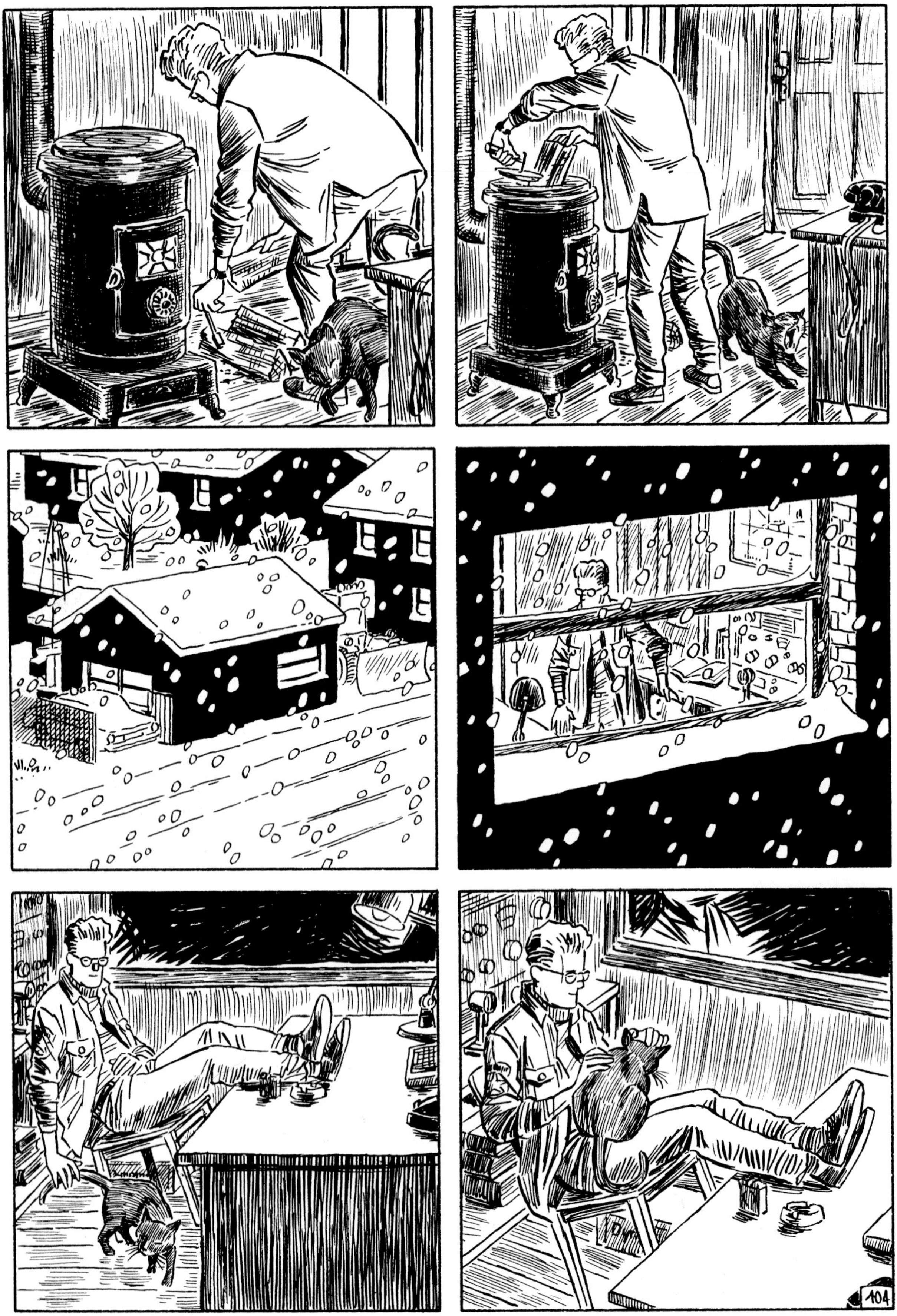

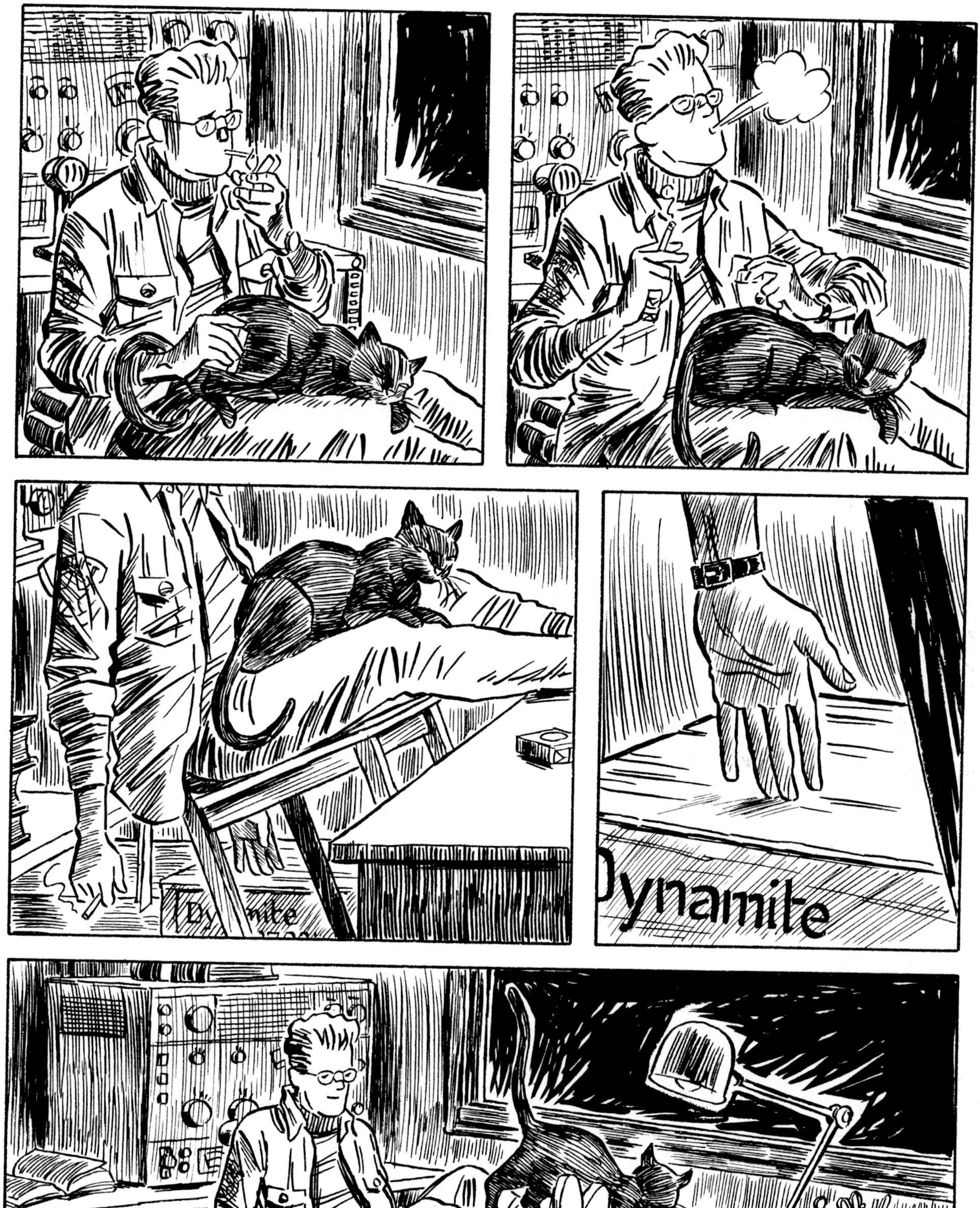
Dynamite

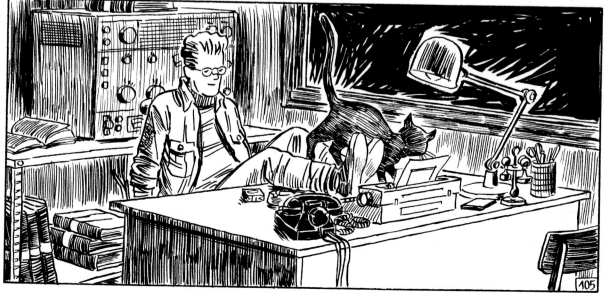

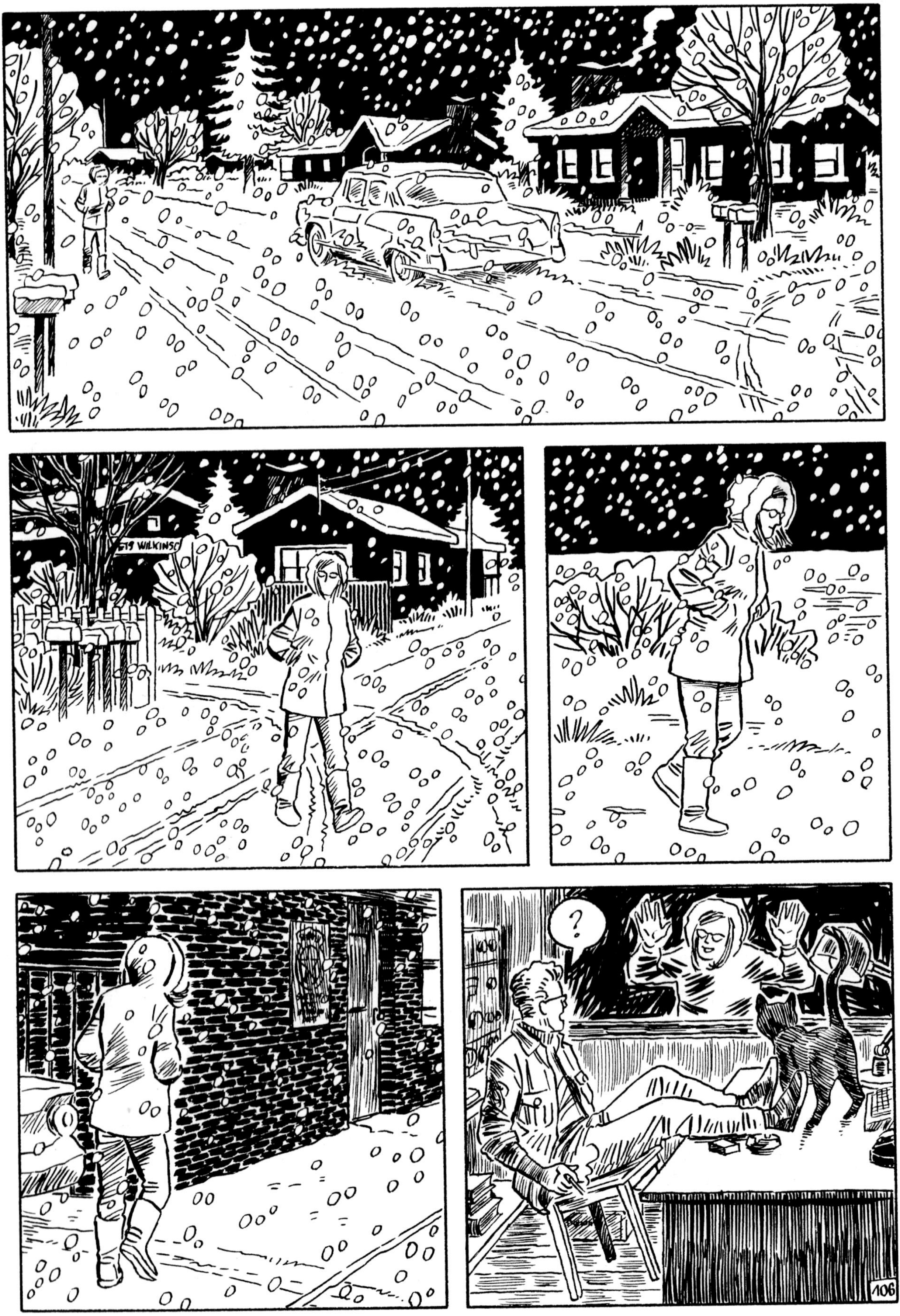
519 WILKINSO
?

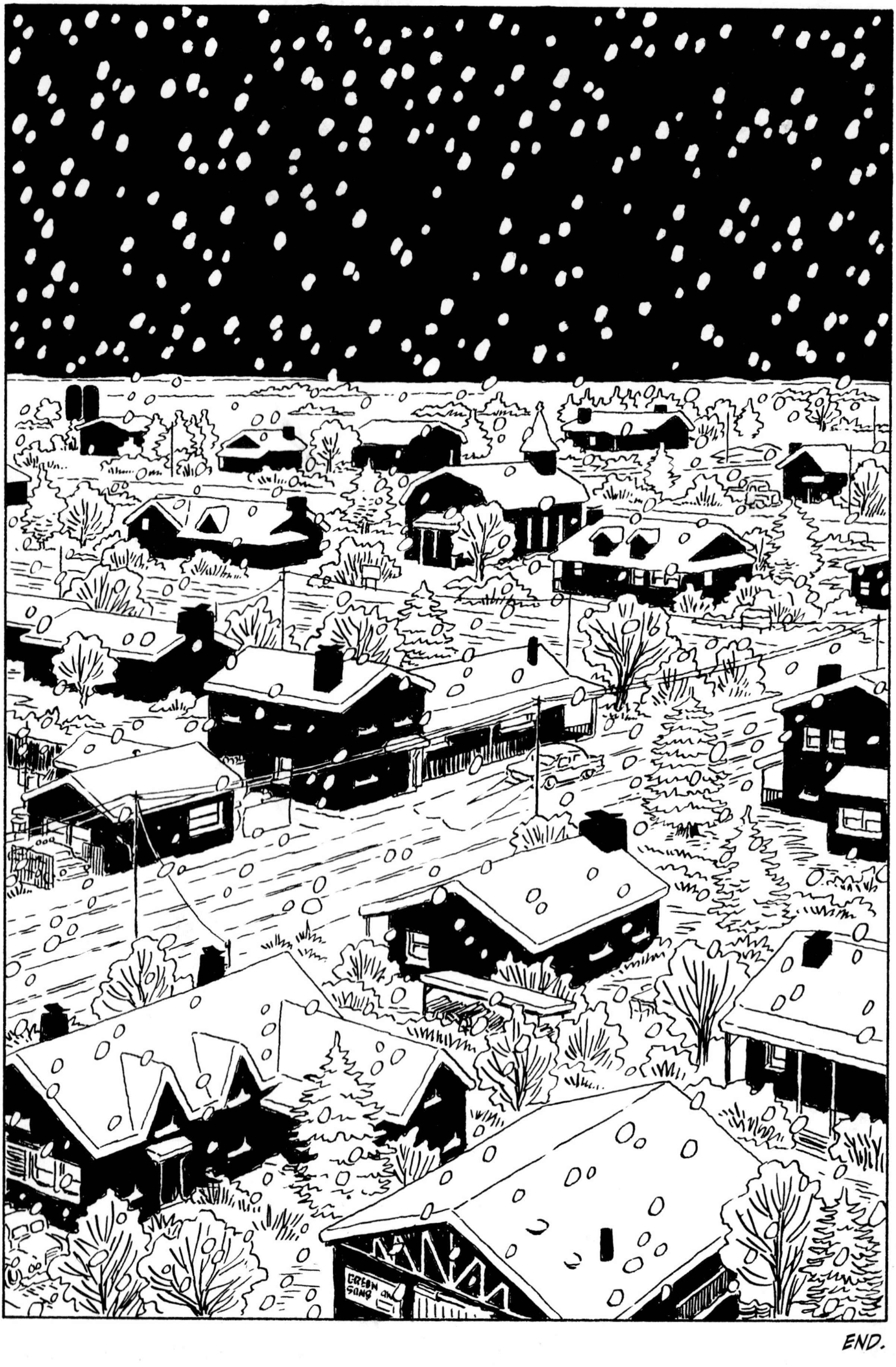

END.